THE DEVIL MADE ME Brew IT

The Devil Made Me Brew It
The Witches of Wayward Bay, Book One
Copyright © 2023 by Sarah Piper
SarahPiperBooks.com

Published by Two Gnomes Media
Cover design by Two Gnomes Media

All rights reserved. With the exception of brief quotations used for promotional or review purposes, no part of this book may be recorded, reproduced, stored in a retrieval system, or transmitted in any form or by any means without the express permission of the author.

This book is a work of fiction. Names, characters, places, businesses, organizations, brands, media, and incidents are either products of the author's imagination or are used fictitiously. Any resemblance to actual events, locations, or persons, living or dead, is entirely coincidental.

v10

E-book ISBN: 978-1-948455-92-3
Paperback ISBN: 978-1-948455-93-0
Audiobook ISBN: 978-1-948455-94-7

BOOK SERIES BY SARAH PIPER

M/F Romance Series

The Witches of Wayward Bay

Vampire Royals of New York

Reverse Harem Romance Series

Claimed by Gargoyles

The Witch's Monsters

Tarot Academy

The Witch's Rebels

Romance Serials

Crescent Hollow

GET CONNECTED!

I love connecting with readers! There are a few different ways you can keep in touch:

Email: sarah@sarahpiperbooks.com

Patreon: patreon.com/sarahpiper

Facebook group: Sarah Piper's Sassy Witches

TikTok: @sarahpiperbooks

Newsletter: Never miss a new release or a sale! sarahpiperbooks.com/readers-club

DEDICATION

For my BOCO Besties,

Kelsey and Stephanie

*who share my appreciation
for the finer things in life:*

*good food, strong wine,
lots of laughs, & smutty books*

CHAPTER ONE

VIOLET

It's official. The Devil is stalking me.

It started last night with a drop-in at the dinner table that nearly *ruined* my grilled cheese and tomato soup. I chased him off with a menacing wave of the spatula, only to suffer a second interruption when he crashed my Charmed rewatch.

Then, the ultimate sin: the jerk shows up in my *bed*, barging in on some much-needed quality time with my emotional support vibrator Mr. Wiggles, who voiced his displeasure by conking out at the *worst* possible moment.

Unforgivable!

Which brings us to this morning's invasion at my magical tea shop, Kettle and Cauldron. At five a.m. On what's supposed to be a capital-B Big day that I can *not* afford to screw up. Not unless I want to lose all the caffeinejonesing customers of Wayward Bay to Mean Beans, the soulless new coffee chain opening across the street.

But does the Devil care about my plight? Nope.

I've just flicked on the lights when I catch him lounging on the counter with that glint in his eyes, his wicked grin as much a warning as it is an invitation. One this witch will *not* be accepting, *thankyouverymuch.*

"Sir, for the last time." I shoot the insolent Tarot card a glare that could shrivel testicles if I concentrated hard enough. "Whatever you're peddling, I'm *not* interested."

Not yet, Violet Pepperdine, comes the ominous whisper of my intuition. *But you* will *be...*

A chill skitters down my spine, but I refuse to cower. Fear is the Devil's language, not mine. My language is tea. Tea that needs to make a big splash today if we've got any chance of surviving Mean Beans mania, T-minus two hours and counting.

"Any more out of you," I warn the Devil, "and I'll incinerate your ass."

That shuts him up, but the silence is temporary. He's part of my late grandmother Gigi's Tarot deck, a beautiful set of magical, hand-painted cards that vanished under mysterious circumstances when she died. But a few weeks after her funeral, the cards started popping up again in the most random places: the pocket of a hand-me-down coat. Tucked between the pages of a library book. Bottom of the kitchen junk drawer at my latest foster home, beneath a mountain of pens, twist ties, and half-spent packs of Marlboros.

It's been sixteen years since Gigi's passing, and the cards have only grown more insistent, pestering me until I heed their every message, whether I want to or not.

Today, I most assuredly do not. All that devilish doom-and-gloom cluttering up my mind? Hard pass. I already know I'm an obsessive, anxious, over-thinking hyper-perfectionist trapped in a prison of my own making. Not exactly breaking news, my guy!

So, turning my back on his maddening smirk, I scan the shelves of teas, spices, and magical ingredients behind the counter, making sure everything's in perfect order.

I came in early to get a jump on things before my nemesis Hoovers up all the pedestrian traffic, but it seems they're already well ahead of me. Peering out my windows, I spy a small army of rosy-cheeked, green-aproned baristas buzzing around like brainwashed bees, ensuring the walkways are swept, the windows Windexed, the grand-opening banner hung straight.

Free hat with every purchase! it proclaims. *Today only!*

Guess they're expecting big crowds. Bigger than poor old Mr. Corto ever got before Beans swindled him out of his lease, forcing him to shutter Corto's Curiosities. Now he's living with his daughter in Phoenix and there's nowhere within a hundred miles to buy powdered dragon scales *or* a lock of hair from a haunted doll.

Goddess, it's enough to crank my simmering anxiety to a full-on boil. The woman who rents me the café space and the adorable apartment above it is an absolute saint, but I've fallen so far behind on rent, not even my unlimited-tea-and-scones promissory notes can save me.

Especially when she's got her pick of big-city chains swooping in with offers to buy at twice the market value and a smarmy realtor nephew eager to make a name for himself. He's the reason Curiosities went kaput. See also: Second Chance Romance, the former book store now pushing trendy wines and linen towels embroidered with such witticisms as *It's Wine O'clock!* and *My Blood Type is Merlot!* He even tried to trick my sweet old aunts into selling their historic Three Sisters B&B, but they ran him off the property with a not-so-subtle threat about turning him into a wart on a toad's dick, which is absolutely a thing they can do, unbeknownst to him.

With its quaint, tree-lined streets, gorgeous Victorian architecture, and all-around small-town charm, *everyone* wants a piece of Wayward Bay and he knows it. He makes sure *I* know it, too—reminds me every week, waltzing in on his aunt's heels and whisper-shouting in her ear while she orders her tea and gives me apologetic smiles. Things like, "The family agrees about selling, Aunt Beverly," and "It's too much for you to manage at your age," and—my favorite chestnut, always accompanied by a pointed glare in my direction—"It's bad business to let tenants take advantage of your naivety."

It's those special times I like to remind myself that harming people just because you don't like them is against the rules of magic and decency both. Lucky for him.

You can't ignore this mess forever, Violet...

The Devil pings my intuition again, raising the hairs on the back of my neck and *super* pissing me off.

"Hey. Dickhead. No means no." I don't wait for a response. Just snap my fingers and incinerate him.

Then I smile, because that trick *never* gets old.

My familiars agree. As the burned-sugar-and-bourbon scent of my magic fills the air, the cats—a sleek black tabby named Grumpy and a fat orange floofball named Sunshine—bolt out from the storage room and pounce on the counter, pawing through the ashes.

"Aww, we love making things go *poof*, don't we?" I scoop them up for a snuggle—a ritual Sunshine adores and Grumpy pretends to hate because he's got a reputation to uphold. "How are Mama's favorite troublemakers today? As mischievous as you are handsome? Yes, I agree. Way more handsome than that mean ol' Devil!"

They indulge me for three whole seconds before leaping out of my arms and bounding up the back stairs to our apartment, where they'll hide out until closing time. Sociable cats, they're not.

With a sense of deep satisfaction, I sweep the Devil's ashes into the bin and scour the counter with sage-and-lemon-balm cleansing spray. The Devil will return—Gigi's magic Tarot cards always do—but for now, I'm a witch on a mission.

I may not have a team of sign-hanging, window-washing minions, but I *do* have magic. From the well-stocked shelves, I select my ingredients—peppermint leaves, cinnamon, grated orange peel, vanilla bean—and stir them into a cauldron of water charged under a waxing moon. Bringing the mixture to a gentle simmer, I close my eyes and envision the café jam-packed with happy customers.

Then I recite the prosperity spell Gigi taught me nearly two decades ago:

> *Luck and good fortune, I call upon thee*
> *To bless me with wealth and prosperity*
> *My door is open, the hearth is aglow*
> *My wishes are granted, above and below*

The invigorating scent of the brew mingles with the sugary haze of my magic, infusing me with confidence as I continue the morning prep: bakery order from Emmilou's Sweet-N-Savories arranged in the case. Overstuffed velvet couches freshly fluffed. Fall vibes playlist floating through the speakers. Flames crackling in the stone hearth along the back wall.

And me, tea witch extraordinaire, ready to rock the fuzzy

fall socks off anyone who sets foot inside. Not with your garden-variety, ho-hum brews, mind you. I'm talking about the real-deal, perfection-in-a-cup wonderdrinks that taste like liquid happiness and cure just about anything from the common cold to a broken heart. And thanks to my empathic magic, I always know which blend a customer needs.

Out on Main Street, the ancient oak and maple trees are aflame with the reds and golds that make upstate New York so enchanting this time of year, the autumn air sweet with the scent of apples, everything bursting with promise and potential. I couldn't have asked for a better day to set my intention for success.

So, trusting the magic, I tighten my apron strings, turn on the OPEN sign, and wait.

I continue to wait, even as the customers line up outside Mean Beans an hour before they're set to open.

I wait some more, spotting a few of my regulars in the crowd.

The minutes pass. The commotion outside grows louder as the chain opens its doors for the inaugural customers. There is much cheering and photo-snapping and free-hat-distributing.

More people arrive by the minute—tourists and residents both.

I give my prosperity cauldron another stir.

Send a quick prayer to the goddess.

And try desperately not to fret as minutes turn to hours

and dark clouds gather in the sky and the line outside Mean Beans wraps around the entire freaking block, impervious to the brewing storm.

By lunchtime, even the cats have wandered back downstairs, certain there won't be a single visitor to disturb them. I'm about ready to call it a day and queue up another Charmed episode when I finally spot a friendly face outside.

A hypochondriac germaphobe with a smile that can light up a room and a laugh that makes even the most brutal town council meetings fun, Mayor Amalie Singh is one of my favorite humans and K&C regulars.

If she bails on me for Mean Beans...

I suck in a steadying breath. Call upon the magic of my prosperity spell, and—

"Hello hello *helloooo!*" comes the chipper call and the tinkling of the chimes over my door. "I've got a tickle in my throat, Violet. Did my assistant tell you? Was it that obvious in the staff meeting?" She flutters her fingers over her neck and makes a delicate coughing sound. "Oh, no... it's progressed from a tickle to a scratch. I'm in back-to-back budget meetings for the rest of the month! I can't afford to be cooped up in the hospital!" She pulls a tissue from her purse and sneezes. "Do you think it's cancer? Oh, dear. It's probably cancer."

"It's probably seasonal allergies, and I've got you covered."

"Oh, honey. You always do." Relief floods her energy field

as I get to work on her brew, scanning the shelves until I feel the intuitive tug that tells me I've got the right blend in mind—green tea, lemon verbena, peppermint leaves, fresh-squeezed lemon juice, fresh grated ginger root, and crushed dried pineapple to sweeten the brew. I'm also adding some essence of blue kyanite to encourage clear communication—that should help with her throat issues.

A pinch of this, a dollop of that, a whispered incantation to lock in the medicinal properties and maximize their potency, and voilà! Behold the marvelous magic of tea.

It is, as my coven sister Olivy says, my witchy zone of genius. And since *her* witchy zone of genius is dark magic and blood curses, I generally make it a point to agree with her in all matters.

Unfortunately, in a town where the majority of the population doesn't know magic exists and the equally uninitiated tourists would rather drink the generic sludge from Mean Beans, I fear my witchy zone of genius is cursed to remain an undiscovered gem.

"Are you all right, Violet?" Mayor Singh asks, her own troubles momentarily forgotten. "You seem... out of sorts."

"What? No. I'm good. Fine. Perfectly good and perfectly fine."

She arches a quizzical eyebrow.

"Just... trying to get used to the new neighbors," I admit. "Business has been slow today. You're my first customer, actually."

"Oh, good heavens." She glances out at the mob across the street and frowns. "I'd really hoped some of the overflow would find their way over here."

Forcing a smile, I top off the tea with a web of elderberry-infused honey, pop on the lid, and hand it over. "Sip it slowly and let it work its magic. You'll be back to full capacity before you know it."

"I feel better already." She slides a ten across the counter and winks, her energy warm and genuine. "Keep the change."

"Thanks, Mayor Singh. Good luck with the budget meetings."

At the door, she stops suddenly, turning back with a grave look in her eyes. A wave of regret pulses outward, taking me by surprise. Despite her constant fretting, I've never known the mayor to be so somber.

"You're one of the good ones, Violet Pepperdine. Wayward Bay is lucky to have you. Whatever the future holds, remember that."

She's out the door before I can even formulate a response.

One of the good ones? Whatever the future holds? What is she talking about? Sure, Beans is putting a crimp in my style —a big one—but I can weather this storm.

Can't I?

A flash of silver and black on the counter, and I turn to find my stalker grinning up at me once again, like this is all a big cosmic joke and he can't wait to deliver the punchline.

Ignoring this will only make it worse. Haven't you learned that by now?

"No. I haven't learned it, obviously." I snatch up the card, ignoring the uncomfortable buzz of magic prickling my fingertips.

Trouble is brewing, Violet...

"You wanna know what's brewing? I'll tell you what's brewing. Coffee. At Mean Beans. Which is apparently the place to be, since all the usual tea-sipping, scone-gobbling customers are lining up around the block for a free hat and an uninspired half-caf, low-foam, cappu-latte sugar bomb made from an industrial-sized container of powdered chemicals, and I'm standing around with a broomstick up my butt just praying to the goddess I don't lose my business and get cast out into the cold, cold world like last week's stinky fish—fish everyone will trample on as they sprint over to Mean Beans. So as you can see, I have enough to worry about without *you* turning up every five minutes with your creepy grin and your ominous warnings and your stupidly handsome face and—"

Movement outside the door catches my eye.

The card evaporates, and I dust off my apron, double-checking there's no trace of the Devil clinging to the fabric. But when I glance up again, there's no customer at the threshold.

Just an official-looking envelope carelessly shoved under the door.

The moment I see it, the energy in the room turns cold and unpleasant, like stepping into a winter slush puddle wearing nothing but socks.

And I know *exactly* who left it for me.

Nathan Pike, realtor from Hell.

No wonder the Devil keeps showing up. Nathan isn't just a passive-aggressive twatwaffle. He's evil incarnate, ready to carve up Wayward Bay and sell it off to the highest bidders, piece by piece.

I pluck the envelope from the floor and tear into it, my heart sinking as the words take shape. No, I wasn't expecting a birthday party invite or a thank-you note for the free scones he pilfers from his aunt, but this?

It steals the breath from my lungs—a full accounting of my past-due rent, plus compounding interest and late fees, followed by several paragraphs detailing his plan to bring in potential buyers and convince Beverly to sell. Failing that, he's working on getting power of attorney over his aunt's holdings, since she's clearly not of sound mind.

Thinking about him criticizing that sweet old woman—sharp as a tack and one of the kindest non-magical souls in Wayward Bay—makes my blood boil.

But Nathan's not done twisting the knife just yet.

There, at the very bottom, shouting at me in all-caps, multiple-exclamation-points glory:

PAYMENT DUE IN FULL!!!! 30 DAYS OR EVICTION PROCEEDINGS WILL COMMENCE!!!!

I waver on my feet, the room spinning.

Thirty days?

Even accounting for the monthly catch-up payments I've already arranged with Beverly, the added interest and fees push my debt into five-figure territory. And while I might be able to scrape together the cash to clear that particular slate, I'm also paying off a hefty small-business loan and back taxes, not to mention a maxed-out credit card. Realistically speaking, I'm probably going to have to hire some help too—especially if I want to compete with Beans.

Which puts the cost of keeping Kettle and Cauldron afloat somewhere in the range of...

$100,000.

Tears sting my eyes, blurring the cozy café into a black smudge.

Crafting magical tea isn't just my job, it's my life's dream. A natural expression of the goddess-given empathic magic that lives and breathes inside me.

It's also my grandmother's legacy.

Gigi raised me from birth when no one else wanted the job. She helped me through school bullies and unrequited love and my first bumbling attempts at spellwork. Then, she taught me to harness and hone my magic until it was my very own. The one thing no one else could do quite like me. The one thing I've always come back to.

More than my memories of our time together, more than her mysterious Tarot cards and the spells she bequeathed to me, tea magic is what connects us. What keeps her close, even in death.

I named Kettle and Cauldron for my favorite things from her kitchen—her floral teakettle and the cast-iron cauldron always simmering on the stove, the orange-and-cardamom scent of her magic welcoming me home after a long day.

And now, after just two years in business, I'm on the verge of losing it. The one thing I swore I'd never, ever screw up.

Outside, the first few drops of rain hit the pavement and a cold breeze shakes the leaves from the trees, whipping them into a red-and-gold frenzy. A flock of tourists exits Mean Beans, smiles wide as they pose for a group selfie in the rain, their matching ball caps adorned with the chain's infamous logo: a cartoon coffee bean punching another bean in the face.

I sink down onto a stool, head in my hands. Nathan's letter spirals to the floor.

Thirty days. Thirty days to find a hundred grand, or my life's dream will go the way of the Devil card and *poof!* right out of existence.

CHAPTER TWO

DEVLIN

One might assume it's hard—no pun intended—to have a lousy time at an orgy. Especially at one of *my* orgies. Perched on an overlook high in the Santa Monica Mountains, my Hollywood Hills mansion is *the* place to see and be seen, offering a veritable buffet of adult entertainment options under one very expensive, very exclusive roof. My nightly fêtes have become infamous—a badge of honor, I'm told, for those who meet the criteria for an invitation.

Namely, being rich and famous and ridiculously good-looking.

Trust me—life as an immortal is far too long to spend it in the company of the dull and ill-favored. Especially when said company is naked.

Lest I be accused of superficiality, there's one more criterion—most important of all. Before stepping a single manicured toe over my property line, aspiring guests must accept the iron-clad terms of service specifying the price of admission:

Their souls.

All signatures are made in person—none of this modern digital nonsense—and require a drop of blood to bind them.

Just a little prick, my bouncers tell them, their Hell-forged demon blades gleaming as brightly as their smiles, *and your dalliance with the Devil may begin...*

The humans laugh and sign the paperwork and dutifully hold out their finger for the nick of the blade, thinking it's all just part of the spectacle, the exclusivity, the eccentric enigma that is Mr. Devlin Pierce.

Cruel? Perhaps. Deceitful? No. I've never lied to them. It's all in the terms, clear as the night is long. If only they read the fine print.

But they're far more interested in getting in the door, hobnobbing with the cream of the California crop: actors, models, singers and rappers, professional athletes, the occasional tech billionaire. Not to mention the latest strain of nouveau riche—the influencers.

I'm still not exactly sure how they make their millions, but they seem to believe I'm one of them—beautiful, entertaining, ostentatious, attention-seeking.

The ruse has worked out well for me. Far better than the previous century's attempts to infiltrate the close-knit circles of the morally bankrupt: politicians, mafia henchmen, clergy.

Not my style, friends. Look at this face—the face of a prince. Social media stardom is a much better fit. The wild parties? Just an added perk. Icing on the Devil's food cake, so to speak. And normally, I'm the first one in line for a bite.

Not so tonight.

I'd only just slipped into my arseless leather party attire—and before you judge, this is bespoke Italian craftsmanship, not some redneck knockoff—when I felt it. No, not the tantalizing sting of a riding crop kissing my exposed backside—as much as I do on occasion enjoy that particular sensation.

I'm talking about that ice-cold whisper between the shoulder blades, the invisible touch of something that lurks beyond the veil, just outside the realm of perception.

I haven't been able to shake it. Something is just... off. Has *been* off, if I'm being honest. And it's not just the bad mojo, either.

I never thought I'd say this, but the task of filling Hell's bottomless coffers has become as unfulfilling as smiting demons for sport. Tonight, not even the promise of debasing the illustrious Hollywood elite can sweeten my sour mood.

The very thought of posing for another selfie with my drunken revelers, of devising one more outlandish poolside stunt to keep the insipid bubbleheads coming back for more, of awakening face-down on my alpaca rug beneath one more nameless pile of naked, sweat-glistened humans with little recollection of how they came to join me...

Demon's *balls*, it's enough to turn my blood to lead.

Most people would literally sell off a body part to score an invitation—and have tried, if the internet rumors are anything to go by—yet here I am, wandering the master suite in my fine leathers, proverbial dick in proverbial hand, bored out of my *bloody* skull. If I could actually die, I'd smash that skull into the wall repeatedly until the job was done, grateful for a change from the stale routine.

Alas, I'm cursed as an immortal. Any head-bashing would be an exercise in futility. Not unlike arseless leather pants (though I'm told I wear them well).

An explosion of laughter downstairs shatters my rumination, reminding me I've still got a role to play. A job to do. Expectations to meet, night after night, if I'm to sign over enough souls to satisfy the terms of my banishment, return home to Hell, and reclaim my rightful throne.

You didn't think I was doing this for fun, did you?

Readying myself for the myriad phones and drones that await, I head out with every intention of donning the glittering smile, the mask of the unflappable rake they love to hate and hate to love. But the moment I step onto the gleaming marble staircase and spot the gyrating, inebriated throngs below, my feet stop working.

I can't do it. Can't take another step.

Can't pretend, even for one more night.

Still unseen by the crowd, I slip back into my suite and

take the hidden staircase down to the kitchen, blissfully ignored by the demon caterers and bartenders on my staff.

I dart out the back and down another hallway, my private sanctuary so close I can almost hear the fire crackling in the hearth. Almost taste the bourbon I'm soon to pour. Almost relax enough to—

A glass shatters. An idiot curses.

Then he stumbles out of the billiards room and right into my arms.

Dreadful heathen.

Also, a highly overpaid professional quarterback. Dressed in nothing but a pale blue ballerina skirt—a jarring contrast to the uniform he dons every Sunday. He stares up at me with the glassy, vacant eyes of a man who's just gone a few rounds with the designer-drug candy bowl.

"Heyyyy," he slurs. "I know *you*!"

"And I you." I set him on his feet, propping him against the wall for support. "If you'll excuse me, I—"

He lifts a finger, as if to put me on pause, and fishes his phone out of... well, I'm quite sure I don't want to know. His skirt doesn't appear to have pockets.

Before I can beg off, he's throwing an arm around me, pressing his cheek to mine and holding up the phone for a few selfies.

Fine, fine. All part of the play. A fake smile here, a thumbs-up there.

He exchanges the phone for a Sharpie.

Again, no idea where that exchange happened.

Again, trying not to think about it too hard. Especially when he asks for an autograph.

On his arse.

Well, Devlin Pierce is nothing if not accommodating. Also, prepared. Retrieving my own Sharpie from an *actual* pocket designed for just that purpose, I flip up the skirt and do the deed on his left cheek, finishing it with a smiley face to let him know just how bloody *ecstatic* I am to make his acquaintance.

I also draw a dick, because who wouldn't? A genuine grin graces my lips as I think about how long Sharpie takes to wash off, and how he'll forget this entire interaction until game day this weekend, when his football mates spot my artwork in the locker room.

"Enjoy your evening, QB One." A quick smack on the arse, and I send him on his way.

Coast clear, I return to the shadows, slinking past door after door—the game room, the sauna, the home theater, the home film studio—each room brimming with the sounds of laughter and revelry and the unmistakably wet slap of flesh on flesh.

Also, the occasional bleating of a goat, and... is that a monkey?

Good grief, I hope he signed the consent form.

It's a full twenty minutes before I reach my destination, ducking and weaving to avoid my guests, stopping when avoidance just isn't an option: another selfie, this time with an upstart congressman. A shot of something pink and overly sweet with a woman matching that very description. The autographing of a bare breast—singer, I think.

And then, just when I'm ready to light myself on fire to avoid another run-in, I reach the elusive door, press my eye to the retinal scanner, and...

I'm in.

The breath leaves me in a rush.

Undisturbed by my demonic staff and magically hidden from human perception, the study is my private oasis when the rest of my home feels like anything but.

In here, there's no pretense. No deejays and flashing neon lights. No crystal bowls filled with pills. No scantily clad beauties vying for attention, no fellow influencers begging for collaboration opps to boost the so-called algorithms.

Just the stodgy leather furniture and built-in shelves of rich mahogany set against butter-yellow walls. A few portraits painted by men long since dead. The stone hearth and a fire that jumps to life at the snap of my fingers.

My black satin smoking jacket hangs on the wrought iron coat rack inside, untouched since my last visit, and I slip it over my shoulders before sinking into a chair before the hearth.

Ah, but there's nothing quite like a fall fire. Staring into the flames, I feel the tension leaving my tired muscles, the knot of worry in my gut loosening.

In the quiet of my inner sanctum, it's easy to believe I'm not an infamous entertainer. For a moment, I might even pretend I'm not the Devil, either. Just a man enjoying a roaring fire, nowhere else to be, no one around to judge his worthiness and find it utterly lacking.

"So sorry," comes the grating interruption. "Is all this drama and debauchery boring you tonight, Highness?"

CHAPTER THREE

VIOLET

"Locusts. That's what the situation calls for. A plague of locusts." Olivy's standing at the window shooting daggers at the neighbors who've turned up for seconds at Mean Beans, all rocking their free hats from earlier.

Salt in the wound, but anyway.

"We'll need a jar of crushed beetles," she continues. "Six rusty nails, broken glass, a handful of graveyard dirt, two vials of blood, and—"

"Locusts are too old-world." Darla sets down the notebook she's been scribbling in and taps her chin with the pencil. "Bedbugs could work, though. Ooh! Should I write that down?"

"No!" All of us practically screech. As a writing witch, Darla has a way with words. A magical, mystical, open-to-interpretation way that more often than not ends in disaster, bless her clever heart.

"What about a flood?" This from Emmilou, of Emmilou's Sweet-N-Savories, who's never resorted to violence a day in her life (other than at last year's Haunted Halloween Ball when she catapulted a dozen homemade powdered donuts at my ex, but that was a well-deserved pelting).

"A flood, yes!" Fiona's stormy gray eyes widen over the lemons she's cutting up for drinks, and an explosive burst of lightning makes the lights over her head flicker. Peak Fiona, psychic witch and drama queen extraordinaire. "I can see it now. The screaming, the running, the repenting... *Very* biblical, Vi."

"Girls." I toss my spent apron and dishtowels into the wash pile and sigh. "No one is cursing Mean Beans with locusts, bedbugs, floods, or any other deluge, apocalyptic or mundane. Darla, drop the pen. Olivy, put that jar back. Those are black caraway seeds, not beetles."

"You never let us have any fun," Olivy pouts, reluctantly replacing the jar. "And *Peen* Beans isn't going to eliminate itself. Be proactive."

"Excellent point, Olivy," Darla says. "Isn't that what Aunt Joslyn's always on about? Magic helps those who help themselves?"

Exhaustion settling in bone-deep, I flick my fingers at the open sign, and off it goes. "Right now I'd kinda like to help myself to a—"

"Magic Mojito Lemonito!" Fiona passes me a glass mug

filled with something slushy, cheerfully yellow, and piping hot, garnished with mint leaves and a sugared lemon slice.

How she managed to make a hot slushy is beyond me, but hey. Magic. Hell of a thing.

"I was going to say a bubble bath and a German chocolate cupcake," I reply, "but this looks even better."

"Witch-N-Bitch Happy Hour is officially in session." She gestures for the others to grab a slushy. "And you guys are going to *love* this. Trust me—it's written in the stars."

"You would know." I wink at my sister and take the offered mug, my bath-and-cupcake pity party plans evaporating.

That's okay, though. I'm glad my coven sisters are here—their particular brand of whimsy with a sprinkle of crazy is just what I need. They showed up right after I got my letter of doom, which is unsurprising. The five of us aren't related by blood, but our connection runs deep. Whenever one of us is in trouble, we all sense it. More accurately, Fiona senses it—a disturbance in the force, as she describes it—and immediately tells the others. Our very own witchy phone tree.

Thankfully, my sister's psychic abilities never reveal the specifics of those disturbances. Exhibit A: my nastygram from Nathan.

Beneath the counter, shoved behind the stack of clean aprons, his letter lingers. It's tucked out of sight, but I can still feel it, every word embedded in my mind, blinking at me like a big flashing sign: *Failure! Failure! Failure!*

"Here's to a better tomorrow," Fiona says, and we all raise a mug to that. "And to Peen Beans getting shut down for unspecified, non-apocalyptic health code violations and/or a flood of terrible online reviews Darla and I may or may not know something and/or nothing about."

"Here, here." I tip the mug back, and down the hatch it goes.

The drink is sweet and citrusy with just the right amount of mint and far too much alcohol, the rum hitting me hard and fast. After just a few sips, the sting of today's disaster starts to dull.

"She's smiling, everyone," Fiona says, and the lights flicker again, this time sending Grumpy and Sunshine bolting back upstairs. We all hoot and holler at that, relocating our happy-hour adventures to the two velvet couches in the back, right near the fireplace.

The darkness snuck up on us early tonight, the storm casting Main Street in an ominous black shimmer. But here inside Kettle and Cauldron, After-Hours Edition, the fire crackles, the familiar laughter of my favorite witches filling the café, soothing me in a way no spell or even a cup of my special tea ever could. This kind of magic is something else entirely. Love and friendship and sisterhood, pure and simple. The balm that heals all wounds.

I didn't realize how much I needed it until now.

"Don't worry, Vi." Emmie pulls me in for a side hug. "After a few days, the newness will wear off, the free hats will be gone, and things will be right back to normal over here."

Her declaration is met with a chorus of nods and affirmations, and I smile and nod right along with them. But through all their encouragement, through all the laughs and Peen Bean jokes, my stomach churns with anxiety. "Right back to normal" is no longer good enough. Not the kind of good enough that can bring in $100,000 in a month's time.

"Besides," Olivy adds with a cool confidence I only *wish* I possessed, "if anyone can handle a little competition, it's Violet *Fucking* Pepperdine."

"You *have* to say that," I reply. "You're my sisters."

"We say it because it's true." Emmie squeezes my cheeks. "Don't let this cute face fool you, friends. Behind the big glasses and shy smile, our girl is a witchy, formidable, tea-slinging badass."

"At least one of those things, anyway." I laugh and swat her hand away, then reach for my mug, surprised to find it empty, one of Gigi's Tarot cards stuck to the bottom.

"Who is it this time?" Darla wants to know.

Glancing at the figure on the card—a beautiful nude woman with long silver hair kneeling beside a stream, a bright seven-pointed star illuminating the landscape—I smile. "The Star."

"Your favorite," Darla says softly. "See? Even the cards know you're going to be okay."

I want to believe it, too. That the card heralds a time of

healing and renewal, of inspiration, the guiding light and north star of my heart. But when I close my eyes and brush my fingertips along the card's border now, I hear only a faint whisper...

If you don't believe in yourself, Violet Pepperdine, how can anyone else?

"Um, Violet?" Olivy says. "Looks like your Star brought a plus-one."

Damn it. I know who it is before I even look at him.

"Didn't we talk about this?" I open my eyes and glare at the late-arriving Devil, all swagger and shine, horns gleaming.

You haven't told them yet, my intuition nags. *You can't run from this forever...*

"Clearly we need more booze." Fiona heads back to the kitchen to whip up another batch of Lemonitos, and for the moment, the conversation fades to a comfortable silence, all of us momentarily seduced by the heady mix of the autumn night—the dance of the golden flames, the scent of fallen leaves and candle wax and vanilla tea floating in the air, the cozy Celtic harp on my latest café playlist.

Safe and warm in my favorite place, surrounded by my favorite people, part of me wishes I *could* tell them the truth. About my crushing debt, Nathan's deadline, all the stupid mistakes I made that landed me in this pickle.

About the new competition across the street being just the tip of the shitstorm iceberg, and how I've been ignoring the Devil for days because he knows all the things I'm not ready to admit to myself, let alone to the people I love most.

But how can I tell them that Violet Fucking Pepperdine, the so-called witchy, formidable, tea-slinging badass, is currently sitting in the driver's seat of the Red Hot Mess Express, one more blind curve away from driving it straight off a cliff?

If they find out how dire my situation is, they'll feel obligated to bail me out. Loans I'll never be able to pay back—loans they'll insist are gifts. Picking up shifts at the café, refusing to let me pay them for the work. Sacrificing time and energy they should be pouring into their *own* businesses and big dreams, not someone else's.

Help is a tricky thing. What starts off as generosity can easily turn into obligation and resentment. And no matter how genuine and well-meaning everyone is at the start, that's precisely the kind of stuff that destroys relationships.

Tears glaze my eyes. I love these witches far too much to become a burden to them. To risk it for even a single day.

This is *my* hot mess. I got myself into it, so it's on me to dig my way out.

"Give me *that*." I grab the Lemonito pitcher out of Fiona's hands, filling up my mug and downing half of it in one go.

"Good goddess, she's mainlining," says Olivy.

"Slow down, Violet!" Fiona reaches for the mug. "Remember what happened last time you overdid it with the booze?"

"Which part?" I ask.

"The part where you chipped a tooth making out with Ol' Aggie," Darla says. "And begged us to let you sleep under the maple tree with her."

Oh, right. Ol' Aggie being the cast-iron statue of Agatha Wayward, the witch who sacrificed the last of her magic to protect the Bay from malevolent forces back in Ye Olden Times. To read the human history books, her three cousins (men, of course) were the real heroes, planting the trees and laying the bricks and brokering trade agreements with the neighboring villages that allowed Wayward Bay to thrive.

But Aggie worked tirelessly on another front, ensuring that women could vote and run for local office, that we could hold property in our own names and work outside the home without permission from husbands or fathers. That's the bit that finally earned her the statue in Founders' Grove in the Town Hall courtyard, along with the official title as a founder, a hundred years after her male counterparts had received the same accolades.

But the witches here... We know the rest of Aggie's story, too. The magical battles she fought. The secret coven she united, the rituals they cast beneath the very maple trees that protect her statue now, ensuring our town would always be a safe haven for witches and other magical folk.

Her magic is still here with us, buzzing through every tree and rock, heard in the caw of every crow. It calls us here, from all the various places we've come. It reminds us that no matter how lonely we may feel, as long as we're true to ourselves as women of the craft, we're never really alone.

Aggie's statue was just dedicated last year.

Hence the upwelling of love I felt on that particular occasion.

"I wasn't making out with her," I clarify now. "Just showing my appreciation."

Olivy laughs. "You literally threw yourself at her like a common hussy. I've got the video to prove it."

"In my defense, it was *faerie* wine." I down the last sip, my head swimming pleasantly, money worries fading away. "Someone should've warned me."

"*Everyone* warned you," says Emmie. "Including both grooms, the entire wedding party, us, the fae bartender, and the waiver you signed before ordering a drink off the 'special' menu."

"Consider me warned anew." I hold up my mug. "No more making out with statues. I promise."

"You sure?" Fiona's brow crinkles with concern, the humor fading from her gray eyes.

"I'm sure." Ignoring the Star and the Devil both, I nod for Fiona to load me up, liquid courage for the win. "Unless you're suggesting Violet *Fucking* Pepperdine, slayer of the competition and glasses-wearing badass, can't handle one more drink."

CHAPTER FOUR

DEVLIN

I decide not to smite the filthy intruder. On account of me being magnanimous and him being my best mate.

"Piss off, Finn," I offer instead, but my tone is giving more exhaustion than ire, which Finn takes as an invitation.

Pouring two glasses of bourbon from the bar, he scans me from head to toe and says, "I can't recall a night when you've remained in your bathrobe so late into the festivities. Are you getting old and impotent?"

"I'm *relaxing*. At least, I was."

"Relaxing. At an orgy. I see." He sips his drink. Adds a bit more from the bottle. "Shall I fetch you a blanket as well? A glass of Metamucil and some cream for your arthritic cock, perhaps? A supple young lass to help you rub it in, sparing you the indignity of—"

"One more word about my cock, and I'll sacrifice *yours* to

Abraxas." I smooth my palms down the lapels. "It's not a bathrobe, you imbecile. It's a smoking jacket."

"You don't smoke."

I flick my wrist in his direction. He ducks just in time to avoid a burst of flame. It hits the oil panting behind him, incinerating it on contact.

"So we're in a mood, then. Excellent." Ignoring the smoldering Picasso and the mood both, Finn hands me the other drink and drops into the adjacent armchair, eyeing me warily.

Dodging his ever-watchful scrutiny, I retrieve my phone and scroll—universal gesture for leave me the fuck alone—but Finn isn't one for subtle cues.

"You know we left the confines of Hell so you could *enjoy* your existence, right?" he says. "Not brood like some emo Hollywood boy-band reject who didn't make it onto the concert poster."

"We left the confines of Hell because my father, in all his infinite wisdom, gave me no other choice, and you were daft enough to follow me. So what does that say about you?"

"I'm trying to look at the bright side."

"One of your less endearing qualities."

"We're in Los Angeles, Dev. Regardless of the circumstances that brought us here... Well, to put it simply, we're already seated at the restaurant. May as well enjoy the buffet."

"I *hate* buffets."

"It's a metaphor, for fuck's sake, and what in the burning lakes are you *looking* at?" He snatches the phone from my hand and inspects the screen. "Witchtok? You're obsessing again, mate."

"I'm *preparing*, and as someone who had front-row seats to the last near-apocalyptic catastrophe brought upon our heads by a witch, I assumed you might be more sympathetic."

"It's been three hundred years. If your witch wanted to track you down again and—"

"*Ex*-witch."

"—attack, she'd have done so long before now."

"You're underestimating the ability of a scorned woman to hold a grudge."

"Pretty sure you were the scorned one there, but who's counting?"

"I was young and foolish." I return my attention to the flames, old wounds slicing my heart anew. "Perhaps I hurt her in some deep, unfathomable way. Something I might have done differently if only I'd—"

"For fuck's sake, Dev. You brought her home to meet Mum and Dad and show her 'round your old stomping grounds, and instead of giving you a blowjob in your childhood bedroom like a *decent* girlfriend, she drugged you, freed the worst demons of the lot, and led them to war against the God of Death—a war that nearly wiped out all of humanity in the crossfire, and *would* have, had your control-freak tyrant of a father not stepped in. And now you're here, scrolling the socials and indulging in a full-on pity party while a *real* party carries on just outside the door, which is a level of meta-fuckery I can't even wrap my mind around. You need help, mate. Years upon years of it, if you ask me, and I'm not sure why you're waiting, considering you can't swing a dead hellhound in this town without hitting a therapist square in the face. Is it an insurance mix-up? Or just you being a complete and utter knob?" He hands back the phone, shaking his head. "My money's on option B. Knob."

"Piss off. Again." Unoriginal, but it's all I've got. The tank, as they say, is running on fumes.

"Witchtok." He sighs as I renew my scrolling. "So this is what it's come to?"

"Have you a better idea?"

"Better than watching humans argue over whose pantheon is the most powerful and who gets to call themselves a hereditary witch. And what is with the obsession with aesthetics? In our day, witches didn't need pretty rocks and incense and T-shirts that say *The Moon Made Me Do It*. They just did it."

"In our day, demons didn't make a habit of provoking the Devil, either. Yet here you are."

"Dress for the job you want, not the one you have." He holds up his glass in cheers, then takes another hefty swig. "Anyway, yes, I *do* have a better idea than doom-scrolling.

Lose the bathrobe and the Broody McBrooderson attitude, and—"

"I'm serious, Finn. I can't afford to be caught unawares again."

"Where is this coming from? Did something happen?"

I recall the feeling from earlier. The cold scrape down my spine, the rattling in my bones. "I just... I felt something. Bit of a tingle."

"A 'damn, these are really good drugs' tingle, or a 'time to see the doc and get a shot before my dick falls off' tingle?"

"Be serious, Finn."

"Personally, I can think of nothing *more* serious than losing one's favorite appendage, but since you're clearly—"

"*Not* in the mood. So if you can't rein it in, then kindly fuck yourself right back out from whence you came. I'm sure there are plenty of vacuous heads in the mansion this evening for you to fill with your special brand of fun."

"Heads, holes. Either way." He turns toward the fire, a blissful moment of silence descending.

The flames crackle and pop, seducing me with their erotic dance. It's at once familiar and strange, like the cover of a song I used to love, the new rendition not quite hitting the mark.

"It's the strangest thing," I admit. "But I just can't shake the feeling that there's... some other place I'm supposed to be."

He glances over at me, his brow furrowing, and for a moment I think he might offer some sage piece of advice.

But then he laughs and says, "Balls deep in one of the twin starlets currently handcuffed to your bed? They had to ditch their publicist in a dangerous high-speed chase through the hills just to make it here tonight, and they're getting impatient waiting for you to notice."

"Like I give a fuck about their publicist."

"Well, that's the whole issue, innit? Apparently, you *did* fuck her, multiple times, in multiple orifices, then ghosted her, despite numerous attempts on her part to arrange for... *ahem*... a re-servicing of the aforementioned orifices. So now she's forbidding her clients from associating with you in *any* manner, public or private. Not that I blame her, what with all the dalliances and disappearing acts you've pulled this month. It reminds me of the summer of 1743—now *that* was a banner year, wasn't it? 1810 is a close second, though..."

Finn rambles on about my indiscretions, a best-of-the-best highlights reel of debauchery that spans the centuries. Normally, I'd sit back and take it all in, pride swelling in my chest, laughing right along with him. *Ah, the good ol' days...*

But that dark, chilly whisper hasn't left me.

"In any case, you shouldn't worry so much." Finn finally pauses for another swig of bourbon. "We're nearly there."

"Nearly where?"

"A few hundred more souls, give or take, and we're back in your father's good graces. Assuming he upholds his end of the bargain, we'll be back in time for the family Christmas party."

I turn to him, my jaw dropping. We've been at the soul-corrupting game for so many centuries, I stopped counting.

After that business with the witch ex-girlfriend, the war, etcetera, my father revoked my title and banished me from Hell, never to return until and unless I completed the task he set forth: Sign over one million souls to eternal demonic servitude, delivering them to Hell upon their deaths.

Well. One million may as well have been a trillion, for all I knew—a cruel, impossible punishment devised by a cruel, impossible father eager to make an example of his errant son.

But now... Is it actually possible we're that close?

"You're certain?" I ask.

"By my last accounting, we only had about five hundred left. And tonight's turnout is stellar."

"One seventy, I believe."

"Precisely." Finn downs the last of his bourbon and shrugs. "At this rate, we could wrap it all up with just a few more parties."

"You really believe that?"

"Put your back into it, mate. Los Angeles, remember? It's precisely why we chose the place. Not exactly a challenge."

I pinch the bridge of my nose and sigh. "Please don't make the fish in a barrel analogy again, Finn. For the love of all that's unholy, don't—"

"Highly immoral fish in a rotten barrel of filth that's *long* overdue for a good scouring. Before you start feeling guilty about it."

"How do you sleep at night?"

"Preferably between two buxom beauty influencers, three on a good night." He grabs one of the couch pillows and mimics some sort of lewd... well, to be perfectly honest, I can't quite tell if he's spanking it or dancing with it or possibly experiencing a medical emergency, but his antics pry a laugh out of me nevertheless.

Ah, Finn. There's no one like my best mate to lift my spirits during the dark times.

Grateful for the levity, I head to the bar to fix us fresh drinks, thinking I might hunt down those starlets after all.

But then, just as I'm plucking an ice cube from the bucket and imagining my bedsheets stained with burgundy lipstick, I feel it again.

That dark whisper of magic kissing its way down my neck, settling right between my shoulder blades.

And this time, it doesn't relent.

"Finn?" I whisper, but he's far too enamored of his own performance to notice the subtle shift in the air. The taste of it.

Witchcraft.

I suck in a painful breath. The icy feeling intensifies, gripping my heart in its cruel fist.

"Finn?" I try again, barely getting the word out as the

magic fully takes hold. The glass slips from my hand, shatters. The pain twists me in half. "We've... got a serious... problem..."

The fire surges brightly, flames dancing before my eyes.

It's the very last thing I see before my world goes black.

CHAPTER FIVE

VIOLET

Did I say one more drink? I meant two. Three *tops*.

Maybe it was four? I lost count after my sisters headed out. See, this is what happens when I'm left under the sole supervision of two mischievous cats, a magical deck of Tarot cards that refuse to respect personal boundaries, and the nonstop chatter of my own mind.

"To *excellent* company," I slur, raising my drink, and I swear the Devil winks at me.

"I'm not talking to *you*." Placing the mug on top of his smug face, I pick up the Star card and gaze into her eyes, letting her soothing energy wrap around me like a hug.

Her earlier message echoes.

If you don't believe in yourself, Violet Pepperdine, how can anyone else?

Girl has a point. And I *do* believe in myself. And the café. And I'm a witch, for goddess' sake, and a damn good one at that. Just because I won't use magic to bring a bad-luck plague raining down on *Peen* Beans doesn't mean there isn't *some* kind of spell that can help me. Right?

The Star's endless well of hope propels me off the couch and straight over to my wall of ingredients. It's all teas and powders, leaves and flowers, moon water and crystal essences, but there's a tall shelf on the right where I keep some of my favorite witchy books and, locked in a drawer beneath them, my laptop.

I boot up the computer and launch the massive spreadsheet that hosts my personal Book of Shadows—a project I've been working on for years, transcribing my favorite rituals and techniques into digital format. It's got everything from my own recipes and experiments to stuff I've come across in ancient witchcraft texts, tips from my sisters and aunts, and random things I've read online and want to try.

But there's one book I've never transcribed. One collection of spells and advice I never wanted to change from its original form.

Gigi's Book of Shadows.

It sits in the center of the shelf, black leather spine embossed with silver moons, cracked with age and love. I trail my fingers down the worn leather, and its magic pulses, a warmth spreading from my fingertips and up my arm, straight to my heart.

Gigi gifted this book to me upon her death, hoping I'd continue to learn from her long after she passed through the veil. I've spent more time poring over the handwritten pages than I can count, absorbing as much as I can, carrying on her legacy. Every time I open the book, I feel her with me, a guiding spirit who's never once doubted me.

But using her magic to get myself out of debt feels different from all that. Like a cheat, somehow. Wrong.

No. Not *wrong*, I realize as the heat chews through my stomach. *Shameful*. Like she might sense my reasons for using it and know that I just couldn't hack it. Not even after everything she taught me. Everything I promised her.

Leaving her book in place, I select a few others instead, and the memory of her smile dims, the sharp edges of grief worn smooth by the passage of time and the alcohol both.

Magical elixirs, in their own way.

Anyway, I don't need Gigi's spells for this. I've got plenty of my own. I just need to find the right one.

Setting the magical mood, I put on some Stevie Nicks, light a black pillar candle, and dig out some clear quartz crystals to amplify my spellwork.

"There has to be something here." I flip through one of my handwritten notebooks, noting a few potential ideas. From between its yellowing pages, a Tarot card slips free.

Yeah. Him again.

"You must be *really* into me." I set aside the book and pluck the Devil from the countertop. "You can't even stay away for more than five minutes."

Ignoring the tingling heat in my fingertips, which is

almost definitely probably *very* likely the alcohol, I prop the card against the black candle and get back to my spreadsheets. Goddess, these spells are a mess. I know I don't use them much, but still. That's no excuse for poor organization. Digital files are just as important as paper ones, and they deserve the same level of care and attention as the most delicate pages in an ancient grimoire.

Maybe that's why my life is in a shambles. The Universe knows I'm unfit for adulting. And budgeting. And magicking. Holding my liquor should probably go on that list too, but that's another spreadsheet for another day.

"Stay focused and keep it simple," I remind my Virgo brain, Chief Executive Overcomplicater. "Right, boys?"

Grumpy and Sunshine leap up onto the counter, pawing and nosing at the laptop—Mama's little helpers.

"Spell to Unlock Your Heart's Desire? Good call, Sunshine. Definitely sounds promising." I copy it into a new spreadsheet—the keepers file. "Or maybe this one—Go Forth and Prosper. If I combine that with a Road Opening spell to increase opportunities and—ooh, here we go. Abundantly Yours. Wait, this one has potential too—Bound and Determined. I'm determined, right Grumpy?"

The tabby, currently licking his privates, ignores me.

No judgments here, dude. Would if I could.

By the time I finish sorting and organizing, I'm down to seven potential spells. There's a lot of overlap, so I cut and paste a few sections from each into a new spreadsheet, filtering first by desired outcome, then by ingredient. But it's still too clunky to use, especially in my current somewhat inebriated state.

"Pivot table to the rescue." I get to work populating the table, arranging everything into rows and columns, muttering pieces of the spells as I'm copying them over.

For every lock, there is a key...

Copy, paste.

The heart's true desire lies hidden within...

The candle flame flickers. Yes! I'm *so* on the right track.

The road ahead is open, opportunity awaits...

Another flicker. My heart skips, excitement welling inside.

Powerful allies, hidden and true...

Bring it on!

Magic and will, returned by three...

This is going to be epic!

And thus we are bound, so mote it be...

With a sharp hiss, Sunshine darts across the counter. I look up from the laptop just in time to see the candle topple, black wax spilling, the Devil card caught in the crossfire. I reach for the card, but before I can save it, it ignites in a burst of blue flame so bright it hurts to look at.

The flame fizzles out quickly. When my vision finally returns to normal, I realize the Devil is gone. The cats are gone, too. Stevie has stopped singing. The fire in the hearth is nothing but embers.

Something is very, very wrong.

"Sunshine?" I whisper, goosebumps prickling my arms. "Grumpy-butt?"

No response. No sound at all but for the pounding of my own heart.

I've barely taken my next breath when a blast of powerful magic whisks through the room, surrounding me in a smoky tempest that claws at my hair and steals my breath. Without another thought, I dive beneath the counter and cover my head.

By the time the magical storm passes and the strange, sparkly blue smoke dissipates, I'm no longer alone.

There, in the center of the café, a man rises from the glittering darkness like a legendary monster from the mists of creation. Horns protrude from a head of dark, silky-looking hair, his eyes glowing red, broad shoulders pulling at the fabric of a...

Wait. Is that a bathrobe? And... some kind of... leather?

All at once, recognition hits. My heart drops right into my stomach.

"Show yourself, dark sorceress!" the Devil bellows, his commanding British tone leaving no room for argument. "And prepare to meet your end."

CHAPTER SIX

DEVLIN

Fire and brimstone. Smoke and ash. My body disintegrates as the universe collapses and reforms, scattering the dust of my bones through time and space and realms unending, through the dawn of demonkind and the end of the human age, then back again, a kaleidoscope of light and dark, life and death, beginnings and endings and beginnings anew, and—

Merciful Hell, I need to lay off the hard drugs.

Where in the seventy-eight lower regions of Hades am I?

I take a whiff, trying to get my bearings. The scent of magic is everywhere, like burned cotton candy laced with expensive bourbon. Not altogether unpleasant, but I learned long ago not to trust the sweet seductions of witchcraft.

Bones thankfully intact, the ground solid beneath me once more, I gingerly rise to my full height. A thick haze of blue smoke slowly dissipates, revealing some sort of... restaurant?

Velvet couches in purple and red, the spent embers of a recent fire in the hearth. Framed artwork covers nearly every wall—moon phases here, diagrams of plants over there, far too many paintings of small woodland animals sipping from fancy teacups.

Not your typical evil-witch-from-the-primordial-swamp aesthetic, I'll give you that. But I won't be fooled again. The dark ones can hide amongst the trappings of humdrum human lives until the end of time, but the Devil waits for no enemy.

"Show yourself, dark sorceress!" I command. "And prepare to meet your end."

A yowling screech and a bright orange and black blur from the shadows is my only answer, and I brace myself for the onslaught, calling upon my last reserves of hellfire. The flame grows bright between my palms, eager to cut through anyone who dare threaten me.

But this is no witch attack. It's... cats.

Two of them. One orange, one black. Both circling me like predators, hissing but wisely keeping their distance.

I hiss right back at them, making their fur stand on end.

"Grumpy, no!" A battle cry cuts through the darkness, soft but mighty, definitely female, followed by a stumble and the felling of several countertop stools. "Damn it," the female mutters. Then, "Run, boys! Run! Save yourselves!"

I follow the sound and the fury to its source. There, tumbling out from behind the fallen stools—a tiny sprite of a girl dressed in denim overalls and a black shirt covered in red-and-white polka-dotted mushrooms. From beneath a cloud of auburn curls that may have once been a bun and a pair of glasses too large for her delicate face, she blinks up at me, blue eyes wide and terrified. Magic emanates from her in faint shimmery waves.

Damn it.

Another witch, then. Likely an apprentice. Clearly not a professional by any stretch.

"P-please don't hurt my familiars," she stammers, crouching down to gather the offending beasts into her arms.

"Where *is* she?" I cross the distance between us in three quick steps, my shadow falling across her face. "Answer me!"

The two feral felines bolt, vanishing into the darkness behind the counter. Still crouched on the floor, the sprite says nothing. Just trembles, those big blue eyes peering up at me, lip quivering.

Well. The delicate flower act won't fly with me. I need answers. *Now.*

I hook my fingers through her overall straps and haul her up, setting her on her feet. She's even smaller than I presumed, the top of her head just barely grazing my collarbone, her narrow shoulders rounding as she hugs herself to fight off a shiver.

My heart gives an unexpected thud, my blood roaring with a fierce and inexplicable need to... protect her?

Damn it. Again.

More witchcraft, no doubt. How these women live with themselves is beyond me. Bloody unconscionable.

"Speak!" I command.

"We're... we're closed," she squeaks out, taking a step backward, then another, tilting her head back so she can meet my eyes.

"Then *un*-close and give me what I need." I close in on her once more. "Or suffer the consequences."

"I... I can't. Everything's already shut down for the night."

"I beg your pardon?"

"You're welcome to come back tomorrow. We open at seven. I can help you then." She takes another step backward, gracelessly tripping over the fallen stools. I dart forward and scoop her into my arms right before she lands and breaks something vital.

She blinks up at me, bewildered, the glasses askew, her heart jackhammering so hard I can feel it. That damnable need to protect her rises anew.

Shaking my head to rid myself of her annoying magic, I give her my most intimidating glare. Exhale loudly through my nose. Set her back on her feet. "Try. *Again.*"

She straightens her glasses and offers what's probably supposed to be an accommodating smile, but looks more like the face you make when you've got a terrible cramp in a very sensitive place. "I suppose I can put the kettle back on, fix you up a little something? Tea, or perhaps a magic mojito lemonito, if you'd like?" She gestures toward a glass pitcher of orange-yellow slush abandoned on the counter, half empty. "Though I should warn you, it's a *lot* stronger than it—"

"What I'd *like* is for you to stop babbling and answer my question before I lose my temper and blast this entire town to Hell."

"No! No blasting. I'll answer your question. Any question. I'm just... what was it, again? The question?"

For fuck's sake. "Where *is* she?!"

"Where is *who*?"

"The evil witch queen who summoned me!"

"Evil witch queen? I... I'm certain I don't know who you're talking about."

"And I'm certain you *do*." Ignoring her baffled expression, I step around her and peek behind the counter—empty. I head into the kitchen and scan the space—a couple of small ovens and a pantry, dried herbs hanging in bundles over a stainless-steel counter, teakettles on every blasted burner, an orange tail peeking out from behind a trash bin.

But no sign of the ancient witch.

"I know she's in here somewhere, skulking about." I lift the lid on the closest teakettle—a ceramic floral piece painted with roses and peonies—and peek inside. Empty. "Very likely biding her time until she can catch me unawares, but that is *not* going to happen tonight, I assure you."

"I think you've got the wrong café." Little Miss Mushroom Shirt is right on my heels, removing the teakettle lid from my grasp and setting it back in its proper place. "Or maybe the wrong witch?"

I lean in close, the air shimmering between us. Her wild curls seem to be reaching out for the lingering magic, like flowering vines longing for the sun.

"Are you asking me," I say, ignoring the sudden urge to twine my fingers into that silky mess of auburn curls, "or telling me?"

"I don't... know?"

"For fuck's sake. You're a witch, are you not?"

"What?" she laughs, as if my asking is the most preposterous thing that's happened tonight. "No!"

I take a deep whiff of her scent. "I can smell the magic on you, woman."

"You can? Right. Of course you can. Okay, *fine*. Yes, I'm a witch. Technically. But not, like, a dark sorceress or evil queen or whatever. I'm just... just a tea witch. An empathic one, actually, and I'm sensing you are *very* angry right now, which I understand, because I've obviously interrupted your evening of..." She trails off, her gaze roaming the length of my smoking jacket, all the way down to my bare feet, then back up. "Something... super important. Obviously."

"*Obviously.*"

"But maybe we should all just take a few cleansing breaths..." She nods and inhales deeply, exhales, gestures at me, does it again, just in case I'm unclear on the concept of breathing. "See? Better already. We'll just calm down and talk this out like—"

"Calm down? A summoning is not a thing to be taken lightly *or* calmly. In fact, it's forbidden dark magic, last I checked, punishable by... by..." A new scent wafts into the space, and I take another whiff, catching the sharp remnants of...

Oh, you have got *to be kidding me.*

"Good goddess, woman. You're drunk."

"No lies detected." Another nervous giggle bubbles out of her, then quickly turns into a hiccup.

"Excuse me?"

"I know! I didn't didn't mean to drink so much, or to drunk-dial you—sorry, drunk-*summon* you. But clearly something went awry tonight—a long line of somethings, actually—and I was hoping it would all just blow over, but then you stood up out of the magical darkness like, *rawr*, I'm the Devil, and—"

"*You* summoned me?"

A nod. Another hiccup. A crimson blush staining her cheeks.

I take in the sight of her again, the mushrooms dotting the shirt, the wild knot of hair making *her* look a bit like a mushroom too, sprouting up out of the ground as if we're trapped in some sort of fairytale forest. It would all be quite whimsical and adorable, if I were in the mood for whimsy and adoration.

"That's simply not possible," I say.

"And yet, here you are. Summoned." She spreads her hands before me and shrugs. Followed by another hiccup. "By me."

"Only the most powerful witches can summon me. *Ancient* witches well-heeled in the dark arts. Which you are *clearly* not."

And if I don't find the witch who is responsible for this, she's certain to track me down and—

"Hate to rain on your know-it-all parade, sir, but I'm the only witch here (hiccup). So unless your all-powerful ancient well-heeled dark arts witch-person has a *serious* GPS problem (hiccup), this disaster is all mine."

The inebriated little witch has the nerve to cross her arms and glare at me. Glare! As if *I'm* the wrongdoer here.

Unbelievable.

And yet... I *do* believe her. Earnestness shines through every fiber of her tiny being. And that scent—the sugar, the bourbon—it's definitely her magic, no trace of anyone else's.

I cast another glance around the café. Candle wax spilled

across the countertop, a black scorch mark suggesting fire magic gone awry. A stack of witchcraft books teetering beside a laptop. The aforementioned half-spent pitcher of something alcoholic.

Her story checks out.

Ah, well. A break from the routine, I suppose, and no head-bashing required.

Alas, duty calls.

"Well then." I flash a no-hard-feelings grin. "As lovely as it was to meet you—against my will and all the laws of witchcraft and sorcery, ancient and new and yet to be invented—I think it's time we say goodnight. Farewell, tiny drunk one, and best of luck with your future spell-casting."

She blows a few curls out of her eyes and offers a sad wave. Again, something inside my chest twinges.

Indigestion. Obviously. Mental note to speak to my chef about preparing a milder sauce for Taco Tuesdays.

"Well?" I demand. "What are you waiting for?"

"Um... for you to... leave?"

"Hellfire help me. You really *are* out of your league, aren't you?" Crouching down so we're eye to eye, I place my hands on her shoulders and speak slowly and clearly. "When a spellcaster summons the Devil, that spellcaster must *un*-cast in order to set him free."

"Un-cast?"

"Release me from the spell. Sooner rather than later, if

you don't mind. There's still a chance I might make my appointment with the twins."

"What twins?"

"Neither here nor there. The un-casting, if you please."

She nods once, face screwing into a look of pure determination that would put even the most brutal demons in Hell to shame, and sweeps her hands toward me several times. "Be gone, evil nightmare. Be gone!"

"What in the name of... Are you *shooing* me?"

"I'm... trying to banish you?"

"Try harder, because it's not working."

"Which means none of this is real. That's the obvious answer."

"It most certainly *is* real."

"Nope. I'm dreaming. Nightmaring."

"You're really not."

"I just need to wake up and this will all be over." She presses her fingertips to her temples and closes her eyes, muttering to herself a string of inane promises about never drinking again, only tea and water, straight and narrow from here on out, she'll even come clean about the money, whatever the bleeding skies any of it means, if only—if *only!*—the goddess will put an end to this crazy nightmare.

I let her go on about it, the temple-rubbing, the babbling and praying, the bargaining, the whole skit-and-skedoodle.

When she finally opens her eyes again, she has the audacity to look annoyed that I'm still here.

"You're no more dreaming than I," I tell her, Bearer of Bad News being one of my many titles.

"How do you know? Maybe this is *your* nightmare, and I'm trapped."

"Trust me, I've had some fucked-up nocturnal encounters, typically under the influence, and this tête-à-tête blows them all out of the wacky waters." I crowd into her space again, backing her against the wall and caging her in with my arms. "You and I have a serious problem, *witch*, and if you value your soul, I suggest you figure out how to fix it."

"I... I don't know how to fix it. I'm not even sure how it happened."

A frisson of panic sparks to life in my chest, quickly giving way to fury. "Do you have *any* idea who you're dealing with?"

"*You*," comes the accusatory response, but it's not from my little mushroom, who's currently staring up at me with her very big, very blue eyes.

"Olivy!" she breathes more than speaks, then ducks out from under my arms in a mad dash for the doorway, where a black-haired witch clad in a deep indigo cape is unabashedly staring at me.

Recognition is clear in her sharp gaze.

Keeping her eyes locked on mine, she lowers her hood and says to the other one, "Are you all right? I was out for my midnight walk and heard shouting."

"I... I sort of..." The little witch turns to me, then back to this Olivy woman.

"Go on." I cross my arms over my chest. "Tell her how we met, *Mushroom*."

"He... Well... I was just sort of looking through my spells, and—"

"Drunk," I add.

"A little drunk, yes. And then there was a flash and some fire and a lot of smoke, and when I looked up again, there he was."

Olivy gasps, her eyes narrowing on me as though she's just caught the scent of her prey and can't wait to pounce. "Violet *summoned* you?"

"No, I just happened to get a midnight hankering for tea and decided to pop on over to the land of pumpkin spice, clear across the country, dressed in arseless leather chaps and a satin smoking jacket and for the love of *Hell*, isn't it obvious? Yes, she summoned me. And while we're on that subject..." I turn my attention back to the spell caster. "Any particular reason, or just looking for some late-night company?"

"I didn't mean to!" Exasperation darkens her cheeks. "That's what I'm trying to tell you! It was an accident!"

"Seriously?" the other woman says. "Violet. How can you summon the Devil by accident? It isn't the sort of thing that just *happens*."

"*Thank* you." I grab the pitcher of yellow-orange slush

she offered earlier. Looks terrible but smells enough like alcohol to get a pass. Desperate times, etcetera. "I'm glad *one* of you was paying attention at witch school."

"I don't know what you want me to say," Violet says, "because it *did* just happen."

"Do you know how much magic a *regular* demonic summoning requires? And this is the Devil. The Devil!" Olivy again. Hand on hip, dark eyes probing. Kind of creepy, if you ask me. Not someone you'd be keen to meet in the proverbial dark alley. "Not to mention a willingness to break every rule of witchcraft in existence and risk your own life in the process. What the *serious* fuck, Vi?"

"Fair question." I take a swig of the booze. Terrible, as expected, but strong. Into the win column it goes. "What in the *very* serious fuck indeed."

"I can't explain it!" she erupts, all fire and brimstone and wild curls. "You were supposed to be a pivot table!"

"A *pivot* table?" I try to recall the term. Not sure I've heard it before, but it sounds a bit like... "Oh! Is that a sexual device? The one with the leather straps and all the different notches for the—"

"It's a spreadsheet function! *Spreadsheets*! My love language! How could I screw this up?"

"Spreadsheets?" Olivy grabs what I assume is the offending laptop, her eyes scanning the screen.

"This is all wrong," Violet says, pacing. "Goddess, I *knew* I shouldn't have had all those lemonitos. One minute I'm enjoying the citrusy-minty buzz, scrolling through my old digital spellbooks, fixing typos, updating ingredients with appropriate substitutions, highlighting rows and columns for future reference, organizing my pivot table, thinking that maybe—just *maybe*—my life isn't such a shitshow after all."

"Take a breather, Vi," Olivy says. "I just need to get a better look at this spreadsheet mess and—"

"There I am, getting all high on life like maybe there's actually some teeny, tiny shred of hope left to cling to," Violet continues, ignoring her sister—wholly unaware of her sister, actually—"because the universe has my back and I've got magic in my blood, damn it, and if I put all these spells into a pivot table, I can sort and export and find *precisely* what I need, right? Because that's how pivot tables work, *right*?"

Blank stare. It's all I've got. "Is this a trick question, or—"

"But is that what happened? Is it? No, of course not! Because one minute I'm sorting and highlighting, happily pivoting, and all of a sudden, a cat and a flash and a fire and bim-bam-*boom*, the Devil. Really, Universe? The freaking Devil? The Aunts are going to murder me, and poor Gigi's probably rolling over in her grave to make room for my soon-to-be-murdered corpse, but hey... bright side?" She whirls around to face me again, her eyes wild, more curls springing loose from the bun, a pint-sized Medusa on a rampage. "If I'm dead, at least I won't have to deal with *you*."

I raise a single eyebrow.

Deal with me? As if *I'm* the reason for this catastrophe? Oh, I think not.

I set down my rum slushy. Roll up my satin sleeves (not as easy as it looks). The gloves are officially off.

My skin turns hot, horns lengthening and twisting outward from my skull, shoulders broadening, a glimpse of my true form flashing beneath the civilized facade. *This* is the real me. The face of death I show my corrupted souls upon their very last breath, the precise moment they realize just how much they've signed away.

Time to show this troublemaker exactly *who she's dealing with now...*

"Well, that depends, *witch*." I take a step closer and grin down at her, feeling every bit the all-powerful monster the legends would have you believe. "Is your soul *wholly* untarnished? Nary a sin nor errant thought in that pretty little head? No lies or secrets, no shame or guilt, no past transgressions? *Or...*" I grip her quavering chin between my thumb and index finger, tilting her face up toward me, her eyes so wide with fright I can see my reflection in them—glowing red eyes, gnarled black horns, teeth as sharp as razor wire. "Might there be a special place in my domain reserved *just* for you?"

Her face pales enough that I *almost* feel guilty for intimidating her. Almost.

"Oh, goddess," she whispers. "Oh goddess oh goddess oh—"

I press a finger to her lips. "Let's not summon another all-powerful being to this soirée, shall we?"

"No, we shall not. Won't not. Definitely not. Um. Olivy?" Darting away from me, she joins her sister at the laptop. "Do you have any valerian root on you? I ran out and my head is killing me."

"Go sniff some lavender and calm your perky tits." The dark witch cracks her knuckles and starts typing, eyes never leaving the screen. "You too, Satan."

"I prefer you not use that term, if you don't mind."

"I don't *care*, does that count? Anyway, no use getting your Devil-drawers in a bunch until we know exactly what we're dealing with and—oh, wait. Oh *no*..."

Fingers pause abruptly over the keys.

Gasps are gasped.

Curses are cursed.

"Is this the spell you cast?" Olivy asks, and the mushroom nods. "For the love of the goddess, Vi. You're lucky the magical kickback didn't disintegrate you."

"Just tell me it's reversible," Violet says. "Please, please, *please* tell me the summoning spell is reversible."

"It's not your run-of-the-mill summoning spell, guys."

I meet the woman's eyes across the glow of the laptop screen, my last hopes for an easy fix evaporating. "On a scale of one to ten, just how fucked am I?"

"That depends." She snaps the laptop closed. Folds her

hands on top of it. Ponders. "Is one the *most* fucked or the least?"

"One is the low end of the spectrum. Best possible outcome."

"In that case, you're definitely a one... *million*." The dark witch smirks at me as if this is the highlight of her week. "Completely, utterly, upside-down and sideways fucked with a broomstick, nary a bottle of lube in sight."

CHAPTER SEVEN

VIOLET

"Here's what we know," Olivy says. "You summoned the Devil with some kind of bidding spell, but there's also—"

"Now that we've got that sorted..." The Devil, horns intact but handsome human face back online, offers us an award-winning smile—probably the same one that tricks helpless victims into signing over their souls. "Kindly reverse it so I can *bid* you adieu."

"I wish I could," Olivy says, "but this isn't *just* a bidding spell. That's what I'm saying. There's also a binding component, among other things."

"How is this even possible?" I ask. "I didn't perform any spells. Not really."

My sister's eyes narrow. "Define 'not really.'"

"I mean, I said a few lines as I was copying them over, and then the Devil card from Gigi's Tarot deck sort of...

caught on fire? When Sunshine knocked over the candle? But I wasn't speaking a full *binding* spell. I wouldn't even know where to start."

"It's not just the words, Vi. It's the intent behind them. The spell itself, the Tarot cards, the candle... all that stuff just amplified your true intention. Which is why you... Oh, shit. *Amplified*." Her eyes widen with some new revelation. "Yep, you've got an amplifier component in here as well, and the quartz crystals called in that magic like a moth to the flame."

The Devil rubs one of his horns. "The moth in this scenario being...?"

Olivy glares. "The left one's looking a little droopy, Horns. You might want to get that straightened out."

"It's straight enough to impale you, should the mood strike. Anyway, if you've got all the spells and components, isn't that enough to create a counter-spell?"

"A spell is much more than the sum of its components." Olivy shakes her head, her dark hair almost blue in the dim space. "Tell you the truth, I don't think I could recreate this spell if my afterlife depended on it."

The Devil puffs out his chest, his eyes glowing red again, lip curling into a terrifying sneer. "And what if it *does* depend on it, witch?"

"Really? We're measuring dicks now?" Olivy crosses her arms and glares at him with a single raised eyebrow, a look half the men in this town have come to fear. "Do you honestly think there's anything in this world I want *more* than to send you straight back to the bowels of Hell from whence you came?"

"I didn't come here from Hell. I came here from Los Angeles, where I was enjoying an intimate gathering of friends in my own home when I was snatched away without warning and—"

"And *what*?" she demands, champion of witches great and small, my absolute hero, refusing to give an inch when the Devil wants to take a hundred miles.

Wisely, he backs off.

Score one for the witches.

Brushing the non-existent lint from his bathrobe cuffs, looking far more elegant than any Devil has the right to, he retracts the horns and says calmly, "I'm merely expressing my desire to bring this evening to a close post-haste so we can all get back to our regular lives. *Separate* regular lives."

"And I'm merely expressing that you're about to be disappointed." Olivy returns to the laptop. "First of all? I've never even *seen* a spell like this, Vi. It's like you combined parts of three or four different rituals and traditions, ancient and modern and some really experimental stuff all mixed in." She continues tabbing through my files. "*Damn*, girl. This is some powerful magic. How long have you been sitting on this stuff?"

"Um... Forever? It's just bits and bobs I've collected over the years. Some of it I use for teas and tinctures. Some I've just been... saving for a rainy day."

A flash of lightning illuminates the space, and I swear I see a chill run through the man, head to toe. But when I meet his eyes, he looks away.

Olivy snaps her fingers, bringing the hearth fire back to life. The room warms considerably.

"So what, precisely, are we dealing with here?" the Devil asks. "I've been summoned, fine. With a possible binding component. But to what end?"

"From what I can piece together, you two are magically bound to each other until—oh, this is good. So fucking good." Olivy grins, practically bouncing. "Until such a time when the truest desire of the witch's heart is unlocked by an unlikely ally."

"Me, being the ally?" he asks, and Olivy nods. Then their two heads swivel toward me, awaiting the answer to the final unspoken question in this night of epic magical fuckery.

Just what *is* my heart's truest desire?

I could tell them I'm looking for a soulmate or for world peace or for someone to fix the potholes on Birchwood Lane.

But the magic would know. It always knows.

"Swear you won't tell the sisters," I say. "Or the Aunts. Or the Peen Beans minions or anyone in Wayward Bay, magical or mundane, or—"

"Violet," Olivy says, "what in the goddess's wine hole is going *on* with you?"

"Swear it!"

She rolls her eyes, then grabs a knife from under the counter and slices her palm, pressing the bloodied hand to her chest. "I swear by the blood upon my heart, what you say tonight stays between us."

Now it's my turn to roll my eyes. "Seriously? Why are you like this?"

"Are all the witches in this town so unstable?" the Devil wants to know.

"Answer the question, Vi."

"His or yours?"

Olivy glares again. She's really got it down to a science.

"Money," I whisper, shame stealing my voice. "My truest desire is a hundred thousand dollars to get myself back in the black, in thirty days, or Kettle and Cauldron is done."

I dig out the stupid letter from behind the aprons and hand it over.

Olivy's face falls as she reads it. "Is this accurate?"

"Yep. Plus the credit card debt and loan stuff and taxes and... yeah. Might as well be ten million."

"Oh, honey." Olivy pulls me into an uncharacteristic hug, which only underscores the severity here. Olivy is *not* a hugger—not unless she needs your blood or hair for a curse. "Why didn't you say something sooner?"

"Shame?" I say. "Fear? Stubbornness? Take your pick."

"But you know we'll help you figure something out. You don't even have to ask."

"I *can't* ask, Ols. I won't. And you can't say a word."

"But this is—"

"You made a blood oath!"

She lifts her hands in surrender, the cut still gleaming with blood. "My lips are sealed. But for the record, I don't like it."

"Noted."

"So this whole magical mishap is about money?" The Devil scoffs. "You're a witch. A powerful one, apparently, despite all appearances to the contrary. Why don't you just..." He makes a wand-waving gesture, as if I can zap away my problems with a flick of the wrist and a "so mote it be."

"That's not how magic works," I say. "We can't create things out of thin air."

"You conjured me out of thin air, did you not?"

"I *transferred* you here from Los Angeles, where you already existed."

"So?"

"It's the same principle. If I magic up a pile of money, it has to already exist somewhere else, which means my spell would be taking that money from another person's possession and transferring it here, into mine."

"I'm... not seeing the issue."

"It's stealing!"

"Ah." He drops onto the purple couch, feet propped up

on the coffee table, hands behind his head like, just make yourself at home, Devil man. "So your problem isn't magic. It's morals."

I smack his feet off the table. "Morals are only a problem for people who don't have them."

"For people who don't have *yours*, you mean."

I swear Olivy snickers. Apparently, we're top-notch entertainment tonight.

"If you're so smart and upstanding and moral," I huff, "why don't *you* give me the money and be done with it?"

"Firstly, I never said I was any of those things. Secondly, I don't have a dime to my name."

"Right. Even your bathrobe looks expensive."

"Smoking jacket. And it *was* expensive."

"How did you pay for it if you're so broke?"

He flashes the textbook definition of a devilish grin, making my insides all hot and gooey. "I don't trade in human currency, witch. Never have. The Devil trades in favors. So, in a very roundabout sort of way, yes, I suppose I *can* solve your problem. The question is—what are you willing to give me in return?"

"Look around. Unless you want some tea and scones, I'm drawing a blank."

"Don't sell yourself short, Mushroom. Even a hot-mess witch such as yourself has something to bargain with."

"Quit instigating her," Olivy snaps. "We all know the price for a Devil's bargain, and my sister is *not* paying it."

"You've summoned me to help you," he says, as if he's trying to reason with a small child throwing a tantrum. "Ergo, you must allow me to do just that. Using my influence is the shortest distance between two points—A, the witch losing her beloved shop, and B, the witch saving it."

"Maybe he's got a point, Olivy."

"He doesn't. Trust me." She brings the laptop over and sits on the red couch across from him. "Anyway, the spell won't allow it. This has to be a genuine, no-shortcuts effort to unlock her heart's desire. Any attempts to circumvent it with magic or manipulation will only make things worse. For both of you."

I drop onto the couch next to him, head in my hands. "As if anything could make this night any worse."

"Is that a dare?" he asks. "I'll give it my best shot, though I'm not sure I can compete with this grade-A cockup. Is there any more rum slushy? The night is only getting longer, and I'm not interested in being sober for it."

"No one cares what you're interested in," I snap.

Olivy snickers again. "Let the record reflect that I called it first, but you two are totally gonna bone. As for the parameters of the spell, there's—"

"You are *literally* the worst," I say. "You know that?"

"I'm not the one who summoned the hellspawn."

"Another point to the dark and creepy one," says the hellspawn. "And excuse me—Hell *King*, if you please."

"If you think I'm calling you highness," I grumble, "you're about to be disappointed again."

"Says the woman who needs my help cleaning up her terrible credit. Which, by the way, I haven't even agreed to yet."

"You don't have a choice," Olivy says.

"The Devil always has a choice," he huffs. "The Devil *makes* the choices."

"The Devil overmuch talks in the third person," Olivy says, "but if he refuses to carry out the spell, then he'll be stuck in Wayward Bay for the rest of his life. Which won't be that long, since he'll also become a mortal and *die*, so we've got that to look forward to."

"Olivy!" I gasp, guilt blazing through my gut.

She rolls her eyes. "Fine. I added in the dying part to drive the point home. But the stuck in WB as a mortal guy part is true. Which means he *will* die. Eventually."

"A *mortal*? In *this* town?" He scowls, pressing a hand to his heart. "A fate worse than death. You probably don't even have a proper airport."

"There's a bus depot," I add helpfully.

"Oh for fuck's... *No*. This won't do. If you and I are to be handcuffed together—not in the fun way, wasted opportunity if ever there was one—then you're just going to have to come home with me."

"Home, as in..." I swallow hard. "Hell?"

"Worse than that, I'm afraid." He grins again, cold and

calculating, far too tempting, reminding me of his namesake Tarot card. "California."

"Hate to burst your bubble again," Olivy chimes in, even though the smile twitching at the corner of her mouth tells me she's really enjoying all this bubble-bursting, "but you two can't leave the Bay. Not until the task is complete and the spell is broken."

"Guess again, Creepy. You say we're bound? Fine. We're bound. To each *other*. That doesn't mean we're stuck here with *you*." The Devil grabs my hand and gets to his feet, hauling me up with him. Then he lifts his other arm, drawing a complicated sigil in the air. Magic sparks faintly, but nothing happens.

He tries two more times. Whatever he's attempting, it doesn't seem to be catching.

"Can't get it up, hellspawn?" Olivy asks. "Pretty sure they make a pill for that."

"Pretty sure I *invented* that pill." He drops my hand and tries again, double-fisting it this time. Still, no dice. "Why isn't my portal magic working? My intention is to bring her with me. Still bound, still enlisted in Operation Heart's Desire. It shouldn't matter where the desire-unlocking happens."

Olivy sighs. "One more time for the folks in the back. The spell Violet cast was an insanely powerful one. It summoned you to Wayward Bay, bound you to her, and wrapped it all up with a wishes-really-do-come-true bow.

The wish being her desire to wipe out her debt and save Kettle and Cauldron, which is also the location where the binding spell was cast. So until that happens, I'm afraid you two crazy kids are stuck. Here. Together." She grins at him, her eyes shining. "Welcome to Wayward Bay, Horns. Try not to blow anything up while you're here."

CHAPTER EIGHT

DEVLIN

I storm out the café door and onto the rain-slicked sidewalk, where—like a swift kick to the nether regions—I'm immediately confronted by the painful reality of my situation.

A three-part awakening, if you will.

One, I have no cell phone. Must've dropped it when the witch zapped me from my study.

Two, I have no pants, and it's bloody cold here, the rain and late hour not helping in that department.

Three, perhaps most tragic of all, this charming greeting card of a town has recently suffered a senseless attack from a roving band of Fall Vibes vigilantes, who've vomited upon every storefront and residential window a nauseating mix of twinkle lights, faux autumn leaves, and your basic Spooky Halloween Starter pack of rubber bats, plastic spiders, and tissue-paper ghosts.

Superb. Not only am I bound to the most annoying witch this side of the veil, but I'm stuck in Pumpkinville.

"Wait up!" Mushroom follows me outside, leaving ol' Caped and Creepy behind, probably to whip up a batch of poison apples for the local schoolchildren. How these two are sisters is a mystery—one I have no interest in solving.

Right now, my only interest lies in procuring copious amounts of alcohol and a suitable pair of pants. Prime directive.

Most of the shops look buttoned up for the night, but I spy a golden light shining like a beacon a couple of blocks down and head off in that direction. Hope springs fucking eternal.

My newly acquired shadow is right on my heels. "Where are you going?"

"To find a purveyor of wine and spirits that caters to someone *other* than a coven of barely legal sorority sisters who should *never* be allowed to practice magic under the influence. Or practice magic at all, really, given the apparent carelessness with which you bandy about your spells. Does the goddess Hecate know what you lot are up to? In my day, she had laws governing this sort of thing. With appropriate magical punishments, eternal damnation being a perennial favorite."

Violet stops dead in her tracks. "Eternal damnation?"

Ignoring her, I keep walking. And fuming. And walking

some more. Only to slam into an invisible wall and be yanked backward by an equally invisible leash.

Ah. So the whole "bound together" bit is literal, then. Well. The hits just keep on coming!

I turn back to find her standing on the sidewalk beneath a streetlamp, sleeves pulled down over her hands, glasses misting up, halo of dark frizz circling her head. Instinct has me reaching for my smoking jacket, wanting to take it off and drape it over her shoulders.

I resist the urge.

"Come *here*," I demand.

She takes a few tentative steps forward. I hold up a hand to stop her, then take a few steps back. Hit that blasted boundary again.

Math isn't my strong suit, but... Thirty feet, give or take. Maybe thirty-five. That's all we've got.

"Bleeding *skies*, you've really got me wrapped around your finger now, don't you? A man can't even go out for a nightcap without his witch attached at the hip."

She rushes toward me. Attempts another one of those crampy apologetic smiles, made more crampy by the chattering teeth. "I'll c-c-come with you. It's fine. I d-d-don't mind."

"Really? And what about when I sleep? Or use the facilities? Will you come with me then?" I lean in close, drop my voice to a seductive whisper. Some things can't be helped, this being one of them. "What about when I shower? Do you have any idea the sort of debauchery I can get up to in there with naught but a bottle of shower gel, hot water streaming down my chest, one hand gripping my wet, hard—"

"Doors!" she practically yelps. "I've got plenty of d-d-doors. Lots of sturdy, well-made, *closable* doors to ensure privacy at all times, even if we've got a limited range."

"Good to know, and by the way, I was talking about my hard back scrubber."

She peers up at me over the rims of her glasses—lashes dark from the lingering drizzle, her eyes even more intensely blue up close—and laughs.

The mushroom laughs.

It's like a song, like a poem, like the chiming of fairy bells... capped by a ridiculously awkward snort, which only sets her off again, both hands clamped over her mouth to try to hold it at bay, no use. The laughter echoes down the empty street, and that thing inside my chest kicks me in the ribs again, Taco Tuesday back to haunt me, and suddenly I want to make her laugh like that all over again.

Which also makes me want to set my own arsehole on fire because wake the fuck *up*, Devlin. This isn't some quaint little rom-com sidequest. I'm trapped here. Which means I'm *not* in Los Angeles, fulfilling my duties to my father. Proving my worth. Earning my right to sit upon the throne I lost so long ago. My right to go back home.

Rage simmers anew.

Turning back toward that golden light, my last hope, I march onward.

So does she. No longer laughing. No longer snorting. Teeth chattering all over the place.

"When I get a hold of Hecate," I grumble, "we're going to have words about this... this... what in the bleeding orifices do you call this town again?"

"Wayward Bay?"

"Yes. That. *Exactly* that. Well, I suppose it does what it says on the tin, doesn't it? Because I've already met two of its resident miscreants, and—oh, Hello, darling. Now *this* looks promising."

Saints and Sinners Fine Wine and Spirits. Source of the golden light and my new lease on life. Never have I ever been so happy to see a liquor store display window (its over-reliance on haystacks and plastic ghost lights as decorative accents notwithstanding).

"Demon-owned," Violet informs me. "Well, demon *and* fae, but Maleek set up shop and picked the name before he met Jovahn."

"Demon and fae? Hmm. Are there any regular humans in this town?"

"Of course. We just have a higher population of magical beings than most other places in the States. One of the town founders was a witch—Agatha Wayward. Her magic is what draws a lot of us here."

I file that knowledge away for later.

"Their wedding was pretty amazing, actually," she continues.

"Agatha Wayward's?"

"No, Maleek and Jovahn. They had all this food from Jovahn's fae court, but his family cast a spell on it so it wouldn't trap anyone in their home realm—fae have weird rules about that sort of thing. The wine was *really* intense, though. I made the mistake of drinking it too fast, and I ended up—"

"Mushroom? As fascinating as the cautionary tales of your casual alcoholism may be, which is to say not at all, let's adopt a new policy." I open the door and usher her inside. "Less talking, more helping me find another liquid coping mechanism."

The shop is small but well-appointed, carrying enough of a selection of higher-end bourbons to meet my immediate needs. I select a bottle (or seven) while Violet greets the demon manning the register—Maleek, I presume.

A wave and a smile for the fine proprietor, then I'm off.

Or... not.

"Um, excuse you?" Violet stares at me, hand on her hip like I'm about to get a scolding, which I'd gladly submit to under different circumstances, but since we're both wearing too many clothes for that, I merely scowl at her.

"Aren't you forgetting something?" she says.

"Am I? Oh! Wait! You're right. Thank you." Shuffling the bourbon bottles over to one arm, I grab a handful of nips from the counter—mixed bag, mostly cheap vodka and flavored whiskeys, but one can never be too prepared for a good time. "Clearly, my head isn't screwed on straight tonight. All set now. Shall we?"

I nod toward the door for her to exit ahead of me, but she doesn't move. She and her demon pal are just standing about gaping at me, brows furrowed, eyes wide.

After a long, awkward stare-off, it finally occurs to me that these two are not actually constipated. They're... expecting me to pay for these spirits.

Fuck. I haven't had to do my own shopping in decades. My staff always handles these things, cashing in one favor or another. I wasn't lying to the witch about my lack of legal tender.

Well. Olivy warned me not to use my influence to help save the shop. Purloining alcohol is not saving the shop. Ergo...

"Maleek," I say hypnotically, gazing into his eyes. "You—"

"Holy shit," he gasps, recognition dawning before I've even had the chance to put the whammy on him. "It's you."

"Holy shit indeed." I grin, basking in his starry-eyed wonderment.

"I... I can't believe you're here," he stammers. "In Wayward Bay. With Violet. This is just... Wow. Well, anything you need, sir. Help yourself."

"You *know* him?" Violet asks the man.

"He's a demon, Mushroom," I explain. "Of course he knows me."

"Yeah, but—oh, goddess. You're his boss."

"In a manner of speaking, yes, but I prefer more of an informal, hands-off approach. You know what they say—an empowered demon is an effective demon. Especially when he knows *exactly* what his boss most needs."

"A calming blend of lavender, chamomile, and lemon balm," the witch says, going a bit starry-eyed herself, though not over me, which is off-putting. "With a fine dusting of cane sugar and a spritz of rose quartz essence. I call it my STFU and CTFD Tea. Works wonders for anger issues."

"Just hearing you talk about it as if it's your long-lost soulmate is *giving* me anger issues, so I'll go ahead and take a pass on that. Maleek, thank you for your service, the spirits are *exactly* what I need."

Maleek nods, some of his earlier bewilderment fading. "How do you two know each other again?"

I feel Violet tense beside me, and when I glance over and catch her eye, she gives me a nearly imperceptible shake of the head.

Right. She doesn't want anyone else to know about her financial woes. A thing that should *not* concern me, and yet...

"I'm helping Violet with some marketing plans for her shop," I say, keeping the summoning snafu to myself for some unnamed reason I don't care to explore while sober.

"Oh, right!" Maleek says. "I heard you're kind of a big deal on social media these days."

"The biggest."

"Seriously?" Violet asks, that happy twinkle returning to her eyes. "The Devil is on MySpace? What will they think of next?"

"MySpace?" Maleek laughs. "Oh my word, aren't you *adorable*? Babe, come out front!" he calls toward the back of the store. "You have to meet this time-traveling witch! She just got here all the way from 2007!"

"Very funny, Maleek." Violet turns to smile at a fae male exiting the back storeroom. "Jovahn's here tonight too?"

"He's helping me with inventory—we're finalizing the liquor order for the Haunted Halloween Ball. Mayor Singh has been checking in twice a day to make sure we've got it covered."

"Don't tell me Fiona ran out of rum already!" The fae—Jovahn—gathers Violet into a hug, which sets my teeth on edge—again, completely baffling. Again, won't be examining until I'm thoroughly inebriated.

"Fiona had *more* than enough rum. Ask me how I know." Violet tries to laugh, but it quickly shatters into a sigh, her body slumping against his chest, and without being prompted, without being asked, without being invited or permitted, he rubs a hand up and down her back and asks if she's *feeling* okay.

Un-fucking-believable.

Before I have the opportunity to explain to this handsy, helps-himself-to-hugs-and-backrubs fae that *yes*, the witch is feeling just fine—that *I'm* the injured party here, and by the way, why are you *still* touching her?—the door whooshes open and ushers in another demon.

One I've never before been so happy to see.

"There you are! Bloody Hell, Dev." Finn pulls me aside, dropping his voice to a whisper. "I've been calling in every favor we've got left trying to track you down. Took some doing, but we finally traced the magical signature." He hands over my blessed phone. "I thought we'd lost you for good. You literally vanished into thin air."

Relief washes over me at the sight of my friend. And my phone. Not necessarily in that order. "Thank you."

"How the fuck did you end up here, of all places?"

"My services were... urgently requested."

"By whom?"

I make a vague gesture in the direction of the mushroom, who escaped the fae's embrace and is now trying—adorably but unsuccessfully—to hide behind a display of regional wines and plastic fall foliage.

Finn's jaw drops. "You've *got* to be kidding me."

"Do I look like I'm kidding you?"

"He's not much of a kidder." Violet peeks out from behind the wines, taking in the sight of the new demon. "Welcome to Wayward Bay! I really, really hope you're not another Devil. But if you are, forget I said that. Actually, forget I said anything, other than the welcome part, because I genuinely—"

"Violet?" I sigh. There's a fine line between adorable and annoying, and she's definitely trampling over it. "We talked about this."

"We... we did?"

I make a zipping-my-lips motion. The slightly more polite version of the shut-the-hell-up motion, which I mostly reserve for Finn.

"Oh! That. Right. Less talking, more drinking. Got it." She mimics the lip-zipping motion, then grabs a bottle from the wine display and pretends to drink, giggling at her own antics.

The corner of my mouth twitches with the flicker of a laugh, but I lock that nonsense down *tout de suite*.

"A word, Highness?" Finn says through clenched teeth. "In private, if we may?"

CHAPTER NINE

DEVLIN

Out in front of the store, I crack open two Fireball shots and pass one to Finn, sharing the details on the summoning.

"What about your father?" he asks. "Did you tell her about—"

"No, and there's no need. I can continue the work here under the guise of my influencer career."

Finn looks at me as if I've completely lost the plot, which... fair enough. "How do you see this working out, Dev? Logistically speaking?"

"Easy. I find a place to host a few gatherings—tea shop, after hours, perhaps—and home in on the most corruptible souls in town."

"Don't hold your breath, mate. This town is straight out of the Hallmark Channel handbook. Literally. I recognize it from that fall rom-com we watched last year—what was it called? Halloween Homecoming or some such? Wait, no.

That was that the college football porno with the cheerleaders dressed up like slutty goblins and—"

"Setting aside for the moment your *exquisite* taste in films..." I down another Fireball shot, then move on to the butterscotch schnapps, equally terrible but doing its part in keeping my buzz alive. "We need to figure it out. According to her sister, who seems to know a good deal about summoning spells and dark magic, the witch and I are bound."

"Bound? What does that mean?"

"We can't leave this town. Or, for that matter..." I take several steps into the street. Hit the wall, nearly stumbling with the force of it. "Each other."

"For how long?"

"Until—and I quote—I unlock her heart's truest desire."

"Sorry, mate," Finn says, clearly *not* sorry, his shoulders shaking with barely contained laughter. "But that sounds suspiciously Hallmarky. I can already see the trailer."

"Don't. For the love of hellfire, do *not* do the movie announcer voice—"

"In a *world* where magic is *real* and dreams really *do* come true—"

"I'm serious, Finn. Quit while you're—"

"One witch has a *dream* bigger than *all* the rest."

"Are you always this obstinate?"

"A burning desire that can *only* be unlocked by a *Prince*."

"You've missed your calling. Truly."

"But it's not Prince Charming riding to her rescue this time. It's... dun dun *dun!* The Prince of Darkness *himself.*" Finn doubles over, and it's almost enough to make me laugh, too.

Almost. If it weren't so damned close to the inconvenient truth.

Fucking *Hell*, what a mess.

"What does the witch desire, anyway?" he asks.

"The usual. Money." I tighten the tie on my smoking jacket, for all that it helps. Hell of a nip in the air, and it's biting relentlessly on my backside. "She's trying to bail out her tea shop—place just a few doors down. Sinking ship."

"Why is it *your* ship to fix? We've got more important things to do than clean up some flighty witch's bad credit."

"She's not flighty, Finn. Just in a bind. It happens."

He watches me a beat, eyebrows raised, and I realize how oddly defensive I sound. How defensive I *feel* when I think of her standing behind her tea counter, curly hair tied back, glasses sliding down her nose as she mixes up her brews, trying to make an honest go of things.

"As I said, I don't have a choice," I rush to add. "The magic has bound us together until the task is complete."

"Which will be when, exactly?"

"However long it takes. Although, she's only got a month before she's evicted from the storefront, so... less than that, I suppose."

"A month? Fuck *me*, Dev. No, that's not an invitation."

"Fuck *yourself*, Finn. That *is* an invitation."

"I'm serious. A month is about how long we've got left to lock in those last five hundred souls. Fail that, and we're all smoked."

My heart drops into my gut as the truth of his words sinks in.

A thousand years—that's all my father gave me. One millennium to sign over one million souls, or kiss the throne, my home, and my immortality goodbye, cursed to live out the last of my measly years as a powerless mortal, subject to the whims of an angry, vengeful god until I take my last breath.

For their unwavering loyalty, all the demons who chose to accompany me to the human realm—Finn and the twelve additional demons currently serving as my staff in Los Angeles—are cursed to the same fate.

If the task sounds impossible, that's because it is. Or should have been, anyway. In all his infinite, Godly wisdom, the old man never expected me to accomplish it. Just used it as a way to profit off my ineptitude—kind of his M.O.

But he severely underestimated me and my demon companions. Sure, none of us believed we could do it—not at first. But now that we're close, I can see it in their eyes. In *Finn's* eyes. The hope they kept hidden for centuries, finally sparking back to life.

"I suppose we'll need to cancel tomorrow's festivities," he

says, the flame in his eyes guttering as the reality of my predicament settles in.

"No. Nothing changes on that front." I down another shot, my mind churning with new plans. I will *not* leave them to further suffering at my father's hands. Not while we've still got a fighting chance. "Can you keep up appearances? Act the happy host, play up my absence as some sort of... traveling publicity stunt?"

"I can try, but we still need someone to recruit the guests. Boots on the ground, so to speak."

"Put Azazel in charge of that."

"Azazel is a vacuous twat."

"A well-connected vacuous twat, which is precisely what we need."

The demon Azazel isn't one of ours, but we've been running in the same circles for centuries. He's currently serving as a movie producer—lives in the neighborhood, loves popping by to partake in our intimate gatherings, always good for a favor or two.

And yes, you've definitely heard of him.

"Fine," Finn grumbles. "But now *you're* going to owe me favors. Lots of them."

"Noted."

The evening storm is finally passing, giving the moon a chance to make her appearance. Finn gazes up and sighs. "Seven flaming rivers, Dev. Of all the times to fall into a witch's snare."

"I *did* warn you," I remind him. "I felt the magic calling to me all evening."

"Yes, and thank your ancient *balls* the copious hours of WitchTok scrolling finally paid off." He rolls his eyes and gestures for another Fireball.

I pass him the shot. "I've got this. Trust me. Everything will work out."

Finn downs the drink. Shakes his head. Curses up at the moon, then at me. And then, finally, a brief nod.

As always, my best friend's loyalty never wavers.

"I'll portal back in to check on you tomorrow," he says. "Bring you some clothing before the Pumpkinville Police arrest you for public indecency."

I grin and bow. "Public indecency is just one of the many services I offer."

"Will you be all right for the night?"

"I'll ask the demon inside to loan me some clothing. Since I can't be more than thirty or so feet from the witch, I'll be staying at her place."

"Aha!" Finn pitches his empty bottles into a trash bin that reads *Keep the Bay Beautiful!* "Silver lining, there it is."

I peer inside the storefront, where Violet is currently chatting with the proprietors, Maleek laughing at something she just said, her face lighting up in response. "If by 'silver lining' you mean the thing that will keep me up night after night and most likely lead to my downfall..."

"I don't know about all that, Dev. She's pretty cute. In that hot nerd-girl sort of way. Perhaps you might come to another sort of arrangement to pass the time."

"*Goodnight*, Finn."

"Yes, yes. I know a brushoff when I see one." Laughing, he claps a hand over my shoulder. "Try not to cause any more trouble tonight. And don't worry about things at home. I'll be sure to keep the company satisfied and the bed warm in your absence."

"*Which* bed?"

"All of them. Floors too. And the billiards table, the infinity pool, the table in the projector room, all seven hot tubs, the croquet lawn, the pool house..." Finn walks down the street, rattling off all the places he'll be happily debasing in my absence, until he finally vanishes into the darkness beyond, a faint trail of Hell magic glowing in his wake.

CHAPTER TEN

VIOLET

The sun has barely graced us when I sneak downstairs and confirm that last night was *not*, in fact, a lemonito-induced nightmare.

Gone are yesterday's first-world-witch problems of finding the Devil card lounging on my counter. This morning, the *actual* Devil is lounging on the *couch*, stretched out in all his gleaming, bare-chested glory, blanket wrapped around his lower half in a way that has me thinking *very* bad thoughts.

Or it would be... If my brain wasn't hijacked by the *second* most impossible sight of the morning.

Grumpy. The cat who *hates* people. Especially men-people. Yet there he is, sleeping on top of all that glorious bare-chestedness, the Devil's hand resting casually on his back, both of them sound asleep, all cozied up like they've been snuggle buddies for a century.

I try not to let this bother me.

I also try not to notice how adorable they look, peacefully snoozing in front of the fading embers of last night's fire, the faint smell of my magic lingering.

Wow. I really did it. I summoned the Devil last night. And now he's here, half-naked on my couch. Petting my cat, which is sadly not a euphemism.

I take a silent step forward, then another, ogling the specimen as I might a newly discovered herb for my tea recipes. Messy black hair just begging to be touched. Perfect amount of dark stubble along his jawline. The long, lean lines of his body, a work of art against the purple velvet. The firm ridges of rock-hard abs and those sexy-as-sin v-muscles disappearing beneath the blanket like a forbidden invitation.

Memories of last night flicker through my mind—the Devil darting out to catch me when I tripped over the stools, those powerful arms lifting me to safety, the scent of him nearly overwhelming, like fire and black pepper and the darkest dark chocolate.

My hand drifts forward, reaching for him without any conscious effort on my part. It's by sheer willpower that I don't accidentally-on-purpose yank off that blanket and blame it on the cat.

Shoving my hands into my pockets, I force myself to do an about-face, tiptoe into the café kitchen, and put on the kettle. Tea time—best way to start the day.

I head back out to my wall of ingredients, eager to make

my selections for my morning brew, but something seems... off. I glance around at the gleaming counter, and that's when it hits me.

This place was a disaster zone last night. Stools toppled, candle wax spilled across the counter, half-emptied mugs from our earlier Witch-N-Bitch all over the place. I was so exhausted after the ordeal, I barely remember getting home from the liquor store, depositing the Devil on the couch, and dragging myself up to bed, muttering something about cleaning up the evidence in the morning.

But now, there is no evidence. He cleaned everything up.

Ignoring the warmth spreading through my chest, and possibly spreading lower, I select my ingredients from the wall—green tea, holy basil for clarity and attention, peppermint to chase off the lingering brain fog, and a dash of black pepper to boost my personal power.

Focus and direction, that's what we need today. No more fuzzy-headed, booze-addled brain calling the shots around here. *And that goes for you, too, libido. No one south of the border gets a say, got it?*

No response. We'll take that as a yes.

I've just started to grind the pepper when she appears in my empty teacup—another Tarot card. Queen of Swords this time, a woman who knows what she wants, cuts to the chase, and takes no shit. She sits upon her throne, sword held high, shoulders squared. Like, *approach me if you must, but don't even* think *about giving me any shit.*

Her appearance makes me smile. It's just the power boost I need, and the perfect magic to bless my new brew—Make Good Choices, You Stupid Bitch.

For my guest, I craft a variant of my traditional Welcome to Wayward Bay blend. Black tea with vanilla, cardamom, and cinnamon topped with a few shavings of dark chocolate.

Each blend gets its own individual serving pot, assembled on a tea tray with cups and saucers and a selection of pastries and fresh berries. I have no idea what the Devil eats or whether he even likes tea, but I've already kidnapped and bound him, so it's not like I can make a worse impression, right?

You've got this, the Queen of Swords whispers in my mind, then vanishes.

Back in the fireplace area, the Devil is still sleeping on the couch like some kind of sex god who miraculously fell out of the skies and landed in my shop, the morning light pouring through the windows and gilding him in a golden sheen that makes him look even more otherworldly than he already is.

An accidental sigh escapes my lips, and Grumpy's head pops up. He catches me watching him, his stone-cold hater reputation ruined, and leaps away without so much as another glance. The movement disturbs the sleeping Devil, who twitches and yawns, rolls onto his side, and slowly blinks awake.

I watch in quiet admiration as he sits up and stretches,

the blanket falling away to reveal the sweatpants he borrowed from Maleek, every movement sending a zing of awareness right through me. It's a miracle I can even stand still, that the cups and saucers aren't rattling on the tray.

It feels like hours before he finally gets his bearings and glances up. I hold my breath and smile, hoping for one in return, or maybe a nod, some tiny acknowledgment that tells me he's not going to smite me where I stand.

But he just watches me, calm and steady. Intense. A million thoughts run through his eyes, all of them veiled, and my *goddess*, he's got adorable morning face. That slightly rumpled hair, pillow marks lining his cheek, eyes the rich, red-brown color of a cup of Earl Grey.

My thighs involuntarily clench. Aesthetically speaking, the man—Devil—whatever—is pure perfection. I bet he doesn't even have morning breath.

He does, however, have morning *wood*—a thing I've only just now realized after the briefest glance downward—and holy *Hell*. For the first time in my mostly battery-operated sex life, I'm starting to understand the hype over gray sweatpants.

"Something I can help you with this morning, Mushroom?" he asks, his smooth voice and sexy British accent like warm honey.

Honey I would love to have poured all over my naked boobs and licked off...

I shove the tea tray at him as if that alone can hide the

beast between his legs *or* my embarrassment at getting caught staring at it.

"I made *tea!*"

I announce it with the same awestricken amazement I imagine Prometheus employed when he brought fire to the mortals, but the Devil doesn't seem bothered by my misplaced exuberance *or* the unabashed ogling—I mean observing.

In fact, the bastard is grinning at me. Grinning! With his adorably rumpled hair and adorably morninged morning face and that firm, firm, *firm* body.

"In that case..." He takes the tray and sets it on the coffee table in front of the couch. "Good morning, Violet Pepperdine."

He knows my full name?

"Good morning, Mister... Um... Devil Man!" I reply. "Hello! The black kettle with the poppy design is yours, so help yourself!"

"Do you always speak in exclamation points?"

"No! Only when I'm nervous! Not that I'm nervous. Mostly. I've just... never had an overnight guest."

He arches a sexy dark brow, a look that makes everything south of my bellybutton melt.

"In the café!" I rush to explain, awkward laughter bubbling out of me like a cauldron spell gone wild. "*Obviously* I've had overnight guests in my apartment. *Tons* of them. I'm a pro!"

Good goddess, somebody hold me back before I die of a self-inflicted mortification wound...

The Devil doesn't say anything to that, just pours himself a cup of tea, his eyes dancing with a humor and lightness I didn't think was possible for him. Especially not after all the brooding and sarcasm last night.

Confused by the contrast, I reach out to sense his energy—nothing invasive on my part, just a light perusal to see if I'm walking into a death trap. His energy is powerful and intense, but I'm not picking up anything negative or malicious. He's definitely guarded, though. And bewildered, which I guess is to be expected.

For now, I'm safe.

Anticipation has me in a tight hold as he lifts the cup and saucer, draws the teacup to his face, and inhales. The steam curls around his parted mouth, but before he can even take his first sip, the words are spilling out of me like an unstoppable river of pure babble.

"Welcome to Wayward Bay," I say. "That's the name of the blend. And also, yes, welcome. I never got to say it last night. Just to your friend. I think maybe you and I got off on the wrong foot, which is entirely my fault, obviously. I don't blame you for being upset. I just... summoning you really *was* unintentional, and I'm so, so sorry. For what it's worth, I never, *ever* sip and spell. I don't even like drinking all that much, to be honest. And I recognize that magic is a responsibility as much as it is a privilege and I don't take that lightly

—I never have. I was having a *super* bad day yesterday—the worst in a long time, actually—and my sisters came over to cheer me up, and I over-indulged. Not that a bad day is an excuse, of course, but I thought you deserved the explanation. As well as my assurances that I'll do *everything* I can to figure this out and break the spell A.S.A.P. so you can be on your way back home. And while I'm not interested in signing away my soul, if there's anything I *can* help you with in the future, I'm totally here for you. Just... please say something. Anything. Even if it's just that you're going to smite me."

The Devil says nothing. Just closes his eyes and finally takes a sip of the tea. Sighs. Takes another sip. Sets the cup and saucer down without so much as a *clink*.

"Devlin," he finally says, opening his eyes. Unreadable, as ever.

"Does that mean you like it? I've got lots of other kinds. I can make you whatever you want. Black, green, herbal, hot cider... Pretty much anything but coffee."

"Coffee? I should think not." His mouth curves into a soft smile. "Devlin is my name, Mushroom. The one I go by nowadays, and I've grown rather fond of it. So you can call me that. Although 'Mr. Devil Man' has a certain ring to it."

"*Devlin*."

It comes out more breathy than I mean it to, and while I register a slight uptick of smug satisfaction in his energy, he has the grace not to tease me about it.

"Despite the drunken summoning," he says, "the non-consensual binding and ensuing non-consensual imprisonment, the appalling lack of free WiFi in this establishment, and the ceaseless pre-caffeine morning chatter..." He reaches again for his teacup and saucer, shakes his dark head, then takes another delicate sip. When he meets my eyes again, his smiles grows even brighter, a pulse of warmth emanating through his energy. "Any witch who brews a cuppa this good can't be *all* bad."

"Really? You like it?" I'm bouncing on my toes at the almost-praise. At the genuine smile he's been keeping in reserve, finally making an appearance.

"I wouldn't lie about something as important as tea." Devlin sets the cup on the saucer, then crosses his legs and balances the saucer on his kneecap, somehow making the sweatpants look as classy as they do sexy. "I accept your apology for the summoning, however inconvenient it may be. Now sit down, pour yourself some of your lovely tea, and tell me why you were having such a bad day yesterday."

His energy still feels genuine, just an honest curiosity, no traps detected, so I perch on the edge of the couch, keeping a respectful distance, lest some part of me brush against some part of him and spontaneously combust.

"The Kettle and Cauldron is on the verge of closing down." I tell him about the back rent, the realtor nephew and his nastygram, Mean Beans, the whole chain of personal calamities that got me here. "And it's totally my fault. I get that. There were plenty of times over the years where I saw the train coming, but I just couldn't get out of the way fast enough, you know? I always assumed I'd figure it out—another credit card with a better rate, or a new tea blend to put this place on the map. But it was never enough. *Nothing* is ever enough. Now I've got a month to come up with a hundred grand, or I'm done. Nothing short of a heist can dig me out of this hole."

It's more than I've ever admitted to anyone, even to myself. Shame simmers inside, but it doesn't boil over. Doesn't send me into a spiral of despair.

For the first time in years, I actually feel... lighter. Hopeful, even.

What is it about sharing your deepest secrets with total strangers?

"Don't despair," Devlin says, the confidence in his voice putting me further at ease. "Believe it or not, I'm quite familiar with dodging oncoming trains."

I let out a mock gasp. "Even the all-powerful Devil makes mistakes?"

"To hear my father tell it, the all-powerful Devil is the *original* mistake."

His energy darkens, a tempest of anger swirling just behind the lighthearted jokes. But before I can ask what he meant, he reaches for a blueberry scone and says, "Speaking of which, I'm actually on a deadline as well—I've got a prior engagement in Los Angeles that I'm keen to get back to. So, the sooner we can wrap this up, the better for all parties."

"Agreed, and I'm totally open to ideas. Other than the heist."

"Yes, you and your pesky morals." Devlin spreads a bit of clotted cream over the scone and takes a bite. "I suppose you'll just have to rely on clever plotting from your new marketing consultant."

"Marketing consultant?"

"Maleek was right—I *do* have a large social media presence. Large enough that some people may recognize me, even here. Sticking with the consultant cover story is a good idea."

"I still can't believe the Devil has a social media presence. What do you even do on there? Throw parties in Hell and post videos of your demon friends doing keg stands?"

"You're... not that far off the mark. I'm an influencer."

"I have no idea what that is."

Devlin laughs, a sound I'm getting far too attached to. "You weren't kidding with that MySpace comment, were you?"

"I've just never been into the whole social media thing. In high school, I didn't even have my own phone or computer. Now, I barely know how to text. Drives my sisters crazy."

"That settles it, then. You really *do* need a consultant, and voilà, here's your man, eager to assess the shop's potential and make a plan. A bit of pro-bono charity work for my empire of—"

"Devlin, no!" Panic launches me off the couch. If word got around that I accepted pro-bono work from a so-called social media star, my sisters and everyone else in this town would know something's up. Namely, that I'm floundering. That I'm screwing up the one thing I'm supposed to be good at. "You are absolutely *not* telling anyone that I'm some influencer's pet project."

"Would you rather tell them you got plastered on rum slushies and drunk-summoned me in a fit of quiet desperation?"

"Magic mojito lemonitos, and no. I would not." I sit back down and sip my tea, trying to soak up those Queen of Swords take-no-prisoners vibes. "I know I don't have the right to ask. But I would very much appreciate it if we could just say I hired you, and leave it at that."

It's possibly the most direct request I've ever made in my life, and I hold my breath, waiting for him to say no. To tell me I'm in no position to be asking for favors, especially when he's got his own business to run and his own life to lead and his own family dynamics to navigate, and getting kidnapped by a drunk witch was most definitely *not* on his bingo card.

But Devlin merely shrugs. "The only way to break the spell and escape our predicament is to work together to unlock your heart's desire, so that's what we're going to do. Call it whatever you want. Fair enough?"

Relief has me feeling hopeful again. "So you're... you're really going to help me save the café?"

"Don't act so surprised, Mushroom. Believe it or not, the Devil *does* know a little something about entertaining people."

"I'm not *in* the entertainment business. I'm in the tea business."

"What is tea," he says with a dramatic wave of his hand, "if not entertainment for the tongue?"

"Oh, no. If that's the best a world-class influencer can come up with, we may as well close up shop now."

"Excuse me?" He shoots me a defensive glare. "It's catchy, in its own way."

"Like a bad rash."

"Well, I suppose you would know, what with all the overnight guests you've harbored." He makes a show of examining the cushions. "Should I have sanitized this before curling up naked last night?"

He says a whole bunch of other things too, but my newly Queen of Swords-sharpened, super-focused mind is now super focused on the 'curling up naked' part of the story, serving up red-hot images of the Devil sprawled out in his birthday suit, the firm ridges of his abs glistening by the firelight, the dark trail of hair leading down from his bellybutton to—

"...donned at first light," he continues. "Didn't want to alarm any passers-by. Or you, for that matter, though it seems I've failed in at least one of those endeavors. Are you all right?"

"Donned... what?" I blink away the images and try to focus on what he's saying.

"The pants. I prefer sleeping in the nude, but wasn't sure when you'd be awake or when your customers would come, so I—"

"Come?" I squeak.

He cocks his head, brow furrowed. "Violet? Do you need to have a lie-down?"

A lie-down with you, in the nude, during which at least one of us comes, yes, what a lovely idea...

"Nope!" I rocket back to my feet and stack all the empty dishes onto the tray. "I'm good. Great! Just... eager to get..." *...away from you before I do something even stupider than the drunk-summoning that brought you here.* "...to work. New day, new ideas, the tea doesn't make itself!"

"Excellent." Devlin rubs his hands together, grinning as if he's hatching some nefarious scheme that will undoubtedly end with my utter embarrassment and/or arrest. "So, when do we open for business?"

"*We* don't open. *I* open. You go upstairs and entertain yourself in my apartment—quietly—whilst devising marketing plans. And we're moving your sleeping quarters up there, too."

"So we're co-habitating now? Isn't that a bit forward?"

"We're putting you on the sofa sleeper to avoid any

potential customer run-ins. And before you say a word, yes, you *will* be wearing pants." I lift the tea tray, grateful to have something in my hands. Hands that might otherwise fondle those abs. "Any questions?"

"Just one." He folds his arms over his chest, blocking my view. "Have you always been this boring?"

"Have you always been this obnoxious?"

"Hmm." He considers the question. Seriously considers it. "I seem to recall a bout of politeness that lasted about fifteen minutes in the seventeen hundreds. It didn't suit me."

"Well, it suits you today." I nod toward the stairs that lead up to the apartment. "Make yourself at home, eat whatever you want, and stay out of trouble. After I close up shop tonight, we'll order a pizza and put our heads together on a marketing strategy. Sound like a plan?"

"It sounds like a death sentence, but fear not." He gathers up his bourbon bottles and grins, wicked and tempting and definitely not helping my south-of-the-border wildfire situation at *all*. "I'm sure I can find *some* way to amuse myself."

CHAPTER ELEVEN

VIOLET

This morning's rush is about as non-rushy as it was yesterday, the difference being that yesterday I was merely anxious with a chance of panic, and today I'm a wild storm of frayed nerves and fizzy insides who can barely hold a teacup without dropping it.

An hour until closing time, Mean Beans is still the hottest ticket in town, I've had less than a dozen customers, burned myself four times, misplaced all my mint and had to call Aunt Althea to bring some from the Three Sisters gardens, and somehow—defying all laws of physics—spilled chamomile flowers in my *hair*.

Also, Olivy keeps sending me texts that I can't figure out how to answer because my phone keeps locking me out, and anyway, I don't speak emoji.

So, given the humdinger of a day, I probably should've known something was up when I didn't hear a peep from

Devlin upstairs—not my television or the old record player, not the pitter-patter of two feral cats chasing dust motes, not even the creak of a floorboard on the old hardwoods above.

It's not until Mayor Singh bustles in with a big smile and the energy of a proud mama bear that I realize there's some serious Devil-induced trouble afoot.

"You've got quite a crowd back there!" She presses a hand to her chest, nearly breathless. "Oh, Violet. I just *knew* business would pick up today! Sometimes you just have to wait out the storm, right?"

"Crowd?"

"I was worried there'd be a line out the door and I wouldn't be able to get my daily dose! Which I'm in dire need of, by the way. Your brew did the trick on my sore throat yesterday, but now I'm so exhausted from all the budget presentations, I need a big shot of something lively. You wouldn't believe these bean counters, Violet. I swear they schedule meetings just for an excuse to impress us all with their ability to do math on command. And Brandt Remington? Who in their right mind put that windbag in charge of the town financials..."

She chatters on animatedly about the budget stuff, but all I can think about is this mysterious back-door crowd.

I've just finished mixing the black tea, cocoa nibs, cayenne pepper, cinnamon, and ginger for her Kick in the Pants brew when the Six of Wands card appears in the cubby where I keep the cinnamon. In it, a man wearing a victory crown rides high atop his horse before a crowd of adoring onlookers.

Hoping she doesn't notice my shaking hands, I hand over her tea. "Where did you say that crowd was, exactly?"

"Right out back. I walked past and figured you were handing out free samples. Maybe it's just tourists—I thought I saw cameras, too." She frowns as she slides a ten across the counter. "I'm sorry, Violet. I really thought it was for Kettle and Cauldron."

"Not this time." I collect her payment, my mind racing. Crowds? Cameras? There's another building across the small parking lot behind us—a paint-your-own pottery studio called Glaze for Days—but they never seem all that busy. Other than that, there's just my service entrance, and—

Oh, no. My apartment balcony.

A fiery pit of dread opens up in my chest. I usher the mayor out as quickly as I can without being rude, then bolt out through the service entrance to find my parking lot packed with...

Nope, not customers who've forgotten where the entrance is.

Not suppliers mixing up our delivery schedule.

Not school kids on a field trip of all the town's historic buildings.

This gathering is composed entirely of women. Dozens of them. All waving and smiling and yes, taking pictures.

Of the man holding court in a lounge chair on the balcony above.

Freshly showered, wet hair curling around his ears, bare chest gleaming in the sun. I can't see what he's wearing on the bottom from this angle, but knowing him, it's probably just a towel.

"Has anyone ever told you," Devlin calls down to his adoring fans, raising a glass in cheers, "that the women of Wayward Bay are among the most beautiful in the world? Take it from someone who's *seen* the world. You're all just so kind and lovely. Truly. I couldn't be more humbled—"

"We love you, Devlin Pierce!" a random fangirl shouts.

"Devlin's my Daddy!" shouts another—yes, definitely a humbling experience for Devlin.

He responds by blowing a kiss and tossing down a handful of white roses. *My* white roses, carelessly plucked from the arrangement I bought myself to brighten up my space two days ago.

That fiery dread inside me explodes into an inferno of rage.

Leaving the shop completely unattended—a thing I *never* do—I rush upstairs and beeline for the balcony. Where I find, in no particular order:

Two traitorous cats sunning themselves on the railing, tails swishing, not a care in the world.

Three empty bottles that once contained bourbon.

One and a half empty bottles that once contained the remnants of my summer wine stash, kept on hand for guests.

The vase containing what's left of my poor roses.

Two of those umbrella lighting thingies they have at photography studios.

A video camera mounted on a tripod, red light flashing, recording in progress.

And the Devil.

Not—as I initially feared—draped in a towel.

No. He's draped in nothing. Nothing at all. Everything he possesses is just... out there. *Really* out there. Taking up space in the world. A *lot* of space. Holy shit. I can't breathe.

"Ah, Violet!" He smiles when he finally sees me. A *genuine* smile, like he's really glad I'm here, and his energy matches. Playful, excited, lighthearted. "Home for an early dinner, darling? Care to join me on the veranda?"

Fully aware of the ever-growing crowd below, and the recording equipment, I grit my teeth into a fake smile and whisper-shout, "*What* in the five elements of witchkind are you *doing*?"

He presses his fingertips to his chest, jaw dropping, like, *moi? Whatever do you mean?*

My mouth opens and closes, opens and closes, but no words are coming out. I blame the shock.

"Wait... do you mean the Chardonnay?" He holds up the glass of golden wine, sparkling in the late afternoon sunlight. "I know it's gauche, but it was all I could find inside.

You really should consider stocking alternate options. A pinot grigio at the *very* least, but reds are a much better choice this time of year. I'd assumed your palate was a bit more sophisticated given the penchant for tea blending, but perhaps not."

I still can't speak. Can't breathe. My heart is about one more beat from exploding into a pile of red goo.

"Violet? Are you all right? Oh, and don't mind the camera. We're not live. Finn portaled some of my things over, and I decided to shoot some B-roll. I may be on the road, but the show must go on, as ever."

"B-roll? *B-roll!*" I'm pretty sure literal steam is pouring out of my ears, cartoon teakettle style, but the Devil keeps on staring at me like *I'm* the one who's lost the plot. "Devlin! You're *naked*! On my balcony! Where people can walk right by and see you! Where people *are* seeing you! Right this very minute!"

He sets the glass on the patio table and glances down at himself, at the people still lingering below, at the camera, at the whole freaking *spectacle* of it.

Then he just... shrugs.

Shrugs! With that stupid beautiful smile and freshly washed hair and eyes like sun-warmed tea and abs so perfect they *have* to be airbrushed.

"Have you nothing to say for yourself?" I demand.

"In my defense, Violet, it's an unseasonably warm day and you told me to make myself at home."

"Right. Because you often sit around the fires of Hell naked with a glass of wine in the middle of the day, holding court for the ladies?"

"Hell? Not since I was asked to leave. But in Los Angeles, yes, naked day-drinking is high on my go-to activities list, right up there with getting stoned with Finn, adult movie night, adult swim, and roaming from one room to the next without so much as a stitch of clothing to slow me down. In fact, when all this is over, you should visit the estate. I'd love to show you around, clothing optional, of course."

Devlin's energy shifts, his earlier excitement dimming.

Still trying to follow what might very well be the most insane conversation of my life, I finally process what he said. No, not the naked-romping-around-the-estate part. The earlier bit.

"Someone asked you to leave Hell?" I ask, my inner rage notching down from inferno to crackling bonfire. "But... who could do that? I thought you were large-and-in-charge down there."

He clams up, a new feeling flooding his energy—one I'm quite familiar with.

Shame.

"Ugh! Long story, very boring, moving on." Devlin downs the last of his wine and turns back to me with another smile, but it doesn't reach his eyes. "The point being, yes, I *have* been known to appreciate the fruits of the vine in the nude, especially when I'm in the excellent company of beautiful women and good lighting and—oh, goodness! How utterly rude of me! I completely neglected to offer you a glass. Of your own wine, no less." He laughs, shaking his head in self-admonishment. "No wonder you're scolding me like an errant schoolboy caught masturbating in the teacher's lounge."

"*What?*"

With his typical fluid grace, he rises from the lounge chair, his glorious physique on full display—a display I can objectively appreciate as an objective appreciator of fine craftsmanship in general, which should always be appreciated, whether in the form of a marble sculpture, human being, immortal Devil or otherwise.

But still. Not appropriate. Whatsoever.

"Devlin!" I whisper-shout again, making a vague gesture toward the crowd.

"Oh, right! Wow, I'm *really* off my game today." He waltzes over to the edge of the balcony, the view of his lower half thankfully shielded by a row of my potted lemon balm, and tosses down the rest of the roses. "Thank you all so much for popping by. I hope to see you all patronizing Kettle and Cauldron in the coming weeks!"

The adoring fans cheer and whistle and shout out their phone numbers. Someone launches something onto the balcony... pretty sure it's a black lace bra, but I can't bring myself to look too closely.

Because all I can see right now is the tattoo on his backside. The *left* side, specifically. Firm, rounded, and inked, impossible to miss.

I narrow my eyes and scrutinize, since that's clearly what the situation calls for. "Is that a... a *pitchfork*?"

Devlin chuckles and turns to face me, still just airing it all out like nobody's business. "Admiring my body art, are you?"

It takes me a minute to catch my breath again.

Is my blood sugar crashing? Do I need more tea? Why am I so light-headed?

Goddess *damn* it!

"Admiring?" I scoff, averting my eyes. "Hardly. It's just impossible *not* to see it when you're flashing it all around like a... a... a big *flasher*... guy. Who flashes everything."

"As big flasher guys are wont to do."

"I can't believe you have a pitchfork tattooed on your butt cheek."

"It's ironic."

"It's tacky."

"Fine line, Mushroom, and I've been known to walk it on more than one occasion. That in itself is a skill. Highly underrated, if you ask me, this line-walking business. In fact, I'm rather—"

"Inside." Still not meeting his eyes, or any other part of his body, I jab my finger toward the apartment door. "*Now.*"

He huffs and puffs and waltzes into the apartment, pausing only to smile and pluck a bit of chamomile out of my hair before heading straight for the kitchen, where he proceeds to rifle through my pantry, cupboards, and fridge.

All without placing so much as a *dishtowel* over his dangling bits.

"You are *literally* a walking health code violation right now!" I follow him inside, Grumpy and Sunshine slinking in behind me because when it comes to the Devil's antics, somehow my formerly antisocial cats have come down with a case of FOMO and can't leave his side. "I can't *believe* you were out there naked in front of all those people!"

"Perhaps next time you'll reconsider inviting me to observe at the tea shop. Which, by the way, is a thing I'll need to do if I'm to help devise a plan to save it. And you. Goodness, what's gotten into your hair?"

I shake out a bit more of the chamomile. "Just work on devising a plan for the money. Leave the day-to-day tea shop business to me."

"The two are intricately bound, Mushroom. Just like us." He grins again, then leans his hip against my kitchen counter and glances down at his fingernails, as if he's contemplating a manicure. "Ah, fate. Such a cruel mistress, is she not? Anyway, back to this health code business—take a breath, love. This isn't a restaurant. And thank the Devil for that, since you have not *one* appetizing thing to offer. No canapés, no caviar, not an imported cheese wedge in sight. Tell me. How are you not starving?"

"Sorry my palate isn't as *refined* as yours. Next time I'll be sure to have some gourmet options flown in from the coast, along with some pants, because for whatever reason you seem to be completely allergic to the ones you have!"

"Your palate isn't the issue, nor is my lack of pants. The issue is your abject refusal to expand your mind and color outside the lines."

"Really? *Really*?" My insides are boiling again, full steam ahead. "You want to see coloring outside the lines? Fine. Buckle up, buttercup. Here we go."

Without waiting for a reply, I stomp off to the spare room that houses the bulk of my non-tea witchy supplies and make a few selections. Bag of salt, black candles, matches, loaded pin cushion, athame, a scrap of black cotton, and a small obsidian bowl. I also grab the vinegar from the kitchen.

Back in the living room, with the naked-ass, tattooed-ass, obstinate-ass Devil watching me in amused silence, I yank the drapes closed and roll up the braided rug, revealing the bare hardwoods beneath. I draw a pentagram in salt, then place a candle at every point and light it. The obsidian bowl goes smack dab in the center.

Grumpy and Sunshine pad over to me, my familiars finally remembering that their mama exists, and together we sit in front of one of the candles.

"*You*." I point at Devlin. "On the floor directly across from me."

"Care to let me know what game we're playing now?"

"The game where we banish you."

Devlin nearly chokes. "I beg your pardon?"

"Olivy said we can't reverse the spell, but maybe there's a way to just... *poof!* Send you away. With a different spell. Like, a spell on top of a spell, not breaking the first spell, so it's not cheating. Right? Right. Sit down, please."

"I have questions, Mushroom. Many, many questions. Namely, how is an empathic tea witch going to banish the Devil? Isn't that a bit of a stretch outside the ol' comfort zone?"

"All witches have inherent magic for things like banishing, summoning, hexing, healing, growing, and manifesting. Depending on where our skills and talents lie, and how we're raised, we're naturally drawn to more specialized areas over time. Now sit down and give me your hand. Oh! I also need a lock of hair."

"But where, exactly, are you banishing me to? And no, *poof* is not an acceptable answer."

"*Away*. The exact GPS coordinates are not my concern."

"Pardon me for prodding, but they're very much mine."

"If I send you *away*, and it works, that means our magical bind is broken. So from there, you'll be free to return to... wherever. Now, sit down and give me that hand!"

His energy flares with worry, but he does as I ask, sitting across from me and stretching his hand out to the center of the salt pentagram. "I hope you know what you're doing."

"Totally. Hold still—just a little prick."

"*That* is a lie! Happy to give you another glimpse if you need proof of—"

"Do *not* move." I grip his wrist, skin hot to the touch, and press the point of the athame to the center of his palm. A quick slice, and the blood wells up. I blot it with the black cloth and drop it into the bowl along with seven straight pins from the cushion.

"Now the hair," I say, handing him the athame.

"No offense, Mushroom, as I'm sure you're a skilled witch in almost *all* endeavors, botched summoning spell and financial mismanagement notwithstanding, but... Isn't the whole blood-and-banishing gig Olivy's area of expertise?"

"I've seen her perform banishing rituals before, so I know the routine. And I've read a lot of books." I've also watched a lot of Charmed and Supernatural, which are now serving as the basis for my dark-magic mojo, but Devlin doesn't need to know that.

Reluctance mingles with the worry in his energy field, but again, he does as I ask, slicing off a small hank of hair and dropping it into the bowl.

I add the vinegar, filling it until the contents are completely submerged.

"Just close your eyes," I tell him. "Take a few deep breaths and relax. And don't make a *sound* until you're gone."

"Poof?"

"Poof."

He holds my gaze another beat, brow furrowed, but finally, his eyes snap shut.

I strike another match. Take a few deep breaths of my own. And visualize a magical cord connecting us across the pentagram, then fraying, bit by bit until it's completely severed and Devlin finally vanishes.

Holding the image in mind, I recite my spell:

> *I call on the darkness, I call on the night*
> *I call on this magic to set things to rights*
> *By salt and by fire, his blood shall now burn*
> *Be gone from here, Devil—to home, you return!*

On the final word, I drop the lit match into the bowl. It ignites at once, a red flame that spirals outward from the center, then explodes in a bright red starburst with a blast so intense it extinguishes the candles, blows away the salt, knocks me flat on my back, and sends the cats racing halfway up the drapes, clinging for dear life.

Red and black smoke fills the apartment but quickly dissipates, leaving behind the scent of candle wax and burned hair.

I wait for my heart to stop racing, my breathing to go back to normal. After a few tense moments, the cats finally return to investigate, prodding me with curious noses and flicking tails and the general air of superiority cats have perfected over the ages.

"No worries, boys," I say softly. "Mama's A-okay. Did our banishing spell do the trick and send the mean ol' Devil packing?"

I sit up slowly, hope rising quickly. A slight ringing in my ears makes it hard to focus, but there across the dim space...

A dark shape takes form.

Well, less of a dark shape, and more of a flesh-colored one. With shiny black hair and broad shoulders and a shamelessly wicked grin.

"Oh, *no*," I whisper.

"Oh, *yes*. You know, Mushroom, far be it from me to hellsplain dark magic to a witch, but I'm fairly certain when you call upon the magic of the darkness and the night, it helps if you do it when it's *actually* night. Furthermore, while I appreciate a fireworks show as much as the next bloke, I really am quite famished, and my glass has been empty for far too long." He rises from the floor in a graceful movement that defies physics, dangling bits a-danglin' in a way that does *not* defy physics, and heads back to the kitchen. "Let's take another look at this paltry wine selection, shall we? See if you've got something that pairs well with the bitter taste of crushing disappointment."

CHAPTER TWELVE

DEVLIN

An hour later, the bitter taste of crushing disappointment is eclipsed by the sweet-and-spicy deliciousness of a bucket of hot wings and a barbecued ham-and-pineapple pizza (yes, pineapple absolutely *does* belong on a pizza, I shall die on this hill, and this particular pie is doing the goddess' work in redeeming the town of Pumpkinville as a quality establishment in my eyes).

After excavating a halfway decent Cabernet from an old holiday gift basket, we load up two plates and settle in side-by-side on her living room couch for some television, me in my favorite black silk pajama pants and smoking jacket (me being fond of the finer things), Violet in an oversized sweatshirt featuring a gnome picking dandelions (her being fond of the woodland realms).

It happens so naturally, this sitting side-by-side thing, it almost feels like we've been doing it for years. Like we're one of those adorably sickening couples who have things like "pizza night" and "our show" and trade food from each other's plates—you can have my olives, I'll take your extra pickle, save the extra sauce for me.

I dare say it's almost nice. If the Devil were allowed to want nice things of the sort money *can't* buy, which I'm not. And don't. Ever.

Anyway.

Midway through the pizza and the television episode both, I chance a quick glance at her, surprised to find she's already watching me. Assessing in that curious way of hers. Wild auburn curls falling out of the bun to frame her face, the enormous glasses magnifying all the shades of blue in her eyes.

The sudden desire to hug her is strong and nearly overpowering, which is obviously *not* something I can act on, nice things not falling within the Devil's purview, see above.

I return my attention to the pizza, peeling off a pineapple ring and popping it into my mouth. "I'm sorry the spell didn't work. For what it's worth, I really believed you'd be rid of me tonight."

Violet sighs her cute sigh, shoulders slumping. "Thanks for the vote of confidence, however misplaced it may be."

"Faith in your abilities is never misplaced. Just because it didn't work out this time doesn't mean you don't have the skill or talent."

Her cheeks darken, the hint of a smile playing on her

lips, but I can tell she's still out of sorts. Still sad, her small frame swimming in her too-big sweatshirt, hot sauce staining the corner of her mouth, chamomile flowers clinging tenaciously to her hair.

Plucking another one loose, I say softly, "You claim your heart's desire is to save Kettle and Cauldron. Is that all you wish for? Truly?"

She sighs again, a tiny wrinkle appearing between her eyebrows. I resist the urge to smooth it away with my thumb.

"It's the only thing I've got that's all mine," she says, emotion filling her eyes. "My dream, my sweat equity, my magic. The money I've invested so far, for all the good it did. I know I made some big missteps, got in way over my head. But I just... I can't lose this, Devlin. Kettle and Cauldron... it's everything to me."

I reach for my wine, give it a swirl. Down it. Conversations like this... I'm not used to them. The honesty. The vulnerability.

I've spent the last several centuries doing my damndest to encourage people to give in to their baser instincts. To follow their darkest urges right off the cliff, straight into the fires of Hell.

Because my father made it a condition of my return. Because I'm good at it. Because some dark, depraved part of me fucking *revels* in it.

Then a witch ensnares me in her trap—accidental, sure, but absolutely grounds for a good smiting. Yet somehow, all I can think about is helping her. Not because I'm bound to it, not because I'm getting something out of it, not because it brings me some twisted sense of pleasure.

But because I genuinely want to.

"If I'm to help you do this," I say now, forcing myself to meet her eyes, to see the pain and hope in them and not shrink away from either, "without my Hell magic or influence, as your sister instructed us, I need to understand what we're dealing with. I need to see you at work, Violet. You can't just lock me away upstairs and hope for the best."

A smile finally dawns. "Clearly that was *not* the best, as you so demonstrated with your naked day-drinking victory speech."

"Not the best? The ladies of Wayward Bay would beg to differ."

"At least one of them will be begging for a new bra. Lingerie is *not* cheap."

"I'm well aware."

The wrinkle appears once more, and Violet rises from the couch, heading into the kitchen for another slice. She returns with one for me as well, takes her seat, and unpauses the show.

At the end of the episode, she finally turns to me and says, "Here's the deal. You can hang out at the shop and take a few notes, maybe give me some pointers. From a safe, non-distracting, non-annoying distance."

"Excellent. I'll be on my *very* best behavior."

"Fully clothed," she hastens to add, which is smart on her part, loopholes being the Devil's love language. "And before you even ask? *No*, leather chaps don't count as fully clothed. Same for gray sweatpants."

"What? They're both perfectly—"

"Fully. Clothed."

"Fine, fine. I'll have Finn portal in with some additional selections from my wardrobe."

"*Normal* selections," she says, gesturing at my current ensemble. "Not this creepy-old-man-lurking-about-the-billiards-room getup you've got going on here."

"Excuse me, but this is imported silk from—"

"No cameras, no lighting, no social media."

"Cut off my right arm, why don't you?"

"There will also be no touching or rearranging of my ingredients. They need to stay in their appointed receptacles on their designated shelves at all times, to be removed and distributed only by me as needed."

"No touching your jugs—I mean, your *appointed receptacles*. Got it."

"And no critiquing my tea blends or playlists."

I raise my hands in surrender.

"And above all else," she states firmly, eyes blazing, "no fraternizing with the customers."

"Not even a friendly hello?"

"No. *Especially* not a friendly hello. I've seen your version of a friendly hello, and I have no interest in starting a catch-and-release program for renegade fangirl bras."

"You really are quite the stickler." I steal the last chicken wing from her plate—a well-deserved bit of thievery, in my opinion. "Well, I can't promise I won't greet the customers, Violet. They'll be expecting me after my balcony announcement today. But I can promise I'll keep it all above board."

"Fine."

"Is that all, then?"

"For now. But I reserve the right to amend the list at any time without notice."

I blow out a breath, cheeks puffing. "Is there a handbook? I feel like there should be a handbook."

"Devlin, I'm not in the mood—"

"You've got a lot of rules, is what I'm saying. I prefer not to get written up on my first day on the job. Sets a bad tone for the whole relationship, don't you think?"

"If you can't take this seriously, the deal is off."

"Oh, I'm quite serious. As you recall, I'm as desperate to get back to Los Angeles as you are to make me go *poof*, neither of which can happen until we save your café. Any shenanigans at this stage would be akin to mutually assured destruction." I gnaw the wing down to the bone and toss the spent carcass onto my plate. Then, spreading my hands like the little mushroom just scored the deal of the century, I say, "You won't even know I'm there."

CHAPTER THIRTEEN

DEVLIN

She *absolutely* knows I'm here.

Can't be helped. In a town where the news is so non-existent they cover elementary school sports, a newcomer will always draw attention.

This, despite my attempts to blend in.

Granted, I've yet to see anyone *else* reading a print newspaper before the fire, wearing a bespoke Italian suit with a rose-colored silk pocket square, so maybe I'm a *bit* rusty in the blending-in department. But Violet *insisted* I wear clothing today—health code violations, public indecency, blah blah blah—and I refuse to lower my standards. When in Rome, yes, but we're not in Rome, are we. We're in Pumpkinville, where flannel is the new black and the Devil is forced to set a higher bar.

Besides, how else am I to evaluate the tourist clientele for a soul or two teetering on the edge of self-destruction?

If I'm to attract the wealthy, the beautiful, and the immoral to my den of iniquity, I must also look the part. Like Finn said, corrupting the townsfolk is probably too much of a stretch goal, but I can certainly send a few malfeasant tourists into a downward spiral. Just a nudge, that's all. Pave the way for them to continue walking the path they've already chosen, one foot in front of the other, straight on to Hell.

By the by... That whole 'good intentions' thing? Yet another lie perpetuated by dear old Dad to keep his flock in line. The path to Hell is actually paved the same as any other—with greasy fast-food containers, used condoms, and broken dreams.

Thankfully, the lovely ladies of Wayward Bay have already spread the word on the socials about Violet's new houseguest, and ever since I established a no-selfies-without-purchase policy, we've been seeing a steady stream of paying customers, including at least two tourists from Manhattan who will *definitely* get a visit from Azazel with an invite to our next Hollywood Hills soirée.

Still, me as K&C's celebrity mascot is not a long-term solution. Once I'm gone, the attention on the shop will wane, unless we figure out how to capitalize on it.

"Pretty good day so far, huh?" Taking advantage of a momentary break, Violet joins me by the fire, cheeks flushed from the morning rush, curls tamed into a low ponytail. Today's shirt features three birds perched atop teacups dangling from a tree branch, stenciled with the message, *Make Like a Tea and Leaf!*

I fold up my newspaper and return her easy smile. "You should've hired me ages ago."

"Right? From now on, I'll keep you on drunk-summon speed dial." She laughs, light and unburdened, that adorable snort popping up at the end. "I think my two new blends are going over well too. And Emmie brought in some new pastries to try—also strong sellers. Things are definitely looking up."

"That they are."

"Anyway, how are *you* holding up? Do you need a cup of tea? With all the unexpected guests today, I didn't even think to ask you!"

"You're the empathic witch. You're supposed to tell *me* if I need some."

Violet laughs again, and damn if I'm not getting hooked on putting that sparkle in her eyes. "Doesn't work like that exactly."

"How *does* it work? Can you sense what I'm feeling right now? What I'm thinking about?"

"It's... complicated. Thinking, no. I can't read minds. Feeling... Sort of? I get impressions of people's emotions and intentions. General things, like fear or happiness or deceit. The stronger they're feeling the emotion, the easier it is for me to sense it. But let's take the fear thing, for example. It's not like I can tell *what* the person is afraid of. Or with deception, I don't know whether they're about to lie to *me* or someone else, or maybe just feeling guilty about something they've lied about in the past."

"Still, you must have some kind of deeper inkling beyond the vague generalities. I've seen you make a different brew for everyone who's come in today."

"Sure. I always try to sense what a customer needs—what will help them at that particular moment, or bring a smile to their face if I'm picking up on stress or sadness. If it's an obvious physical ailment, like a cold or a cough, I focus on that. Most of the time I'm just offering a cheerful pick-me-up. A little warmth on an otherwise cold day, you know?"

"Wayward Bay is lucky to have you looking out for them."

"Mayor Singh tells me the same thing. I'm just waiting for the rest of the town to get the memo."

"They will. We're going to make sure of that, yes?"

Violet tucks a loose curl behind her ear and nods.

"So tell me," I say. "What does the Devil *most* need at this particular moment?"

She scrutinizes my face, that tiny wrinkle forming between her eyebrows—her contemplative face, I'm coming to learn.

"You're lonely," she whispers, and we both gasp, as if the revelation is as shocking for her to discover as it is for me to realize how transparent I am.

"Oh, goddess." She covers her mouth. "I'm sorry. I didn't

mean to blurt it out like that. I'm probably way off base. It's... not always a perfect science."

Sounds pretty damned perfect to me. In fact, it feels like an accusation. A knife pressed too closely to the tender heart behind the bone, and I recoil, shuffling my paper open, scanning the headlines for an escape from this conversation.

"I quite enjoyed the cup you made on our first morning together," I say brusquely, not meeting her eyes. "Perhaps another of those, if it's not too much trouble?"

"That was my Welcome to Wayward Bay brew—with a few minor customizations."

"Sounds delightful. I'll take a double."

"Devlin?"

"Hmm?"

She's quiet for so long, I'm certain she's shuffled off to make the tea. But when I glance up again, I find her still standing there, just watching me. Calm and sweet and sincere.

"I just wanted to say... thank you." She offers that cute shrug. "I know you *have* to help me in order to break the spell, but still. I appreciate you being so chill about the whole thing. I'm... working on another plan to set you free."

"We *have* a plan, Mushroom. Wrangle up some business, make some money, save the shop—Bob's your uncle, we're on our way."

"A *different* plan. You'll see." She tries to wink at me, fails miserably, laughs again, and then she's off.

It doesn't take long for her to brew the tea, but before she can deliver it, the next wave of customers sweeps in. I'm contemplating getting up and retrieving it from the counter myself when someone *else* does the honors instead, delivering it to me with a dark, foreboding glare, no extra charge.

"How's it hangin', Horns?" the woman says.

Olivy.

I fold up my newspaper and sigh. "Has anyone ever told you, you're a bit spooky?"

"I don't know, *Satan*. Has anyone ever told you that?" She sets the cup and saucer on the table, then sits across from me, uninvited.

"Don't you have a job? A hobby? A body to hide beneath your floorboards?"

"You'd think so, right? Alas, I'm on team good-guy. I help the cops take down assholes who hurt women. Which is, not coincidentally, why I'm here." She folds her hands in her lap and grins, interview style. "So tell me, Devlin Pierce. How do you feel about keeping your cock attached to your body?"

"I'm very much attached to the attachment." I sip the tea—perfection, as always, almost enough to dim the threats. "How can I help you, Olivy?"

"We need to have a chat about this whole 'unlocking the heart's desire' business. Lay some ground rules."

I don't bother hiding my derisive snort. "The only rules I'm beholden to, *witch*, are those set forth by the laws of magic. I've also agreed to honor your sister's wishes as a courtesy I rarely offer. Beyond that—"

"Beyond *that*, if you value your *attachments*, you'll hear me out."

"Oh, for fuck's..." I place the folded newspaper in my lap and give the vile witch my full attention. "Carry on."

"I don't know how much Violet told you about our family, but we're a tight bunch. Five of us girls—sisters by choice. And the Aunts."

"The Aunts?"

"Joslyn, Althea, and Lorelei. They run Three Sisters B&B up on Raven Hill."

"Sisters by choice as well?"

"They're our aunts by choice, but the three of them are blood-related. Waywards, actually, descended from the town founder, Agatha Wayward. And like I said, we're close. Closer than blood."

"Which explains why you're threatening to chop off my favorite appendage to use in your dark workings."

"Dark workings?" A lopsided grin twists her black-painted lips. "Do you have any idea how much I could get for the Devil's *actual* dick on the dark web?"

"*No*, and I don't want to know. Merciful Hell, why are you so vicious? Your sister makes a calming tea. Perhaps you should indulge in a cup. Or eight."

"And dull the edges of my sharp and scintillating personality?" Olivy laughs, but it fades quickly. When she speaks again, her voice is soft, laced with a tender affection I didn't even know she was capable of. "Violet... She's the best of us. Biggest heart, biggest dreams, first in line to help an old lady across the street, first to fall in love, first to get crushed when life drops a bomb on her head. It *kills* me that she's in this predicament with the café, but you heard what she said—I'm bound to secrecy. She won't let her family help her. Which means it all comes down to you."

"Your point being?"

"No offense, but I don't trust *anyone* outside the inner circle."

"As well you shouldn't."

"I don't want her to get hurt. Period."

"You've got nothing to worry about there. The spell prevents me from harming so much as a hair on her head, lest the magic think I'm trying to cheat my way out of our deal."

Her eyes blaze—an even more terrifying sight than her black lipstick. "That's not the kind of hurt I'm talking about."

It's admirable, the way she looks out for her sister. Which is the only reason I'm even entertaining this conversation instead of roasting her alive. Loyalty goes a long way with me.

"I'll say this, Olivy, but only once. You have no reason to trust me, but despite the circumstances of our meeting, I harbor no ill will toward Violet. I'm not sure whether the Devil's word is worth as much as his severed cock on the internet, but I'll give it to you anyway. I promise I'll take care of her and do everything in my power to help unlock her heart's desire, whatever that entails."

"Fair enough."

"But you need to do something for me in return."

"A Devil's bargain?" She laughs. "I don't think so."

"No. A sisters' bargain." I extend my hand. "Don't count Violet down and out just yet. Yes, she's in a bind, and yes, I'm going to do everything in my power within the confines of the spell to help her. But she's a strong woman in her own right. She's already brainstorming new ideas, coming up with new brews, making an effort to analyze her competition. So no, saving the shop does *not* come down to me. She's a fighter, and she's bloody well *got* this. Understand?"

Her eyes widen, then drop to my hand. She stares at it a few beats, brow furrowed as if she's having some raging internal argument with herself. Then, finally, she shakes.

"No mission creep," she adds. "Like you said, you'll operate within the confines of the spell to help her unlock her desire and save the shop, but that's *it*. No other... entanglements."

"Olivy." I return to my paper and laugh, not out of derision this time, but genuine amusement. "What other entanglements could there *possibly* be?"

CHAPTER FOURTEEN

DEVLIN

If ever I believed my celebrity was a given, that the presence of my company was an experience for which people would offer up a firstborn child, the good folks of Pumpkinville have thoroughly disabused me of that notion.

Talk about a swift kick to the nether regions.

By the third day of my Kettle and Cauldron mascot-ship, the bloom has fallen off the rose. I'm no longer the sexy spectacle for the locals I once was—in fact, they're all treating me as if I'm one of them, nothing to see here, moving right along, which is appalling on at least six different levels—and the tourists have flocked back to Mean Beans, leaving the café a veritable ghost town.

What's worse, since I haven't been posting on my own channels, the views and engagement metrics are down across the board, and Finn and Azazel are threatening to obliterate each other over party planning creative differences. If I have to field one more inquiry about wrangling live lawn flamingos...

"Fucking disaster," I mutter, scrolling through the social media footage from last night's event. My home is a mess (lawn flamingos left un-wrangled will do that), the guests leave much to be desired, and although I adore my best mate... *Ugh*. When it comes to playing the playboy host-with-the-most, there's just no besting the original.

"I wouldn't call it a disaster, exactly." Violet flops onto the café couch next to me, her curls bouncing. "More like an apocalyptic wasteland."

"I was speaking of something else, Mushroom. Kettle and Cauldron is neither disaster nor wasteland. Just a bit slow."

"It was fun while it lasted, huh?" In the absence of human witnesses, she flicks her fingers toward the fireplace, calling the smoldering flames back to life. "I wish Mean Beans would disappear. I'll never understand why places like that are so popular."

"People are drawn to the comforts of sameness and predictability. At Mean Beans, they know what to expect, whether they're halfway across the world or right in their own backyards."

"That's what's so crazy to me. Why travel anywhere if you're just going to do the same things you do at home? If I took a trip somewhere—even just one town over—I'd want to try all new foods, all new places, talk to new people."

"Not everyone is as adventurous as you."

"I'm the opposite of adventurous, which is why I *don't* take many trips." She laughs. "Not since I was a kid, anyway. Guess I like predictability in my old age too."

"Says the woman who summoned the Devil."

"Oh my goddess! Stop!" She gives me a playful smack on the thigh. "I told you! You were supposed to be a—"

"Pivot table, yes, I recall."

"Not to brag, but I'm actually known as the spreadsheet queen among my sisters. When I'm not drinking, obviously. Just wait until I show you my inventory and budget sheets—prepare to be impressed."

"I'm already impressed." I wink and drain my third cup of tea of the day, each one even better than the last, improving my mood in ways that alcohol, orgies, and social media stardom never quite can. "Mean Beans is just a bump in the road. This tea is too divine to fail—mark my words."

"I keep trying to tell myself that, too. But honestly?" Her face falls, the teasing sparkle dimming from her eyes. Even her curls seem to droop. "It's not just the coffee chain, Devlin. I've been struggling to stay open for a long time now. Even if I tripled the business overnight and kept it steady for months, it wouldn't be enough. For whatever reason, I don't seem to have what the customers ultimately want. I don't know... maybe my teas aren't that special after all."

"Do you really believe that? Wait, don't answer." I rise

from the couch and extend a hand. "Time for an experiment."

Her gaze narrows, but she takes my hand and allows me to lead her behind the counter.

"A request, if you please." I turn toward the impressive wall of teas and spices behind us. "May I—just this once for demonstrative purposes only—fondle your canisters?"

"*What*? Why?"

That doesn't sound like a *no*, exactly, so onward we march.

"I'd like to give this tea blending thing a whirl. Special brew, never before attempted in this realm or the next, it'll be all the rage." I grab the black tea and scan the shelves for some additional inspiration, ignoring her tut-tuts of protest. "Violet, be a dear and put the kettle on, will you?"

"Excuse me, *sir*. I don't know how they did it in *your* time, way back before dinosaurs roamed the earth, but these days the craft of tea blending is a bit more involved than pouring a pot of water over some leaves."

"Correct me if I'm wrong, as my advanced, *advanced* age might be ushering in a bit of hearing and/or memory loss, but I could've sworn you *just* said your teas are, and I quote, 'not that special after all.' If that's true, then it stands to reason any know-nothing twat off the street ought to be able to cobble together a brew, and here I am, far from a know-nothing, farther still from a twat. Now stand aside and let me work."

She leans back against the counter, arms folded across her chest. "Point made."

"Not yet. Put on the kettle."

"Devlin, seriously." She grabs the tea, tucks it back into its cubby. "Go back to the fire and relax. I've got this."

"Really. You've got this." I remove the tea once more, undeterred by her huffing and puffing. "Is that why you've had four customers in the last two hours, one of whom you didn't even charge, despite the fact that he had tea and *two* muffins?"

"Mr. Moriarty is on a fixed income!"

"Keep it up and *you'll* be on a *zero* income."

She glares at me, nostrils flaring. I glare right back, letting my horns show, my irises glowing red.

The mushroom rolls her eyes. "Fine. I'll allow this little experiment, but there are rules, Devlin."

"Of course there are."

"First, you need to wash your hands. With soap. And put on an apron. I don't care *how* much it clashes with that expensive suit, either, which, by the way... Who wears a thousand-dollar suit to hang out in a tea café all day?" She reaches under the counter and fishes one out for me, which I dutifully tie around my hips, poor fashion statement be damned. "Oh, and be sure to put back each ingredient *exactly* where you found it, jars clean of smudges and debris, facing forwards."

"Ten thousand-dollar suit, and are you, perchance, a Virgo?"

"And proud of it. So watch your tone, or I'll put Mr. 10K Suit in a fifty-cent hairnet."

"It's dreadful of you to even suggest such a thing. Now please, for the last time, go put on the kettle."

One more huff, another pointed glare, the stamp of a small but determined foot, and she's off to the kitchen, leaving me to follow the whims of my muse.

Black tea, check. Pink peppercorns... hmm. Fairly certain that's the name of a woman Finn once dated, very keen on sharing as I recall, so we'll toss some of those in as well. Dried cherries, grated ginger, oh *yes* this is going to be perfect. And, ah! How could I forget, king of all spices both magical and mundane, cinnamon!

"You're getting fingerprints on the bottles!" she cries.

"I'll polish them all once my masterpiece is complete." I locate the cardamom pods, pop a few of those into the mix, then back to the cinnamon for another go.

"Devlin! You can't just add things willy-nilly like that! You're using too much cinnamon!"

"You know, you're right. I should try the cayenne pepper instead." I find the bottle and add copious amounts of that too. "When it comes to spice, more is *always* more, am I right?"

"No! You're not right! You're so not right, just standing next to you is giving me an anxiety attack!"

"Then take a few calming breaths and go stand over *there*." I nod toward the exit. "Problem solved."

"That's it. We are *done*!" She marches to the front of the shop, peers out the window in both directions, sighs mightily, then locks the door and flips on the *Be Back After Lunch!* sign.

She's clearly a witch on a mission, stomping back behind the counter and nudging me and my super-brew out of the way without so much as a word, grabbing teas and tinctures and herbs off the shelves, muttering spells and curses under her breath—hellspawn this, chain-breaker that—as she sprinkles and dashes and pours things into a fresh pot, working so fast a veritable dust cloud forms around her.

The kitchen kettle hasn't yet boiled, and I watch in shocked silence as she pours the barely steamed water over the foulest-smelling concoction this side of the River Styx, her face blotchy with anger, curls trembling, lips still muttering who knows what.

Just as I'm beginning to fear the fumes alone will peel the paint from the walls, she gives it a swirl, strains it into a cup, and shoves it toward me.

"Drink this."

I take a step back, hands up. "Never have I ever intentionally ingested something handed off by an angry, beautiful woman and accompanied by the words, 'drink this.' Just a personal policy honed over centuries of hard lessons learned, thanks."

She rolls her pretty blue eyes. "I'm not trying to poison you, Devlin. Just trying one more thing to break our invisible chains. Hail Mary, down the hatch."

"Have we learned nothing from the other night's ill-informed dance on the dark side?"

"That was a banishing spell, which is not—admittedly—my forte. This is tea. Totally different situation."

"I see." I give the brew a tentative whiff—bad idea on my part. "And what is the name of this one, may I ask, and also, may I have a shot of something stronger to chase it?"

"Devil Be Gone. Smells awful, but ultimately harmless." She flashes a wide smile, glasses slipping down her nose. "Just like you."

"I'm far from smelly *or* harmless." Holding my breath, I close my eyes and lift the mug to my lips. Down the hatch it goes, because for some reason I trust this witch, which is an entirely new level of fuckery I didn't realize existed before today, yet here we are. Tea-brewing. Witch-trusting. What's next? Doing good deeds? Giving up drinking? Going to *church*? Apparently, anything goes in the topsy-turvy world of Pumpkinville!

The brew slithers down my throat and settles uncomfortably in my stomach much in the same way I imagine straight battery acid would.

"Well?" she demands. "Anything?"

"Tell me I've vanished," I say, eyes still closed. "Tell me

I'm back in the bowels of Hell, for there's no other reason such a culinary calamity should ever be endured."

"Damn it."

"I'm serious, Mushroom. I feel as though I've spent the better part of the week licking a camel's arsehole—an ill-advised trend I swore off for good after the dark ages."

"Okay, first of all? You need therapy. Second of all... ugh. I need therapy too, because my tea didn't work and you're still here and now you're talking about dark-age camel butts and I'm just in a *very* fragile state so if you don't mind, I'd—"

The door chimes, and a male voice cuts through the bickering.

"Vi? You open, babe?"

What. In the ever-loving. Fuck.

CHAPTER FIFTEEN

DEVLIN

I open my eyes to see a dim bulb of a man jiggling his keys free from the front door. The one Violet most definitely locked.

"*Babe* is most certainly *not* open." I tamp down a surge of irritation. "The sign on the door should've been a dead giveaway. See also, the *locked* door. And yet—"

"Can I help you with something, Brandt?" Violet asks, her annoyance as sharp and pungent as her Devil Be Gone brew.

Clearly, she knows the man.

Clearly, not as well as he'd *like*, judging from the hungry way he's staring at her... canisters.

It shouldn't bother me. But suddenly I'm picturing this dead-eyed Neanderthal stark-raving naked with a pole up his arse, churning like a rotisserie chicken over one of Hell's many fires.

"I was just in the neighborhood." His beady brown eyes flick to me, then back to her. "Everything okay?"

"Just in the neighborhood of your own office less than two blocks away?" Violet laughs. Not her real one. "Yes, what a mighty coincidence. I see you've brought my keys back—you can leave those right on the counter for me, then show yourself out."

"I don't mind hanging on to them. Checking in every once in a—"

"Keys. Counter. Now."

He sighs and pouts in a way highly unbecoming for a nearly middle-aged male, but does as she asks, removing two keys from the ring and sliding them across the counter, his finger still holding them in place.

"You, uh, going to the Halloween Ball?" He flashes her what I suspect is his A-game grin, but I'd bet a small fortune it's the exact face he'd make for the whole rotisserie-pole-up-the-arse scenario, so... hard to tell.

"Always do," she says.

"Dressing up?"

"Halloween Ball, Brandt. Kind of a thing."

"Got a date this year?"

That smarmy grin again. The dull brown eyes. The unchecked desire as he runs them up and down her lithe frame.

Unable to remain a passive witness, I lean across the counter. Grab his wrist. Forcibly remove his hand from the keys and sweep them into my apron pocket. "Thanks *ever* so much for stopping by, *Brandt*. As you can see, Violet and I are quite thoroughly engaged in another matter. So, if you're not here to make a purchase, it's time to make like a tea and *leaf*."

Dim bulb just gapes—really, we're talking twenty watts between the ears, at max—but Violet's snickering behind me, the precious snort filling me with unchecked glee.

Rubbing his wrist, Brandt nods at the dregs of her failed banishing brew, still sitting on the counter between us. "What's *that*?"

"Posterior essence of Camelus bactrianus," I declare with a smile, taking great pleasure in unleashing another of Violet's snorts, try as she might to hide it.

"Is that... some sort of spice?" Twenty Watt wants to know.

"Experiment gone bad," Violet says.

"And this one?" He turns his attention to my abandoned creation, a pile of tea and herbs no one in his right mind would even look at, let alone ask about.

But again, dimness reigns supreme.

"Also bad." Violet tightens her apron strings and sighs. "So, if there's nothing else I can do for you, Brandt—"

"Actually, that one is quite good." Offering a mile-wide customer-service grin, I dump the mixture into a fresh teapot. "Crafted it myself. It's got a bit of a kick, granted, but if you're not sensitive to spice, you might enjoy it."

"He hates spice," Violet informs me. "All kinds of spice."

This shouldn't please me as much as it does, but I'm a petty, petty man and hey, I take my kicks where I can get them.

"I *love* spice," he snaps. "You don't know everything about me, Violet. Not anymore."

Ohhh.. Now this *is getting interesting...*

"Of course you like spice, Brandt." I offer a conspiratorial wink, like, *just one of the guys, we're all friends here, you know how the womenfolk get these* crazy *ideas in their heads*. "But as I mentioned, this particular blend *is* fairly intense. Brand new, hot off the presses. Only for the most *discerning* of customers."

"Yeah? What's in it?"

"Trade secret, but it's called The Devil Made Me Brew It."

"Is that... like... a pun?"

"Oh, it's quite literal. I assure you." I head to the kitchen to fetch the kettle, Violet right on my heels.

"Seriously?" she hisses. "What are you doing? I'm trying to get him out of here!"

"Just having a bit of fun, Mushroom," I whisper. "Experimentation is good for the soul."

"Do you even have a soul?"

"No, but we *do* have a *most discerning* customer, one who's clearly seen you naked at some point in the not-so-distant past which FYI I will *very* much be inquiring about later, and

I'm in the mood to be a complete and utter prick. So! Off we go."

I leave her gaping behind me and head out to brew his tea. The steam curls eagerly from the pot, the scent nearly as pungent as Violet's earlier brew but ever-so-slightly less offensive.

"So, you new in town?" Twenty Watt asks, conversational mastermind that he is. "I wasn't aware Violet had the budget for an employee."

"I'm a consultant, actually." I snap the takeaway lid onto his cup. "Best of the best, very exclusive, years-long waiting list. Anyway, here you are, all fired up and ready to go."

I slide the cup his way. He gives it an indelicate whiff, then recoils, barely smothering a cough.

"Too spicy for you, then?" I laugh. "No worries. Not every man is man enough to handle the Devil's Brew."

"Just getting used to it, is all." He takes a full sip. Coughs and sputters emerge. Eyes water. Face turns the color of a ripe tomato. Very entertaining, the whole hot mess of him.

"It's... it's good," he wheezes, fumbling for his phone and swiping it over the payment screen. He does not, I notice, leave a tip. "Real good. Anyway, I have an important meeting with important people, so..."

"Yes, of course. Oh, and Brandt? Good luck when that brew hits the other end."

He's gone before he can even draw his next breath.

"I don't want to talk about Brandt Remington the Third,"

Violet announces, locking the door behind him. "So don't even ask."

"Brandt Remington the Third?" I laugh. "Poor bloke was bound to be a cunt. No getting 'round it with a name like that." I retrieve the keys from my apron and hand them over. "Anyway, I'm pleased to report that *my* tea-brewing days are officially over, but yours most certainly are not."

"Jury's still out on that." She blows a breath into her curls and collects the kettles and cups from the counter, carrying them into the kitchen. When she returns, she double-checks her bottles and jars, turning them this way and that, carefully putting everything back in its exact right place.

I watch her straightening and polishing, spraying down the counter, cleaning everything to a high shine. She's meticulous and focused, leaving everything she touches better than how she found it.

Yet the pride of a job well done isn't enough to bring the smile back to her face.

"I've got some thoughts for your consideration," I say softly, "if you're ready for them."

"Ah, yes. The official assessment from my best-of-the-best consultant." She tosses a towel over her shoulder and takes a seat at one of the counter stools across from me, drumming her fingers nervously. "Let's have it, then."

"The good news is… It's not the product. Your teas are fabulous, even without my added contributions. And who doesn't love a scratch-made scone with genuine clotted cream?"

"My sister Emmilou makes them for me. She traveled to London and took classes from some famous pastry chef."

"It shows. And the location? Prime real estate. Plenty of pedestrian traffic, easy to get to on foot or by car, ample parking to boot. And you've definitely got the witchy, kitschy, cat-loving, pumpkin-spice vibe on tap that makes *everyone* want to believe in magic, so put that in the win column."

"I'm... not sure if that's a compliment or an insult, but—"

"It's just the facts, Mushroom. You have all the ingredients you need for a successful tea business right here. The thing that's holding you back isn't the product or the place or even the competition, as much as Mean Beans is a thorn in our side."

"Then what *is* the problem?"

"Simple." I spread my hands and grin, like, *ta-da!* "It's... you."

"Okay, now *that* sounds suspiciously like an insult."

"Tell me something. Why do you craft your teas?"

At long last, the smile returns, and behind her glasses, the spark in those blue eyes re-ignites. It changes her whole face, top to bottom. Even the way she holds herself is different now—sitting up straight, shoulders squared, tall and proud. Happy. "I do it because I—"

"Stop. See, I don't even need the words." I circle her face with my finger. "That look says it all. Tea is your absolute passion. Your purpose. The most natural expression of your magic. Even the act of *thinking* about it lights you up from the inside out."

Emotion glazes her eyes. "Yes! That's exactly it. Goddess, you get it."

"I do. And that's *precisely* where we need to start. Not with a marketing plan or a budget review or a social media strategy. But with you. Your *why*."

"My what?"

"No, your *why*. Why you're doing this. What inspires you to wake up at dawn nearly every morning, work yourself to the point of exhaustion, drain your bank accounts, and keep going day after day when the going gets tougher and tougher, all for a chance to share your gifts with Wayward Bay. Basically, all the stuff that's in your heart, waiting to be unlocked."

"You're losing me here, Dev." She shakes her head, thumb tracing a groove in the countertop. "People come for the tea and the food, first and foremost. The vibes, yes, that's a close second. But no one cares that it's my passion. My purpose. My *thing*."

"Then it's your job to make them care." I reach across the counter and grab her hands. "Having a business that serves the public—whether it's tea or a restaurant or sketching caricatures on the street... It always requires a bit of a performance."

"I can't be fake, Devlin. That's not who I am."

"You don't have to be fake. Some of us excel at it, not to name names, *ahem*, but more often than not, the most successful businesses are those whose proprietors find a genuine way to channel their passions and present some aspect of *that* to their customers. Whether it's an author writing a story they personally relate to, or an actor borrowing from a devastating real-life experience to better portray a grieving character, or a tea witch infusing a bit of her unique magic into every cup... People connect with authenticity, Violet. But you're almost preventing them from doing it."

"I am?"

"You're literally hiding out behind the counter. Yes, you talk with some of your neighbors, but when the tourists pop in, you keep your head down and do it like it's a job."

"It *is* a job. I'm making their orders. That's what they pay for."

"I understand that, but you need to let them in a bit. When you're brewing the tea, your back is always turned. They can't see what I see—the way you bite your lip when you're concentrating on selecting the perfect ingredients, the way your eyes shine when you know you've just crafted the ideal brew. The smile that lights up your face when you pop the lid on the takeaway cup or set the spoon on a saucer—the final step before you're about to make someone's day better."

Her cheeks darken, and she turns her hands over, lacing

her fingers through mine. The movement sends a jolt through my arms, my skin heating at her soft touch.

"I... can't believe you noticed all that," she whispers.

"How could I not?" I lean closer. Release a hand just so I can tuck an errant curl behind her ear, silky soft, coiling around my finger like a vine. "We've already proven this endeavor is much more than tossing a few leaves into a pot. What you offer here goes *far* beyond that. Your magic, you, all of it. You need to believe that for yourself, and let your customers connect with it, too."

"My why."

I nod, still fingering that perfect curl, still holding her hand, not wanting to let go of either. "I'm bound by the spell to help you unlock your heart's true desire. You said it was to save the shop, but no. That's just the ultimate goal. Your true *desire* is what lies deeper than that—the magic, the passion."

"I get what you're saying, but... I have no idea how to do that."

"I'll help you."

"You will?"

"I promise you, Mushroom. I'm in it to win it. But the spell requires me to unlock your heart's desire. So, as much as I hate to say it—and *you* might hate to hear it—I *really* need to understand what makes that heart tick. Because that's it, love. That's your why. And if we can bring it out of hiding, we might just figure out how to save Kettle and Cauldron from the chopping block."

Another smile, and she tightens her grip on my hand, renewed hope singing through her touch. "You really think so?"

"I do." I finally release her, mostly because if I don't, I'm going to kiss her, and that can only end in disaster. So, turning on another smile of my own, I lean back against the shelving, cross my arms over my chest, and give her a once-over. "Now *please* put a pre-dinosaurian Devil out of his misery and tell me what you *ever* saw in Mr. Twenty-Watt Dildo the Third."

CHAPTER SIXTEEN

VIOLET

This is a bad idea. Possibly worse than the summoning itself. And the failed banishments. And allowing Devlin to wear a suit to the café, looking so fine it's almost as distracting as his patio-day-drinking birthday suit.

It's worse than pretty much any idea I've ever had since the dawn of Violet Pepperdine. Well, except for dating Brandt last year. Nothing will ever top that in terrible life choices.

But... Devlin's right. We need more than a marketing plan to save the shop, and if he thinks I'm the problem—that I'm getting in my own way and hiding out from my "why"—then it's time for a new tactic.

So this is me, cracking myself wide open for the Devil.

Which sounds *way* more sexy than it is.

Unfortunately.

Because the way I *melted* when he grabbed my hands,

when he touched my hair, when he saw right down to the core of me...

Head in the game, Pepperdine. Head in the game.

Anyway. We started our new mission immediately, no time to waste. Closed up shop at five, headed upstairs, fed the kitties, and now it's official—no more company behavior. No more politely shuffling past each other on the stairs. No more Devlin sitting in his expensive-suited fabulousness while silently observing me at work. No more me watching Charmed or reading alone in my room while he retreats to the purple couch downstairs (and steals my feline reading companions, not that I'm bitter).

From this moment forward, Devlin gets the real me, live and uncut.

And I get the roommate from Hell. Literally.

Goddess, this is crazy. But I'm in too deep now to turn back.

"Consider yourself lucky," I say. "No one outside the inner circle gets my homemade grilled cheese and tomato soup." I slide the sandwiches off the griddle and onto our plates, cheese bubbling out the sides, the bread crisped to golden, buttery perfection. "This is my favorite comfort meal, especially as the weather turns colder." I glance out the window, the rain blurring the trees into a stained-glass tapestry of reds and golds. "There's just something so cozy about it. All that buttery goodness, the gooey melty cheesiness, the tang of the tomatoes."

Eagerly waiting at the small table in my kitchen nook, Devlin laughs. "Well. Now you've gone and hyped it up to the point where it can't *possibly* meet my over-inflated expectations."

"Just try it." I ladle the soup into bowls and set everything on the table, taking the seat across from him. Then, dipping a corner of the sandwich into the steaming soup, I say, "Like this. Only way to do it."

He casts a wary eye, but dunks his sandwich and takes a bite. The moment his teeth sink into the crispy bread, the pretense of culinary discernment drops away. His eyes flutter closed, a glob of melted cheese dripping down the corner of his mouth.

And he moans out loud. Multiple times.

"Mmmm. Oh my... oooooh, *yes*. That's it, right there. Right *fucking* there. So, so good. *Mmmm...*"

My thighs clench in response to the obscenely sexy soundtrack, to the way his tongue darts out to lick the runaway cheese from the corner of his mouth, and something buried inside me—deep, *deep* inside me—thrums back to life.

Is it my primal magic? An unbreakable bond to my ancestors, calling out across the veil? The ancient witchcraft singing through my blood and bones?

Nope. It's...

Hey girl! This is your vagina speaking, what is UP? Sorry I've been out of touch for the past twelve to thirteen months... I was off looking into early retirement options—I mean, after the whole Brandt debacle, I really thought we were closing down for good this time. But then along comes Mr. Hot, Broody, and British, going at that sandwich like tonguing is an Olympic event, and hell-oooo! I'm baaaack! Pretty sure I speak for both of us when I say it's high time we climb aboard that D-train and ride it all the way to Pound Town, round-trip on the daily and twice on Sundays, let's gooo!

"Violet?"

"Hmm?"

"I asked what your secret is?"

The one about your orgasmic reaction to my comfort food bringing my vagina out of hibernation and turning her into my own personal Downtown Pep Squad?

I cross my legs. Ignore the throb. Send that bitch back into hyper-sleep and smile through the pain. "Smoked gouda. A smear of roasted red pepper hummus. Two grinds of black pepper and a dash of Himalayan sea salt to tie it all together. Oh, and butter. Copious amounts, all sides of the bread. You can never have too much butter."

"Indeed." He blots his mouth with the napkin in a way that has me wishing I was born a napkin. "Would it be too much trouble to ask for another? I've still got quite a bit of soup left, and it seems a shame to let the opportunity go to waste."

Are you going to make those sounds again? Because if you are,

I might need to excuse myself for about ten to fourteen minutes to... um...

"No trouble at all!" I say brightly, picking up his plate and carrying it back toward the griddle. "I'm glad you're enjoying yourself."

"Enjoying myself? Mushroom, this meal is downright orgasmic."

I drop the plate into the sink with a clatter. Then I crack up, because what the hell else can I do at this point? The Devil is at my kitchen table, eating grilled cheese in a way that ought to be X-rated, maybe even illegal—definitely a health code violation of some sort, considering what's going on between my thighs right now—and all I can say is, "Second orgasms, coming right up!"

"I *knew* you were a fan of multiples. It's always the quiet ones you have to watch out for."

Fuck the grilled cheese sandwiches! Cries the Downtown Pep Squad. *Girl, it's high time this man butters* our *bread and stuffs us full of his hot, melty—*

"Water?" I choke out. "I mean, would you like some more? For the grilled cheese. You know, because it's... really cheesy."

Devlin smiles, eyes twinkling, the raised brow locked and loaded like a weapon about to go off and obliterate me. "If by water you mean wine, absolutely. But you just focus on the griddle. I'll get the bottle."

Somehow, despite his close proximity in my tiny kitchen,

not to mention the sultriness of the rain pattering against the windows, I don't burn the sandwiches. Which is more than I can say for my panties.

Goddess, why does he have to smell so good? Smoky, sweet, and spicy all at the same time—a deadly combination that's making me even hungrier than the sizzle of butter on the griddle.

Dinner, round two, is another smash hit, and by the time we're finished, the rain has turned into a deluge and my mind has devolved into a hardcore porno starring the naked bad-boy Devil and his naked grilled-cheese-flipping witch (in fact ,that's the title of the film, could anything be more perfect?), cheese melted over various lickable places, spatula getting up to all sorts of shenanigans, and all I can say is thank the underworld *gods* Devlin offers to do the dishes, because I'm pretty sure I need to have that lie-down.

Oblivious to the plight of my perfectly innocent, perfectly ruined panties, Devlin sends me off to the living room to quote-unquote "relax" and "do whatever it is you do on a random evening."

So, while he's washing and drying with his sleeves rolled up—yes, still with the white dress shirt—and I'm trying desperately not to think about those forearms flexing as they pin me down on the mattress, I settle into an approximation of my usual routine, curling up on the couch with my latest book obsession. Sunshine bounds over immediately, Grumpy making me wait for it, and eventually my two familiars are both snuggled up on my lap, eager to hear what's next for our favorite storybook couple.

I snap my fingers to dim the lights and ignite the candles, the scent of my cinnamon simmer pot floating on the air, the rain sluicing down the windows in a thousand tiny rivulets.

Perfect romance-reading vibes? *Engaged.*

"Now. Where were we?" I scan the page and clear my throat, then begin, right where we left off. "Lennox couldn't bear to know he hurt Savannah so grievously. She was his soul mate, his better half, the woman who'd picked up his broken pieces and glued them back together. Her love made him a better man, and now that she was back in his arms—"

"I beg your pardon," Devlin says, and I yelp, startling both cats. I didn't even hear him approach, but suddenly he's right behind the couch, looking down from high above like the dark, brooding god of hotness he is. "But are you reading a romance novel aloud?"

My cheeks flame, and I close the book at once. "Don't judge me."

"To your *cats*?"

"Why is that a problem?"

"It's not a problem. Just a bit..." He grins that maddening grin. "...quirky."

"Grumpy and Sunshine *love* romance novels. Why do you think I named them Grumpy and Sunshine?"

"Because one's an arsehole and the other one's the furry equivalent of a clown on speed?" He comes around to the front and lifts my legs, taking a seat next to me and placing my feet in his lap.

So now I'm paralyzed with fear, lest my fuzzy-socked foot accidentally twitch and rub his—

"Aww," he purrs, and it takes me a second to realize he's talking to the cats, who've abandoned me for their new bestie. Rubbing Sunshine's ears, he says, "Did you hear me talking about you, baby? I meant a *nice* clown on speed. Not a scary one."

Even Grumpy is nudging Devlin's hand, sniffing around for some love. The two cats can't get enough, and now we're all just piled on the too-small couch together like a too-big dysfunctional family, and when Devlin leans down and kisses Grumpy's head, my heart lurches.

That... can't be good. Hopefully it's just a heart attack or something. Because I *can't* be crushing on this man. Devil. That's just not... possible.

"Carry on, Mushroom." Devlin taps the book still clutched in my hands. "Don't leave poor Lennox hanging."

I glare. A thing I've really perfected since the Devil entered my life. And he gives me the sexy eyebrow arch. A thing *he* probably perfected when humans first crawled out of the primordial muck.

"If you're going to mock my hobbies," I snap, "then you can forget the whole thing and go back downstairs. Alone. Without me *or* the cats *or* my grilled cheese."

"No cats or grilled cheese? Please don't banish me so,

mistress." He presses a hand to his heart, his eyes glittering like amber in the candlelight. "I'll behave. I want to hear the rest of the story. Truly."

"You're just saying that."

"I'm not." He stops petting the cats and squeezes my foot, thumb pressing against the arch, a touch that shouldn't feel so damned erotic but does. "Please, continue."

Sparing him one last glare, and also trying not to let the tingling warmth of the impromptu foot massage travel any farther north, I open the book and start again.

"Now that she was back in his arms, Lennox would *not* let Savannah slip away—not even for a moment. Laying her down in the hayloft, he climbed atop her quivering form and unfastened the buttons of her nightdress, recalling their first time so many years ago. He was a gentler man then, the war stripping him of almost all tenderness. Now, he loved her the only way he knew how, furiously and without restraint—"

"Wait, wait, wait." Devlin shakes his head. "Loved her *furiously*? How does that even work?"

"Um. Figure it out?"

"Is he angry about the loving of this woman?"

"It's a euphemism, Devlin."

"In a *hayloft* besides? *This* is where he chooses to bed his so-called soulmate? In a place where farm animals fornicate and def—"

"...*furiously* and without restraint," I continue, giving him a swift kick in the thigh. "A wild storm breaking upon the shores of her body, the desperate tide of him rising higher and higher, until—"

"Stop. Right. There." Devlin shoves a hand through his hair and sighs, as if the whole thing is giving him a headache. "I think what the author is *trying* to say is Lennox and Savannah fucked each other's brains out in the barn. Yes?"

"Yes, only the writer chose to be slightly more eloquent about it, unlike you."

"The *writer*—and I use the term loosely—is mired in purple prose and badly in need of an editor. Or a match and some gasoline. Also, a career counselor—never too late to turn over a new leaf, I always say."

"Ambrosia Divine is a New York Times bestselling author!" I slam the book closed. "I suppose you think you could do better?"

"Oh, I could absolutely do better than *Ambrosia Divine*. That's not even her real name, obviously."

"Is that so, *Devlin Pierce*? I don't see *your* fake name on any book covers. Obnoxious hashtags, sure, you've got that market cornered. But literature? Please."

"You don't even know what a hashtag is. That aside, I'm not talking about *literature*, Mushroom. I'm talking about the fine art of seducing a woman."

"No, you're not. *We're* not. We're not having this conversation."

He folds his arms across his chest and scoffs, forearm

muscles flexing, gods be *damned*. "Don't tell me you read romance for the plot."

"That's part of it, yes. I like a good story."

"A good story. Really."

"Absolutely! I want the whole emotional roller coaster, the character struggles, their day-to-day, all of it. Right up to the hard-won happy ending. *That's* what I read romance for."

"Oh, of *course*. The emotional roller coaster. The happy ending. The white dress and white picket fence and beautiful babies bouncing on the hip. But mostly..." He plucks the book from my hand and tosses it aside. "You read it for the smut. Stand up."

"Excuse me?" I sputter.

"Stand up and let me show you something." He's already on his feet, hand outstretched, leaving me little choice in the matter, what with that stern British daddy vibe that's making me feel some type of way, new kinks unlocked, holy freaking *Hell*.

I take his hand and rise from the couch, knees wobbly but resolve steely.

Until he steps closer. And closer. So close I can see every fleck of gold in his spilled-tea eyes.

Then, in a sultry whisper that has me quivering like poor ol' Savannah in the hayloft, he says, "The key to seducing a woman lies not in overt sexual prowess, although that certainly helps things along." He slides his hands into my hair and cradles the back of my head, his lips so close to mine I can't even breathe. "It lies in seducing her mind."

"You... have a point, but..." I lower my gaze, unable to match his intensity. *Goddess*, why does his touch feel so good?

"It is said that some women can climax with words alone," he whispers. "No physical contact of the genitals whatsoever."

Okay, way to ruin the mood.

"Excuse me, but no woman is getting anywhere *near* the big O when her lover uses words like 'climax' and 'genitals.' You sound like a doctor. And not the hot one, but the bumbling sidekick who barely passed the boards."

I'm good with the words climax and genitals! the Downtown Pep Squad pipes up. *Especially when he says it in British! In fact, I'm pretty sure if he says it again, I'm going to climax right now!*

"Yet the point remains." Devlin lowers his mouth to the side of my neck, breath stirring the fine hairs on my skin. Every cell in my body is working in tandem to hold back the ensuing shiver, to keep me from melting into a puddle on the floor.

"A proper lover knows better than to go in for the kill too quickly." His dark whisper is a danger, a drug, another weapon in the Devil's bottomless arsenal that strips me bare as he drags his mouth to my ear. "A proper lover makes certain his partner knows just how exquisite she is, first and foremost. How utterly *enchanted* he is by the softness of her skin, the warmth of her touch, the light in her eyes. That the barest scent of her desire drives him *mad* with wanting, and if he doesn't claim her right this very *instant*..."

Without warning, he spins me around and pins me face-forward against the wall, wrists bound above my head in his powerful grip, his body pressed against my backside, my heart thundering wildly, breath jagged and desperate.

"—and then he loves her the only way he knows how," he teases, lips feathering the shell of my ear. "Furiously and without restraint, a wild storm breaking upon the shores of her body, the desperate tide of him rising higher and higher, until... Well. Until it does whatever it does, I suppose."

Devlin releases me and returns to the couch, plopping back onto his seat with the cats like this is all just a friendly game of charades, not some freaking multi-dimensional out-of-body experience that leaves me riled up and ready to rock.

"That's how I would do it, anyway." He picks up the cast-aside book, opens to our page. "Though, as we've already demonstrated, there's no accounting for taste. Shall we return to the hayloft, then?"

My mouth goes completely dry, hands and feet tingling with the same sensation I get when I'm having a panic attack. Which is not *exactly* the kind of attack I'm having right now, but something is definitely attacking me from the inside out, the deep depths, as we've mentioned, because there, sitting on my couch in his white shirt and suit pants, Devlin is...

Hard as stone.

Oh, gray sweatpants. You ain't got nothin' on a black suit...

I gape. Devlin notices. And he glances down at his lap, then at me, and says, "So your feline familiars are allowed to appreciate a romance novel, but I can't? Who's being judgy now, miss judgy pants?"

"I didn't say you couldn't appreciate it. Just that... maybe... you could do your appreciating in private? Where I can't see it? You, I mean. Where I can't see *you*." I swallow hard. Force myself to look out the window. To watch the rain running down the glass, very soothing, yes, exactly what I need. Soothing little raindrops, all in a row...

"Distracting you, am I?" he asks.

When I don't respond—which is a thing I literally can't do because my face is on fire and my throat has closed up and I'm seeing stars from lack of oxygen to the brain—Devlin laughs and says, "I always forget how uncomfortable humans get over basic biological functions. Ah, well. I'd offer to cover up with a blanket, but what's the point? No putting *that* genie back in the bottle. Anyway, back to Lennox and Savannah. Where were we?"

CHAPTER SEVENTEEN

VIOLET

Four days into Operation Cracked Wide Open By The Devil (And All I Got Was This Lousy T-Shirt and a Serious Case of Lady Blue-Balls), and we're officially addicted.

Devlin to melty cheese and cheesy romance, exactly in that order.

Me to...

Well, I won't say I'm hooked on *him*, exactly. But the way he makes me feel? *Goddess*. He's just so damn magnetizing—that's the only word for it. Not just because of the obvious reasons—hello, sex on a smoldering stick with a side of more sex, and more sticks, all of them sexy and smoldering, Smokey Bear would definitely *not* approve—but the subtle reasons, too.

Like the way he focuses on me so intently when we're talking and remembers all the details I share with him—from the big stuff like the café's profit-and-loss projections to the tiny stuff like which Charmed episodes are my favorite, and the names and magical focuses of all four of my sisters, even though he's only met Olivy. And if a more cat-friendly male exists, I've never heard of him. I'll be lucky if Grumpy and Sunshine don't pack their bags and hitch a ride with Devlin when the spell finally breaks.

And the laughing? Forget it. I'm doubling over so much these days I've almost got abs now. Like, full on lady-six-pack, here we come.

Devlin is definitely a performer—easy to see why he's so popular on social media. But the more time we spend together, the more I'm starting to realize that the public side of Devlin Pierce is mostly just for show.

It's here in my home—in these often silly, always fun moments together—I get to see the other side. The side of a man with deep emotions and even deeper battle scars. A man with an immortal life marred by loneliness and regret. A man who's just as funny and kind as he is naughty and sinful.

And a man I really wish I could get to know better. One who isn't bound to leave me the moment we break the spell.

I know it can't go beyond that, though—our magical bond, the arrangement. My brain gets it. My heart gets it too. Unfortunately, the vag is completely opposed to the idea that Devlin and I have an expiration date. Fully out of hibernation now, she's serving up non-stop fantasies day in, day out.

And Devlin's antics are *not* helping matters. Every touch

and whispered innuendo may be a joke to him, but even when he *doesn't* go full-on Ambrosia Divine, acting out passages with a passionate exuberance that leaves me wet and weak and wanting, he's still riling me up.

Tonight, after reciting a particularly intense passage between Lennox and Savannah that leaves Devlin just as breathless and turned on as me, I'm so wound up I feel like I'm about to implode. If I don't do something to take the edge off, I'm worried I'll do something *completely* reckless.

Like... just spitballing here... Stripping bare, mounting him on the couch, and *begging* him for a onetime deposit?

Yeah. *That* kind of reckless.

So, after yet another reading session followed by not one but *two* cups of my Shut the Fuck Up and Calm the Fuck Down tea, which does *nothing* to calm the fuck down *me*, I realize there's only one solution.

I haven't booked a self-care session with Mr. Wiggles since Devlin's arrival—feels kind of weird getting off when the object of your naughtiest fantasies is right outside the door—but if ever I needed the support of my emotional support vibrator, it's now.

After triple-checking that Devlin is asleep on the couch, the television droning softly in the background, I close my door tight, light a few candles with the flick of my wrist, strip off my bottoms, and climb into bed.

The vibrator comes to life before I even touch the button, good ol' Mr. Wiggles, the sound and feel of that familiar buzz triggering the clench of my thighs, the hardening of my nipples, everything in me *so* ready for this...

Closing my eyes, I slide one hand up my shirt, fingertips delicately circling my nipple, then pinching it *just* right, my other hand drifting lower, thighs parting, the tip of the vibrator buzzing a teasing path down my clit that sends tiny jolts of pleasure straight to my core.

"Devlin," I whisper, his image dancing through my mind as I recall his every teasing touch, the warm honey of his voice, the light in his eyes when he laughs. I picture him stretched out on my living room couch now, less than fifteen feet from the door, and I wonder if he knows what I'm doing in here. Who I'm thinking about.

Maybe he's not asleep. Maybe he's out there tossing and turning, the desperate ache keeping him awake just as it keeps me awake, everything inside him wound as tight as a drum...

I slowly tease the vibrator inside, imagining it's him filling me up instead, his mouth at my ear, whispering all the filthy things he thinks about when we read together. Then, blazing a trail of kisses down my belly, down one of my thighs, right back up again to settle in *just* where I need him...

The vibe pulses to a higher speed, higher still as I drag it back out, then push in again, out and in, imagining the scrape of Devlin's sexy stubble on my skin, his tongue circling my clit, then dipping inside, deeper, deeper still...

Mr. Wiggles downshifts, throbbing against my G-spot in a way that's got my hips bucking, back arching off the bed, oh goddess, right there, *right* there...

"Devlin!" I gasp, a dark thrill zipping through me and... holy *hell*, "Yes! *Yes!*"

The orgasm rips through me like lightning, a white-hot explosion that spreads from my center outward, tingling heat racing up and down my legs, my whole body singing with it, and—

"Violet!" Devlin bangs on the door. "Are you all right? What's wrong?"

"Nothing! I'm... I'm good! Just—*ohhhh fuck...*" I haven't even stopped twitching from the aftershocks of the last bomb when another ignites, set off by the sound of his voice, a hot wave of pleasure crashing right through me, and then—

"That's it, Mushroom. I'm coming in."

"No, wait!" In a move so fast I nearly break my back, not in the fun way, I whip Mr. Wiggles out and toss him into the nightstand drawer, slam the drawer shut, and yank the covers up to my chin, bolting upright and plastering on a smile just as the bedroom door swings open.

Devlin, disheveled and wild-eyed and sexy as sin, shirtless, black silk pajama pants hanging low on his hips, those v-muscles begging for a *thorough* tonguing...

"You're panting," he announces. "I thought perhaps you'd... hurt... something."

"It was just..." I blink up at him, still smiling, dazed and —yes, brilliant observation—still panting.

It's like when the Devil card showed up that first night between the sheets, only this is so much worse, because the candles are lit (an obvious sign) and I just came—twice— and I've got Self-Care Sex Hair (yes, it's a thing), and the literal Devil is standing at the foot of my bed, taking in the whole scene with wide, all-knowing eyes that have seen it all before and can't wait to see it all again.

And I can't stop wishing he'd drop the pretense, climb in here, and bring me right back to the edge for round three with his hot, demanding, filthy mouth...

"Just a bad dream," I say firmly. Then laugh. And snort. *Oh, goddess, kill me now.* "So, um, why are you here, exactly?"

"You called out for me. Twice. The first time I couldn't be certain, but then... I thought something happened."

Oh, shit. I said that out loud?

"Well, as you can see, all is well!" I pull the blankets even higher and snuggle in deep, faking a yawn. "So *tired*. Phew! Anyway, goodnight, and thanks for stopping, but I'm totally good. Great. Fab—"

Bzzz.

Devlin's eyes narrow. "Do you hear that?"

Bzzzzzzz bzzzzz.

"Nothing!" I nearly shout. "I mean, no, I don't hear a thing. Anyway, thanks again for—"

Bzzzzzzzzzzzz.

"Shh." Devlin cocks an ear. "There it is again. A buzzing of sorts. Sounds like it's coming from the nightstand."

"That? That's my phone. Notifications just blowing up, as the kids say. Pow!" I make a starburst with my fingers. "Someone needs to learn how to leave a message and let it go, am I right?"

"*This* phone?" He picks up my *actual* phone from the dresser by the door—right where I left it—and glances at the screen. "No missed texts or calls. In fact, I think the battery has drained. You really should keep it charged."

Bzzz bzzz bzzzz.

Devlin crosses the room. Right over to me. Leans directly over the buzzing nightstand for the outlet behind the lamp where my charger is currently plugged in, and hooks up my phone.

Bzzzzzzzzzzzzzzz! says Mr. Wiggles, just going for the gold in there, and Devlin's somehow keeping a straight face.

He starts to walk away—thank the universe for small favors—but does an about-face at the last second, then marches right back to me and sits. On the edge of my bed. Just outside the covers, beneath which I'm naked from the waist down—and *very* wet.

"There's nothing to be ashamed of," he says softly, straight face intact but humor dancing in his eyes, bare chest gleaming in the candlelight like full-on romance-novel crack. Or porno crack. There's a fine line, and I'm not sure which side this moment falls on, to be honest. "Lots of people enjoy sex alone. In fact—"

"I'm not *ashamed*, Devlin!" I pull the blankets up over my head and pray to whatever monsters may be listening, *please just open up a pit in the ground and swallow me whole*! "I'm just... not having this conversation with you right now. Or ever. Okay?"

"But you—"

Bzzzzz...

"Oh my goddess, go away! Both of you!"

"Fine. If you'll just answer me one question—honestly and without hesitation—I'll kindly leave you to it."

I peek out from beneath the blanket, knowing I'm going to regret it but unable to stop myself. "What's so important that you need the answer right this very instant?"

Bzzz...

"Were you fantasizing about Twenty Watt?" His stern face breaks into a smile, hand pressed to his heart. "Tell me the truth, Mushroom. I can take it. I will be absolutely devastated and a good bit disgusted and *wholly* disappointed in you, but I can take it. *Ugh*. Go on, rip off the Band-Aid."

"You think I was getting off to... to Brandt? Head rower on the Olympic douche canoe team ten years running?" I can barely say his name in this context without gagging. "Gross! No! I was just... relaxing. Alone. Now leave."

Bzzzzzz bzzz bzzz.

"Wait, one more question. Why does your sex toy keep clamoring for your attention? Has it not finished the job?"

"That's two more questions, and..." I sigh and sit up straight again, tucking the blanket tight around my waist. No way out of this but through it. "It's haunted. Okay? Now go back to the couch and pretend this was all a dream."

"Your vibrator is haunted?" Devlin stares at the buzzing drawer. Then at me. Tries desperately, *desperately* not to laugh again, which, okay, I give him at least ten points for trying.

"Objects get haunted," I say defensively. "Sometimes."

"I've seen a lot of possessed objects in my time, Mushroom, but a haunted sex toy is a definite first. How is this even possible?"

"I'm not sure," I say honestly, because yes, I *do* have a spreadsheet tracking all the research I've done on the subject, and the nerd in me can't help but respond to the genuine curiosity pulsing through Devlin's energy. "Haunted objects are typically the result of the previous owner having some sort of intense spiritual attachment to the thing—like if it was the bed where they gave birth to all their children, or the fire poker they got murdered with. But I bought this thing brand new, *obviously*, so I don't know how it got possessed."

Bzz bzz bzzzz.

Devlin taps the buzzing nightstand with an elegant finger. "Does it frighten you?"

"What? No way. Mr. Wiggles is the sweetest, most hard-working—"

"I'm sorry, did you say… Mr. *Wiggles*?"

Oh, fuck… I did say that. Batting a thousand tonight, girl. Truly.

"That's his name," I say defensively.

"The ghost, or the toy?"

"The toy. The haunted part isn't a ghost, per se. *That* would be creepy."

"Right. Of course. When discussing haunted vibrators, the last thing we want is for things to get creepy." Devlin finally lets out that laugh, and even though I'm 150% sure I'll wish I was dead come tomorrow morning, right now his laughter is so contagious, and the situation so ridiculous, I can't help but respond in kind.

"No ghosts," I clarify. "Just some kind of stuck spiritual energy."

"Stuck energy. Stuck in a pink dildo. That gets stuck in *your* pink—"

"*Devlin!*"

"Just saying, it's not a bad way to spend the afterlife. I might look into it myself as a potential option. One can never plan too far in advance for these things."

"Thankfully, you're immortal."

"And this is one of the rare times I'm regretting it. In any case, just how hard-working is this Mr. Wiggles fellow?

Perhaps he could use an assistant. Share the *load*, so to speak. Pun most *definitely* intended."

"Share the *load*? Are you kidding me right now?"

"It's a perfectly legitimate line of inquiry. Not to mention an excellent pun."

Bzzzzzzz.

"We talked about this! Use sexy words, not gross ones! Goddess, you belong in the locker room with a bunch of frat boys."

"I beg to differ. Load is a *highly* sexy, not-at-all-fratty word."

"It's literally the second worst word in the romance-novel dictionary after *moist*."

"Ambrosia Divine would disagree. In fact, if I pulled one of her books off the shelf right now and flipped to a random page, I bet I could find a sexy scene with the words load *and* moist." Devlin presses his hand to his heart again, voice softening to a breathy impersonation of Ambrosia. "Days after their tragic farewell, *again*, which he should've seen coming but never does because his brains are in his balls, Lennox lay alone in their very special hayloft, naked, hay poking his most tender orifices. Just beyond the scent of his own desperation, and a good bit of cow shit, he could still smell Savannah's perfume, could still feel her warmth in all that soiled hay. He recalled the way her body glistened in the moonlight that first time, the soft curve of her breast against his mouth, the tight, silken feel as he slid into her hidden depths, his balls tightening, begging for release, and now he stroked himself harder, faster, right there, *so* fucking close, and then... *mmmmfuuuuck!* He spilled his moist, aching load all over the hay and—"

I smack him dead in the face with my pillow. "Get out. Right now."

"But we've only just reached the good part!"

"No! This is not a good part! Mr. Wiggles is silent, which means you've offended him so grievously he'll probably never work again."

"Perhaps Mr. Wiggles is just jealous of Lennox's moist—"

"Do *not* finish that sentence. You are hereby banned from ad-libbing any new romance scenes. As well as reading the existing ones."

"You wound me, Violet." Devlin pulls a frown. "Reading together is one of our most cherished pastimes."

"Not anymore. Now it's going into cold storage, where it will never be spoken of again."

"Lennox Steele will find a way back into your heart. His war-hardened love and/or manly appendages will not be thwarted so easily. Not by Savannah's questionable loyalty or the sound of mating bovines in the barn below, and certainly not by a stubborn little tea witch trying to face off with the Devil in a battle of wills she's destined to lose, if for no other reason than she's naked on the lower half while *I* have retained my pants throughout the entirety of this conversation, so who's in a better battle stance now, hmm?"

He's got me cracking up so hard there's no room left for embarrassment—barely even room for air—which is so freaking *Devlin* of him I shouldn't be surprised.

Yet somehow, I *am* surprised. Every day, it's something new. Another layer peeled back. Another ridiculously fun moment. Another glimpse at an immortal man longing for understanding and connection, just like the rest of us mere mortals.

"Thanks," I say, finally catching my breath. "For the laughs *and* the gallant rescue attempt, even though it wasn't needed."

"Yes, I very nearly saved you from another orgasm. What a gent, happy to oblige, I'll be sure to send you a bill." He salutes, then gestures for me to lean forward, replacing the pillow I smacked him with behind my head. "But Violet, really. If you insist on screaming *my* name during your evening rituals, perhaps—"

"Oh my goddess, get *out*!"

"I'm just saying, perhaps you might wait until I'm well out of earshot? In the shower, or focused on some other task, preferably while wearing Violet-orgasm-canceling headphones? Just so we avoid another miscommunication? On the other hand..." He reaches under the bottom of the blanket and finds my foot, pressing his thumb into the arch in that oh-so-perfect way of his. "There may be another solution to this. One that doesn't require batteries."

"Oh, I can't *wait* to hear this."

His fingers draw delicate patterns over my heel, then my ankle, slowly trailing up my calf, sending shockwaves of pleasure racing up my leg. "We don't have access to a hayloft, but—"

"So magnanimous!" I kick him away and yank my foot back under the blanket, out of reach from his too-hot touch. "So chivalrous! I'll call Mayor Singh tomorrow, see if I might get you the key to the city!"

"Mock if you must, but the offer stands." He finally rises from the bed, then double checks my phone charger and blows out my candles—safety first. "I'll be right outside the door if you need me. Literally right there—I'll just go ahead and move the couch a bit closer so I can shorten the distance. Get here faster in your time of need, should such a need arise again, which I'm sure it will, what with Mr. Wiggles' naughty temperament."

"For the last time, go *away*." Laughing, I slink down into the blankets and burrow in. "I need sleep. I have to get up early tomorrow."

"I thought we were closed tomorrow. Your one day off for the month."

"Kettle's closed. But I've got knitting circle with the Aunts on the last Sunday of the month."

His eyebrows jump—both of them at the same time—possibly a first. "*You* knit?"

"Don't look so shocked! I'm a witch of many talents."

"I'm well aware. I just didn't realize knitting was one of them."

"I didn't say I was any *good* at it. But the Aunts let me and Emmie participate because I make the tea and Emmie brings the treats and they love trying to teach us so-called 'kids' their magical, mysterious, old-lady ways, and—no. Devlin, just *no*."

"No, what? I haven't even said anything!"

"You're saying it with your eyes, and I'm responding with my lips: no freaking way are you coming to knitting circle."

"You've kept me in the closet long enough, Violet. Any longer, and I'll start to think you're ashamed of our affair."

"It's not an affair! It's an arrangement."

"Potato, po-tah-to."

"Devlin!"

"I'm serious. I will *not* be locked in a drawer like your haunted battery-operated boyfriends. I have feelings, Violet. Real feelings. Also, we're stuck together. Remember? Where you go, I go."

I sigh. *Shit*, I forgot about that part.

One more flash of that devilish grin, and then he's finally —finally!—stepping back through the doorway. "See you in the morning, darling. I'll be sure to bring my own balls."

"*Devlin!*"

He laughs. Then, eyebrows wriggling, "Balls of *yarn*, you brazen harlot!"

CHAPTER EIGHTEEN

DEVLIN

The shower in Violet's apartment has become my very own personal torture chamber.

Every time I step inside and catch the faintest whiff of her homemade shampoo, I'm instantly hard for her.

Rock fucking hard.

And that's the problem. Because on the *rarest* of occasions, sex can lead to attachment. Even for me. And my situation with the tea witch is much too untenable to risk *any* sort of attachment—especially the emotional sort.

Fuck.

Where in the bleeding fiery lakes is this even *coming* from? I can't recall the last time a woman stirred anything in me beyond lust and annoyance. And in recent years, even the lust part has waned, every interaction feeling exactly the same as the last, a countdown to some final end that never, ever arrives.

Yet here comes this witch, *stirring*.

This may be shocking to hear—it's shocking to admit, even to myself—but I've not had so much as a single wank since Violet and I crossed paths. Oh, I've thought about it, for sure. Came pretty damn close on more than one or two (hundred) occasions.

But something always holds me back.

Because for as many mistakes as I've made—and trust me, listing them would fill an entire library—I do know this:

As long as Violet is on my mind, *any* form of sex—even sex of the lone-wolf nature—is too dangerous. Comes too damn close to triggering those pesky attachment issues, and then where the fuck will I be? Fast-forward a month. Violet, tea shop bustling, heart's desire unlocked, everything set to rights. Me, alone in my study, hiding out from our party guests, longing for things that were never mine to want in the first place.

Or worse. Me, cursed to a mortal life because I couldn't meet my father's demands. Cursed to die, like everyone else, with nothing but a cracked heart stuffed full of anger. Full of regret.

So. Celibate I've remained. Self-control I've mastered.

But fucking *Hell*. Tonight, after what I just witnessed in her bedroom?

Call me weak, call me a fool. But I can't hold back another moment.

The poor, sweet little witch. Mortified doesn't even *begin* to describe it. The crimson color of her cheeks set off her bright blue eyes in a way that will haunt me for eternity—a moment frozen in time to revisit again and again, long after I return to Los Angeles. To Hell, if I ever make it back there.

By sheer force of will and all the Hell magic I could muster, I kept from ravaging her tonight. But there's no way I can sleep like this. Fuck, I can barely remember my own name.

Everything in me aches as I wish her goodnight and close her bedroom door behind me, my cock pressing so urgently against my silk pajamas I'm certain they'll tear. It's a wonder I can even make it to the bath, but somehow I do. Lock the fucking door and turn on the water, full steam ahead.

Stripping bare and stepping in behind the glass door, I get that first heady whiff of the shampoo, like lemons and coconuts and sunshine, deadly fucking combo, and my fist is already wrapped tight around my stone-hard cock, imagining her on her knees for me, the feel of her soft mouth taking me in, my fingers tightening in those wild curls as she licks and teases and sucks...

Mmm... it's almost too much to imagine. Too fucking indulgent, but I'm in too deep to turn back now.

Catching her like that tonight... Knowing she was just behind the door pleasuring herself... Wondering above all else if she was thinking of me the same way I've been thinking of her...

It's enough to drive me to the brink of madness.

I tighten my grip and stroke, one hand braced against the tile, eyes squeezed shut as I picture those soft pink lips, her innocent blue eyes gazing up at me as she loses herself in her own secret fantasies, the good witch who longs to be bad, just for one night...

Fuck, yes...

One more stroke, another, faster, harder, and... *fuuuck*... I hold my breath and come with a shudder that leaves me trembling and spent and slumping against the tiles, waiting for my heart to return to my body.

Despite the solo act, it's still the best bloody orgasm I've had in years, my muscles relaxed, everything inside me warm and content.

But not, I realize, wholly sated.

Bloody *Hell*, she's still with me, and this shower-time dalliance has brought me no closer to getting her out of my mind than I was the first time I gathered her into my arms and drew her close, inhaling the scent of her lemon-coconut hair and burned-sugar magic.

Fuck. Me.

I turn the water as cold as it will go, pruning my skin and shriveling my balls, damn near turning myself blue, and still, the woman won't leave me.

It's not just her intoxicating scent or the damned romance novel scenes we're narrating nightly, either. It's not even catching her unawares tonight during her most *private* moments—an event so thoroughly burned into my memories, I'm declaring this day a national holiday.

No. Something *else* about this witch is chipping away at me. Several somethings. Her bright eyes and the awkward laugh that always tells me my joke hit the mark. The quiet concentration written all over her face as she selects the ingredients for her next brew. The warmth in her eyes when a customer compliments her. And the shirts! Don't even get me started. Gnomes and fairies and animals sipping tea, and the original mushrooms too, all of them conspiring to kill me with an overdose of adorableness that should make me want to *strangle* someone but instead only drives me wild with need.

I'm in dangerous territory here, and I've no bloody idea what to do about it. Because every day that passes, our arrangement feels less like a magical obligation and more like something I look forward to—something I want to *keep* looking forward to.

Spending time with her... It's almost enough to make me want to remove the mask for good. To stop fucking pretending for once in my *literal* God-forsaken life and just... just be.

Right. Talk about an impossible fantasy.

The ugly truth of it is... For all the outrageous favors I grant, for all the favors I'm owed, there's one thing the Devil can *never* have for himself.

Love.

So instead, I turn off the water, grab a towel, and do what I do best.

Take all of it—the fantasy, the desire, the inconvenient *feelings*—and shove them down in that rusty locked box inside me, right next to the abandonment issues and addictions and all the scars that can't be seen, and instead I don the mask, plaster on a nothing-can-touch-me smile, and head back out into the world for another fucking go.

CHAPTER NINETEEN

VIOLET

Three Sisters Bed and Breakfast sits atop Raven Hill like a dark, sentient guardian. A stunning three-story black Victorian with pink gingerbread trim and an unobstructed view of the town and the Bay beyond, the house is a federally protected historical landmark—the original home of the Wayward founding family, passed down and lovingly cared for by my aunts—Joslyn, Lorelei, and Althea.

"Wow." Devlin lets out a low whistle as we head into the foyer and guest check-in area—gorgeous black marble floors, a massive mahogany staircase that leads up to an open balcony area, artwork lining the ruby-red walls. "This place should be a museum."

"It is, actually. I'll give you a tour if you'd like. After knitting circle."

"It's a date, love."

Love? My stomach fizzes. I ignore it. Getting to be a thing, these annoying bodily reactions to his mere existence. "It's an *appointment*, Devlin. Not a date."

"As you wish, Mushroom." Devlin tugs on one of my curls, then waltzes straight back to the kitchen, where the warm, doughy scent of Emmie's fresh-baked magical scones is a beacon to road-weary travelers everywhere.

"Oh my goddess! Devlin!" Emmie, flour-covered and adorable, doesn't even remove her oven mitts. Just pulls Devlin into a hug and mouths "fucking hot" at me over his shoulder. "Olivy mentioned Violet's new friend, but she was weirdly tight-lipped about the details. We've been waiting *forever* to meet you!"

"I'm afraid your sister keeps me chained in the basement most days," he says. "I had to gracelessly invite myself to knitting circle just so I could meet her family. Can you imagine?"

"Goddess, the accent. The sass." Emmie fans herself. "The aunts are going to *love* you! Come on. I can't wait to introduce you."

Grabbing a freshly plated tray of her still-steaming scones, Emmie escorts us to the sunroom beyond the kitchen, where my aunts are already assembled in their respective armchairs, knitting projects and gossip session in full swing.

"Did you hear about Hortense?" Althea's saying. "She's closing the fabric store. Landlord sold the building, and she can't afford the new rent."

"Happening all over town." Joslyn shakes her head, knitting needles clacking angrily, the usual gravel in her voice pitching even lower. "Everyone's caving to that reptile realtor and his banker cronies. He's been here twice already, wheeling and dealing. Thinks he can convince the town to revoke our historical designation and pressure us to sell. Why? So they can turn our family legacy into a condo complex?"

"Look who's here, aunties," Emmie says, ushering us inside.

Their faces light up when we enter, but Althea's eyes laser in on me fast, narrowing with a scrutiny that makes my skin hot. I shouldn't be surprised—an expert herbalist and former nurse, she's always been the caretaker of the bunch. "Violet, are you all right, sweetness? You look like you haven't slept in days."

"That would be my fault," Devlin says, and all three heads turn to him at once, their eyes twinkling.

Great. The aunts are already enraptured. Five words in, and he's got the septuagenarian set on lock. Might be a new record.

"I've been keeping her up until the wee hours," he says with a charming wink.

"Now *that's* a story I'd like to hear." Joslyn releases her knitting and waves two fingers, her needles magically continuing to work. Hands free for the moment, she pulls out her ancient pack of clove cigarettes and sticks one in her mouth, unlit. Thanks to a cancer scare in the nineties, she hasn't smoked in decades, but she kept the oral fixation. Claims it calms her.

"Olivy didn't fill you in?" Devlin takes the chair between Joslyn and Althea, unpacking his knitting. Yes, the man brought his own balls, just as he said he would. And needles. And a project already partway in the making.

Because of *course* the Devil knits in his spare time.

"She told us Violet had a handsome *visitor* staying at the café." Joslyn shoots me a glare that says we *will* be discussing this later. Whether she means me having a handsome visitor, me not introducing him, or him being the Devil, I have no idea.

"Guilty as charged," he says.

Beneath her silver-gray movie-star pin curls, Joslyn—glamor witch and self-proclaimed dame of Wayward Bay community theater—arches a delicate, painted-on eyebrow. "If I'd known the King of Hell was walking among us, I might've worn a nicer dress."

"Your dress is beautiful, Aunt Jos." I lean in to kiss her cheek, pointedly ignoring the plunging neckline of her black dress, far too formal and scandalous for knitting club or pretty much any occasion ever hosted in Wayward Bay, but Jos wouldn't get caught dead in anything less.

Devlin laughs. "I try to keep the true identity under wraps. Awkward at parties otherwise. The fire, the brimstone, the torture. *Ugh.* Lots of stereotypes, as you can imagine."

"Well, any friend of Violet's is a friend of ours." Althea pats his knee. "No matter how many people you've flayed and boiled alive."

"And on *that* note, I'll go put on the kettle." I turn to Devlin and mouth, "*Behave* yourself."

Emmie follows me back to the kitchen. "Way to keep a secret, Violet!"

"It's not a secret! Goddess, you're as bad as the aunts." I retrieve the brew I concocted for today—Family Ties, a green tea blend made with blueberry and coconut for protection, a whisper of cinnamon for love—and fill the teapot. "He's just... consulting."

"Consulting! Is that what the kids are calling it these days?"

"Stop trying to live vicariously through my non-existent sex life. Your non-existent sex life is bound to be highly disappointed."

"Sorry, but I can't rely on the other sisters. Darla's always got her nose in a book, Fiona won't date because she knows it's not going to work out before they even kiss, and Olivy hates everyone. So that leaves you."

"And the aunts. My money's on Jos."

"You're filthy. You know that, right?"

"Learned it from watching you!"

Laughing, the two of us catch up on our various news—

Emmie, learning how to make wedding cakes, her next frontier. Me, insisting the shop is doing just fine—while we wait for the tea to steep, then assemble the tray and head back to the sunroom.

Aunt Lorelei, a weather witch who's more comfortable talking to trees and storms than people and saves up all her words until she's got a bomb to drop, smiles as Emmie and I settle in. "Tell me, Devlin," she says in her sweet, somewhat warbly tone. "How long have you and Violet been fornicating?"

"Oh, we aren't fornicating at present," he says casually, as if she asked him whether he's got any food allergies or dinner plans. Emmie's laughing her ass off—meanwhile, I'm just sitting here choking on my tea and bursting into flames, don't mind me!

"At present..." Lorelei's eyes light up. "So, you're saying there's hope?"

"No!" I blurt out.

Devlin grins at me, his eyes glittering, clearly enjoying this. "Violet and I are... We're... business associates, really."

"He's *consulting*," Emmie says, making air quotes around the word.

"I didn't know you had associates, sweetness," Althea says.

"I don't have *associates*! Just... just the one. Devlin's helping me with some things for the café."

"What things?" Joslyn taps her unlit cigarette into the

ashtray at her side, lips rounding into an O and miming an exhale so perfect I can almost see the smoke. "I didn't realize Kettle and Cauldron needed help. Why didn't you mention it?"

"It doesn't need help," I say. "Not *help* help, I mean. We're just... trying some new marketing tactics. Getting ahead of the trends. Devlin's in the... entertainment business now."

"You're a male escort?" Lorelei sets her knitting in her lap and looks at him, no judgments, just curious.

"Not that kind of entertainment," I say, at the same time Devlin blurts out, "Not anymore."

I shoot him a death-glare, but of course this only encourages him.

"Don't be so judgmental, Violet. Sex is perfectly natural, in all its many forms. With a partner or multiples, paid or otherwise." He winks at me over his knitting. "Or with oneself, as the case may be. Battery-assisted, perhaps."

Yes, I'm still here, still bursting into flames!

Goddess, I *knew* I should've canceled today. What was I *thinking*?

"Sex work is a legitimate business endeavor," Althea adds.

"The oldest one in the book." This, from Joslyn, who's finished her non-cigarette and is now wrestling with her own magic to regain control of her knitting needles.

"I'm not judging sex with *anyone*, paid or otherwise!" I widen my eyes at Devlin, like please please *pretty* please, shut the hell up! "I'm just saying that it's... not the job I hired you for."

"As I recall, you didn't *hire* me for anything. We're bound to—"

"To work together really, really closely until we see some measurable results. More tea, anyone?"

"I've got a few functions coming up," Jos says, patting down her curls and shimmying her shoulders like she's sixteen instead of sixty-eight. "I usually fly solo, but I'd love to bring a manpanion for a change. What do you charge?"

"I'm flattered, Joslyn, but I'm no longer in that line of work. However, I'd be happy to attend as your date—unpaid, of course—if you're interested in—"

"She's not." I set down my teacup and saucer, harder than I intend to. "I mean, *you're* not. Available, that is. You're not available because we have a thing that night."

"But I haven't said which nights," Jos says.

"I'm sure I could get away for a few hours," Devlin says, knitting away like this is just something we do every month, the knitting and the tea and the conversation with my aunts.

"I'm sure you can't." I smile, my jaw aching from clenching so hard. "You and I are *stuck* together, I'm afraid! Really, *really* stuck." I sigh through my nose and glare at him again, like, *throw me a lifeline, buddy!*

Because there's no way I'm playing third wheel while he gallivants around town, living out his twisted senior citizen fetishes with the aunts. Goddess, what is *wrong* with this man?

"No need to get jealous, Mushroom." He reaches over and pats my leg. "Devlin Pierce is nothing if not a crowd pleaser, and there's plenty of me to go 'round. And round again, if I'm being honest."

"I do love a man with stamina," Jos says, peering over at Devlin's knitting. "What a clever pattern, Devlin. They look like little snakes wearing halos."

"Put your glasses on, Jos." Lorelei laughs. "Those aren't snakes. They're dicks with cock rings in the end."

"Very astute, Lorelei. I'm making a tea cozy." Giving me a wink, Devlin sets the X-rated knitting project on a side table and reaches for his cup and saucer, balancing it on his knee like he always does, casual yet elegant. "I was just thinking, Violet. Maybe we should host a post-Halloween soirée at Kettle and Cauldron? Nothing ostentatious, of course. Just something to show off the new product line."

"No," I snap.

"There's a new line?" Jos again.

"What new line?" Althea.

"Ooh! I'll make cupcakes!" Emmie, who's definitely going on my shit list now. "Great idea!"

"I thought so too," Devlin says, "but Violet looks as though she might dismiss it on principle."

I roll my eyes. "Yes, the principle being that we don't have a new product line."

"Because you pooh-poohed that idea too, even though my Devil's brew had merit." He clucks his tongue. "Which is kind of a theme with you, Violet. A reluctance to take risks."

There's nothing malicious coming through his energy. Just a genuine playfulness. But I can't for the life of me figure out what he's up to.

So what the hell games are you playing, Devlin Pierce?

"Can I see you for a moment?" I ask through my plastered-on smile, jerking my head toward the front of the house. "In *private*?"

CHAPTER TWENTY

VIOLET

"Look. I appreciate that you're magically obligated to help me, and yes, that's *entirely* my fault, and something I hope to make up to you once we straighten out this whole heart's desire thing. I *also* appreciate that you're going the extra mile to get to know me and help figure out how I can better connect with my customers. But seriously? Why are you pushing me so hard in there? What's your end game?"

Devlin leans back against the check-in desk, arms crossed, totally relaxed. "It's no game, Mushroom. I'm pushing you because behind all that passion for tea, behind all your words about saving the shop, you're stuck. Something is blocking you from truly tapping into your magic. Your potential. That elusive heart's desire we're supposed to unlock. And I'm trying to get you unstuck. So, you tell me." He steps closer, backing me against the wall until I've got no choice but to look up and meet his eyes. "Why are you pushing so hard to resist me?"

There's nothing but honesty in his gaze, in his energy.

I sigh, the secrets inside me swirling, searching for a crack in the facade. A way out, just this once.

"It's not you I'm resisting, Devlin. I just don't want to talk about the shop's troubles with my aunts."

"But... they're your family, are they not?"

"Not by blood."

"I didn't ask if they were your relatives. I asked if they were your *family*. There's a difference."

Compassion floods his energy, the tenderness in his voice slipping behind my walls, edging closer to my heart.

Something about this conversation is getting to him. I can feel it. Hear it. See it in his eyes, full of concern and understanding both.

It makes me wonder what he's gone through in his long, long life. Does the Devil have a family? Siblings? Does he get along with them? What was he doing in Los Angeles? Why was he asked to leave Hell?

I know the religious stories about the so-called Devil are just that—stories. An invention of flawed men too stubborn and proud to admit their own faults, fabricating a clever bit of fiction so they can blame some scary supernatural force for everything that goes wrong in their lives.

But what I *don't* know about the so-called Devil... Goddess. *Those* stories could fill entire volumes. Libraries.

And all this time... The bickering, the grilled cheeses, the romance novel reinterpretations, the days in the shop... All the time he's been putting in, trying to figure out what makes my heart tick...

I never even asked him what's going on inside *his*.

"Devlin, is your family—"

"Don't deflect," he says, his energy spiking with sadness. "Tell me why you don't trust your family."

I search his eyes, search for a way back into his heart, but I can tell he doesn't want to talk about it.

Maybe he never will.

I sigh and lean back against the wall. "It's not that I don't trust them. I just... I have a hard time asking for help."

"You don't say." He smirks at me, but it's not snarky or annoyed. Just patient. Probing, but not prying.

"I spent a bunch of time in the system."

"Funny, you don't strike me as an ex-con."

"Not that kind of system."

"What kind, then?"

"The kind where you learn that messing up gets you noticed—and not in a good way. The kind where asking for help brands you as needy and helpless. A burden at best. A target at worst."

I lower my gaze, hoping he can't see the memories flashing behind it. All the moving around I had to do as a teen, keeping my head down, my mouth shut, my magic on lockdown, hoping I wouldn't commit some unintentional infraction to upset the balance. To get kicked out of whatever temporary home I'd been shunted off to. And Mr. Roach, the aptly named social worker whose favorite after-school activity was leering at me over his grimy glasses while reminding me how difficult it was to place teenage girls because all of us were just a bunch of—and I quote—money-grubbing, backstabbing whores-in-training.

No, not all the foster placements were horrible. Some of the families really did want to help, and tried their best to make an impossible situation slightly more bearable. But none of them knew about my magic, none of them lasted for long, and none of them ever felt like *home*. Not like the one I'd lost when Gigi died, and not like the one I eventually found—thank the goddess—in Wayward Bay.

"I ran the minute I turned eighteen," I say. "I was in the midwest at the time, and something just told me to head east. I had no money, no friends or family, nothing but the clothes on my back and a few things my grandmother had left me—things I guarded with my life. So I followed that tug inside me, made it all the way to a diner about an hour from the Bay. The waitress took pity on me—brought me a meal on the house. Told me to hang out until closing, so I did. I thought she might offer me a place to stay, but then, a few minutes after closing, Althea showed up. She said she was a witch, like me. That she and her sisters knew I was coming—they'd been waiting for me and asked the waitress to keep an eye out."

Devlin's eyes soften. "You're lucky to have them in your life, Violet."

"All of us are. My sisters... That's pretty much how we all ended up in Wayward Bay over the years. Each of us finding our way, following the magic. The Aunts say it calls to us, right when we need it most." I swipe a lone tear from my cheek and smile. "Coming here, to the B&B, meeting the other aunts, my sisters... It was the first time since Gigi died that I felt like I was home. Truly home. And no matter what happens, I can't... I can't risk it."

"Risk what, love?"

"Messing up again."

"Ah. I see."

"See what?"

"You're not afraid of messing up, Mushroom. You're afraid that if your family—the women who've *chosen* you after years of the rejection you endured as a child—discovered that you're ever-so-slightly *less* than perfect, they might abandon you, just like all those other so-called families did."

His words are a volley of arrows that pierce my heart, but I'm shaking my head anyway. "It's different," I insist. "Totally different."

"How so?"

"I'm not a needy child anymore, Devlin. I'm a grown woman who owns her own business. I'm a witch with access to magic most people only dream about, and unlike that lost and lonely fourteen-year-old girl, *I* know how to harness it. I should be able to figure this out on my own."

"Says who?"

"Says... everyone?"

"Even if that were true, don't you think making mistakes along the way is part of figuring it out?"

"I don't have time for mistakes. I let my financial situation get out of hand, and now I'm in one hell of a mess."

"It's okay to be messy. *Life* is messy. That's part of what makes it worth living."

"Says the immortal with no fear of death."

"Death, no, you've got me there." He tucks a finger under my chin, forcing me to meet his gaze again. Then, in a soft whisper that almost breaks me, "But loss? That's something we're *all* faced with, Mushroom. Even me."

Another tear escapes. He catches it with his thumb.

"You don't have to be perfect, love," he whispers. "You just have to be real."

I shake my head. "I made her a promise, Devlin."

"Who? Your gran?"

I nod. In Gigi's final days, I slept on a cot in her hospital room, right next to her bed. She was pretty out of it by the end, but one night, I woke up at three a.m. and found her watching me, her gaze as sharp and clear as it had ever been.

"I need you to promise me something, Lettie," she said, the nickname she'd given me as a baby when I couldn't say my own name. And just like her gaze, her voice was suddenly clear. Intentional, even in its softness. "There are many times in life when our heads are louder than our hearts—so loud they can overwhelm us, make us lose our way. But dreams? They *thrive* in our hearts. Follow them, and you'll never be lost."

I tell him the story—one I've never shared with another living soul.

"I promised her I'd always follow my dreams. That I'd never let anything push me off my path, whichever path I chose. And now, every time I think about losing Kettle and Cauldron, I feel like I'm letting her down, and I... I can't..."

I turn away from him and grab a tissue from the desk, wiping away my tears and forcing a fresh smile.

"Anyway, the foster stuff... it's all in the past now. Yes, it sucked at the time, but ultimately, it molded me into the woman I am today. A perfectionist—okay, yes, occasionally problematic. But also a woman who dreams big and doesn't give up easily, even when the deck is stacked against her. How could I not be grateful for that?"

Devlin smiles, but it's as sad as his energy, heavy with the weight of his own losses, his own fears. "Being grateful for the outcome doesn't mean we can't acknowledge the pain of the experience. That, too, is part of figuring it out. No way around it, I'm afraid."

Tears prick my eyes again, and I look away before they can spill.

It's taken years of practice, but these days, I can typically sense the edges of people's energy fields. The border where their feelings end and mine begin. But something about Devlin blurs everything in a way where it all just feels like... like *ours*. This vast, shared experience and wordless understanding you can spend your whole life searching for with another person and never, ever find it.

And somehow, I've found it with the Devil.

I turn back to him, overcome with the sudden urge to hug him.

He returns the embrace, one hand cradling my head, the other holding me close, just... just *being* with me.

"I'm sorry for hurting or embarrassing you in there, Violet," he whispers, stroking my hair. "The last thing I want is to put that worry in your heart or drudge up painful memories. But I can't sit back and let you succumb to—"

The front door swings open, and I'm swamped with the energy of... well. A swamp. That's exactly how it feels. Cold and fetid. Stale. Teaming with things you don't want to look too closely at.

I know at once who it is.

"Brandt?" I turn to face him, my lip curling involuntarily. "Why are you *here*?"

He takes in the sight of me and Devlin, still wrapped up in each other's arms. Clearing his throat, he says, "I'm meeting a friend from New York. He's staying at the inn a few days, checking out some properties in town. Why are *you* here?"

I fold my arms over my chest. "Um, my aunts live here?"

"Oh! That's right. I knew that." He glances at Devlin, offers a bullshit man-nod. Another awkward throat-clearing, then back to me. "I'm actually glad I ran into you again. We never got to finish our conversation the other day."

"I'm ninety-nine percent sure all our conversations are finished, Brandt. So what, exactly, are you talking about?"

"The Halloween Ball? I figured you wouldn't have a date, so I thought I'd do you a solid and offer to take you."

"Do me a *solid*?"

Devlin leans close and mutters into my hair, "Really sweeping you off your feet, this one."

Ignoring Devlin's comment, Brandt sighs and shakes his head. "Violet, why are you always making things so difficult? I'm offering you a chance to go to the ball as my date. Lots of women would kill for the opportunity."

"We best alert the police commissioner," Devlin says, "lest the murder rate skyrocket overnight." He wraps an arm around my waist, pulling me in close again. "Very kind of you to offer, Brandt, but your services won't be needed. Violet and I are attending the ball together."

My heart jumps into my throat, but I don't dare contradict this breaking newsflash. Watching Brandt's face contort like melting candle wax is its own reward.

"So you two are, like... a thing?" he asks, still with the melty face.

Devlin wraps his hand around the back of my neck,

giving it a possessive squeeze that sets off a string of sparks all the way down to my—

"We're, like, *many* things," he says. "Would you care for the full list? A diagram, perhaps?"

"Excuse me?"

"Violet is a rich, complex woman, Mr. Remington cubed. One *thing* would no more encapsulate her than it could the vastness of the world's oceans."

Brandt's jaw drops, but before he can unearth a witless comeback, his so-called "friend" finally plods down the stairs, calling his name. Middle-aged guy, cheap suit, hair the color of hair—yes, he's that boring—and off they go, with no more than a cursory nod goodbye.

"I can't believe you said all that to him!" I turn around to face Devlin, my smile wide. "Did you see his face? Goddess, Devlin. Never thought I'd say this, but you're my hero. Truly."

"I get that a lot."

"I'm sure you do."

"I have to ask, Mushroom. What on *earth* did you ever see in that man?"

"A question I would be asking myself, if I gave even one iota of a molecule of a shred of a *shit* about him." I shake my head and bite back a gag—I still can't believe I let that absolute *mollusk* into my bed last year. "You know how some girls go through a bad-boy phase? I was the opposite."

"Ah, yes. The old khaki-pants-wearing, laptop-bag-slinging, personality-of-a-wet-napkin-boy phase that has fathers locking up their daughters all over creation."

"Pretty much."

"The safe choice is the boring choice, Violet. Write that down. Preferably *not* on a wet napkin."

"Forgive me if I don't make any plans based on *that* excellent life advice." Laughing, lighter than I've felt all day, I head back to the kitchen and steal a fresh scone from the cooling rack, because nothing chases off the oogy-ex-boyfriend vibe like a boatload of sugary carbs. "And speaking of plans... Were you serious? About going to the party together?"

Devlin plucks the scone right out of my hand and downs it in two bites. Then, with a mouth full of crumbs and a sparkle in his eyes that reignites all the desperately throbbing parts inside me, he says, "Are you serious about entertaining the idea of allowing me to accompany you?"

"Hmm. Is this the thing where you try to surreptitiously find out if you've got a chance before you officially invite me, just in case I say no and feed into your deep-seated rejection issues?"

"Violet?"

I select another scone from the rack. "Yes?"

"Are we going to this hometown hoedown together or not?"

"It's not a hoedown."

"But is it a date?"

"Yes." I bite into the pastry—sweet, crumbly perfection.

"Yes?"

"Yep. But not a *date*-date."

"A date-date? Who said anything about a date-date? Absolutely *not*!" Devlin laughs, then taps his lips. "It's... it's a... there's a word for it, but it's not coming to me—"

"Work function," I supply. "Two professional colleagues attending an event together. An event that has a *calendar* date, but is not a date in and of itself."

"Ah, a team-building exercise."

"Yes! *Very* good for morale."

"Exactly."

"Precisely. As long as we're clear." I shove in the last of the scone.

"*Crystal*, little Mushroom." Devlin swipes a crumb from the corner of my mouth, then licks it off his thumb. "Absolutely crystal."

CHAPTER TWENTY-ONE

DEVLIN

On the night of the Haunted Halloween Ball, after an exhausting afternoon passing out candy to non-paying, goblin-faced children during the town's annual shop crawl, I wait for my non-date down in the café.

There, in the fine feline company of Grumpy and Sunshine, I enjoy a glass of mulled wine by the fire—a simple pleasure I've sorely neglected in recent years. The purring cats and the dance and sway of the flames lull me into a sense of peace so complete, I don't even hear Violet coming until she's already descending the final stair.

I rise from the couch when I see her, and across the quiet space, she smiles at me, and something in my chest warms and expands as though it might at any moment burst.

She enters the room like a princess from an enchanting storybook, floating toward me as if her feet never touch the ground. Her face is dusted with glitter, her hair free of its usual bun, a cascade of loose chestnut waves falling over soft, bare shoulders. The dress is exquisite—a perfectly fitted beaded white bodice over skirts that fall to her feet in shimmering shades of silver and white, as though the fabric was spun from moonlight. A pair of gossamer wings bloom from the back, so fine and lovely it's a wonder they're not real.

"You look..." My ability to speak in coherent sentences evaporates in the wake of her ethereal beauty. Eons upon eons roaming this earth and all the realms above and below, yet this one moment—this one *woman* reduces me to a bumbling adolescent with a hard-on and a fat, clumsy tongue that can only manage one more word. "...Nice."

Nice. I ought to be drawn and quartered. Even the cats are looking at me as if I need lessons on how to speak to a woman from Ambrosia Divine.

Yet the little mushroom doesn't seem bothered by my ineptitude. Quite the opposite, actually.

"Yeah?" Her smile brightens as she smooths her hands over the skirts, then twirls for me, the wings fluttering behind her, iridescent fabric glittering in the firelight. "I took some liberties with the whole fairy thing. Fae don't actually look like this. Only in kids' books, you know? But I figured it would still work for Halloween. Right?"

"Right," I say, because at this particular moment, she could ask me if I'd like my balls removed and I'd probably just smile and nod, what a fine idea, let's do *exactly* that.

Her effect on me is utterly stupefying, and after far too

many moments of blatantly staring, I finally force my eyes back to the flames and tip back the last of the wine.

She walks a circle around me and takes stock of my outfit, a smile quirking her lips, laughter dancing in her eyes.

Bleeding skies, what I wouldn't give to put that look on your face every night...

"You're not the only one who took a few liberties in the costume department," I confirm, smoothing a hand down my lacy black slip. It stops just above the knee, with a flirty slit up one side trimmed in red and topped with a dainty bow. The black silk is embroidered with words in a fine, white script: Id, Superego, Transference, Regression, Oedipal Complex, and my personal favorite—Penis Envy, to name a few.

"Interesting interpretation," she says. "I'll give you that."

"It's a Freudian slip."

"So I gathered."

"Too clever?"

She laughs her sweet little laugh-snort, the jarring shudder making the glasses slide down her nose, the wings flutter. "Not exactly the word that springs to mind, no."

I push the glasses back where they belong. "What *is* the word that springs to mind?"

"Probably best kept to myself." She tries to wink at me, fails miserably, laughs again, and I'm about ready to suggest we abandon this whole Halloween Ball idea and celebrate the holiday alone. In bed. Without costumes. Which is problematic on several levels, none of which I'm interested in looking at right now, so into the dungeon of denial they go, thank you very much, Dr. Freud!

"Anyway," she says, "I'm just glad you're not naked."

"I'm quite certain you're the only woman in the history of womankind who's ever said that to me. Shall we?" I hold out my arm. She tucks her hand into the crook. For the span of several heartbeats, I can't move. Can't breathe. All I can feel is the warmth of her touch, the certainty of it. The familiarity —no pretense, no hesitation. It's just like the night we ordered pineapple pizza and sat together on the couch watching her witchy show, and all the Ambrosia Divine laughs we've shared since.

Like something we've done a dozen times together. A hundred.

Something I want to *keep* doing with her every night for an eternity.

"Devlin?" She blinks up at me with those big blue eyes, and the air fills with the burned-sugar scent of her magic. I feel it wrapping around me, entangling, enticing, a bittersweet reminder of what this thing between us actually *is*.

A spell to break. A task to complete. A little fun along the way.

So why does my chest hurt when I think about getting the job done? When I think about leaving her to the tea and pumpkins and sister-witches and saucy aunts that comprise her life in Wayward Bay?

"You feeling okay?" she asks, because of course she can sense it. The sudden heaviness. The regret for something I haven't quite lost yet, but will, all too soon.

So once again, I don the mask. For her. For myself. For the father so sure I will never be anything but the careless, irresponsible, worthless playboy.

The Devil.

"It's Halloween, darling," I say with a laugh and a dramatic flourish. "How could I be feeling anything but positively *ghoulish*?"

CHAPTER TWENTY-TWO

DEVLIN

The Wayward Bay Town Hall is only a few blocks away, and we take it on foot, happily dodging even more goblin-face children who are as eager for candy as my own party guests are for their multi-colored pills, and now I understand how it all begins, peanut butter cups being the obvious gateway drug.

Inside, the rotunda has been transformed into a veritable All Hallow's Eve extravaganza, vendors showcasing their wares, children and adults alike begging for candy at every turn, the Pumpkinville Pumpkin Spice Brigade once again doing their civic duty in vomiting up every sort of fall decoration imaginable. Pumpkins and ghosts. Bats and spiders. Cottony cobwebs and spooky flashing lights. Yet somehow, on this night, it all seems to work.

Arm-in-arm, my fairytale princess and I follow the tide of costumed witches and comic book heroes and zombies, from the ring-toss booth to the hot cider booth to the mulled wine booth—much better, that's more like it. Then, past all the snacks and kids' games, we spot a booth where you can paint your own mugs, which Violet is excited to try.

"Glaze for Days is right behind Kettle and Cauldron," she says. "I've never even been in there. Should we give it a go?"

"I'll paint one for you if you paint one for me."

"Deal." She beams at me, eyes sparkling behind the glasses. "But no peeking. I want mine to be a surprise."

The proprietress—Ricci, if the name tag pinned to her black cat costume is anything to go by—hands us each an unglazed white mug and a small kit of paints and brushes, gesturing for us to take a seat at one of several hightop tables set up for this purpose. "Bring the mugs up front when you're done. I'll be firing them back at the shop—you can pick them up in a few days."

"Thank you," Violet says. "I've been wanting to try this place forever!"

"You're Violet, aren't you?" Ricci asks. "From Kettle and Cauldron? I'm so sorry I haven't gotten a chance to pop in yet."

"No worries." Violet laughs. "I was just telling my friend Devlin the same thing—I've been meaning to check out your studio for ages, but I hardly ever leave my shop."

"Story of my life."

I shake the woman's hand, compliment the costume.

"Nice to get out from behind the counter for a change, is it not?"

"I've got one more hour at the booth, then I'm putting on my dancing shoes." Ricci laughs, her cat whiskers wiggling. "Oh! Speaking of being an absolute workaholic... Violet, did you hear about the small business grant thing?"

Violet's eyes light up. "Grant thing?"

"Apparently, the town council is trying to give local businesses a boost, so they're starting up this whole Keep the Bay Beautiful for Business push. I heard Mayor Singh rehearsing her speech in the coat room—I guess she'll be announcing it tonight."

"Well, now that the *cat's* out of the bag," another woman says, coming up behind the cat in question. "I suppose I can let you girls in on the secret."

"Mayor Singh!" Violet leans in for a quick hug. "You look stunning!"

"Oh, this old thing?" The woman, dressed like some sort of pumpkin queen, complete with tiara and scepter, fluffs her hair and smiles. "It all came together kind of last minute. Anyway, as Ricci said, we'll be announcing more details later, but we're teaming up with Remington Capital to award five grants to local businesses. $75,000 each! So keep an ear out, ladies. I'm expecting you *both* to apply."

The mayor bestows blessings upon their heads with her scepter, then anoints me as well, her eyes roving me head to toe, lingering on the legs. Perhaps I should've worn stockings. Alas...

"Sir, can I just say," she just says. "I *love* your costume! You know we celebrate all walks of life here. And love, in all its many forms. Good for you for speaking your personal truth! Brave and handsome. I'm just tickled."

"Is she... hitting on me?" I whisper out of the corner of my mouth to Violet.

"No, she's just... pontificating. She does that."

The mayor continues oohing and ahhing, posing for a few selfies with Violet and Ricci, then one with me and my legs, before finally leaving us to paint our mugs in peace.

I keep my word and avoid spying on Violet's work-in-progress, but I can't avoid spying on the mushroom herself, the way her nose scrunches up as she concentrates on the painting, the flush in her cheeks, her dark waves spilling over her shoulders.

Demon's balls, what I wouldn't give to kiss those shoulders. To press my lips to that soft, warm skin. To taste her. To peel off that dress and—

"Hey!" She looks up, catching me in the act. "We said no peeking!"

"I didn't see a thing. I swear."

"Then why are you staring at me like you just got busted with your hand in the cookie jar?"

Because I just got busted with a full-on erection under nothing but a scrap of silk and if I move too quickly I might sprain something vital...

"I was... wondering what you thought about the grant program. You haven't said a word."

She snorts, but it's not the cute one that comes with her genuine laugh. This one is derisive. Disgusted, almost.

"I was all in until she mentioned Remington Capital." Violet sets down her paintbrush and sighs. "That's the bank Brandt's family runs. They bill themselves as a small-business bank, but they're impossible to work with. I've applied for loans with them in the past—before Brandt and I started dating, I mean. And I always got denied, no explanation given. Plus their credit card rates are ridiculous."

"Unsurprisingly douchey, but that shouldn't stop you from applying for a community-based grant."

"No point. Brandt's on the voting committee—that's how these things work. Mayor Singh said it herself—his bank is putting up the cash. He's not going to pick me."

Now it's my turn to snort. "Because you wouldn't be his date for the ball?"

"That, and the fact that *I* was the one who broke up with *him*. He's never forgiven me. No, not because he ever really cared about me. And no, not because he misses the sex. He was literally the *worst* at it."

"Please don't make me think about him naked, Mushroom. It's just not good manners."

"Sorry." She picks up her brush for another go.

"So you wounded his pride, then. That's it?"

"Oh, you should've heard him. '*No one* breaks up with Brandt Remington the Third! *He* breaks up with *you*!' It was at last year's ball, actually. We'd gone together, but he kept ignoring me for his investor buddies, and then he got super drunk and I overheard him telling them he was just stringing me along for a good time—that I wasn't really serious girlfriend material."

"Fucking imbecile."

"I was basically done with him months earlier—just never worked up the nerve to end it. I didn't want to hurt him. Well, that was the final straw. So, I pulled him aside and suggested we part ways—permanently—and he lost it. Literally chased me out into the courtyard, ranting and raving like a total idiot, making a huge scene. That's when Emmie hit him with the powdered donuts."

"I would've paid good money to see that show."

"It was pretty epic. But now?" She shakes her head. "He'll definitely vote me out of the running. But not before reveling in the fact that I need to apply for his stupid grant in the first place. He always told me Kettle and Cauldron was a waste of time and resources. Tea is *boring*—he actually said that to me. Can you believe it?"

"Mushroom, that man wouldn't know excitement if it crawled up his arse and licked him from the inside out. The fact that you need to apply only proves you're *already* a successful businesswoman. You just need a bit of capital to get to the next level. This isn't the sort of thing a so-called boring waster of time and resources does for herself." I put the finishing touch on my mug, then drop the brush into a cup of rinse water. "Mortal life is far too short to let a useless cunt like Remington make you doubt yourself. Pardon the crass term, but it's fitting."

"Agreed. Also, mollusk," she says with an adorable smirk. "In my head, I call him the mollusk."

"Even more fitting."

Finished with our masterpieces, we've just turned our mugs over to Ricci when we're surrounded and dragged to the dance floor by a trio of green-faced cackling witches, all dressed in the traditional pointy black hats and the slightly *less* traditional scandalous black dresses.

"Lovely to see you again, Joslyn," I say, kissing her and the others in turn. "Althea. Lorelei. My word, I've never seen such breathtakingly beautiful witches."

"Stop flirting with me, Devlin." Joslyn gives my backside a smack, then a firm squeeze—much stronger grip than I gave her credit for, that one. "We'll make the kids jealous."

"We're always jealous of you, Aunt Jos." This from Emmie, who sweeps into our gathering in an adorable bumblebee costume, followed by two other women—a zombie nurse and a dragonfly, respectively. Finally, last in line, dressed like some sort of goth vampire, which is actually not so far off from her usual attire, my dear friend Olivy.

All of them are staring expectantly at me and Violet.

"Okay, so you've already met the Aunts and half the sisters." Violet loops her arm through mine. "But the zombie nurse is my sister Fiona. Darla's the dragonfly."

"Ah, the psychic and the writer," I say. "A pleasure to finally meet you both."

"You are *sooo* going in a book," Darla says, plucking a pen out of her hair, which Violet quickly steals.

"No, he isn't." Violet drops the pen into the bag of a passing trick-or-treater. "Best not to mess with fate on this one, Dar." Then, to me, "My sister's stories have a tendency to come true, but not always in the way she writes them."

"Literary magic leaves a lot open for interpretation," Darla confirms. "The muse is fickle sometimes."

"I wouldn't mind being written into a story," I say. "Especially if it involves haylofts and—"

"Hey!" Violet smacks me.

"Exactly. Hay, and—"

"I mean, *hey*, you're not allowed to talk about Ambrosia Divine anymore. We had a deal, remember?"

Fiona laughs, then leans over and whispers something to Olivy, who nods and says, "Check your crystal ball if you want, but I called it on day one. These two are definitely going to—"

"*Olivy!*" Violet glares at her sister, then takes my hand, leading me away. "Let's dance. Quick, before one of my sisters says something she *shouldn't*. Looking at you, Ols."

"You can run," Olivy says with a dark chuckle that would

frighten most demons, "but you can't hide! Oh, Devlin, that reminds me. Someone was looking for you earlier."

"Who?"

"Didn't catch his name on account of me not being your secretary, but... Hot demon guy? Dark hair, green eyes—"

"Finn?"

"Maybe? He said he tried the café first, but you weren't there, then the liquor store, same deal, so he followed the crowd here."

"Where is he?" I scan the scene, but there's no sign of my best mate.

"Portaled out through the men's room—*super* classy. Said he couldn't wait—he had somewhere more important to be than, and I quote, Hallmark Halloween Central. So I told him to go fuck himself, to which he said, 'Or what?' And I said, 'or I'll dip you in wax and light your dick like a birthday candle.'"

I roll my eyes. "Who hurt you, Olivy? Goodness, the threats. Honestly."

"Your friend didn't take it as a threat. He asked me to marry him, actually." She laughs. "Sick fuck."

"Yes, that's definitely Finn. So when's the big day?"

"Two weeks from never. Anyway, he asked me to tell you that you've got eighty-seven left, whatever that means. I assume brain cells."

"You're a gem, Olivy. Has anyone ever told you that?"

"Has anyone ever told *you* to jump into a pit of boiling tar naked?" she asks sweetly. "Oh, and check your fucking phone. That's him saying it, not me."

I left my phone at the café on account of having no pockets tonight and no interest in getting creative with my personal carryons like my footballer guest from long ago, but no matter. If Finn says we've got eighty-seven left—souls, obviously—that means he doesn't need me weighing in on tonight's affairs anyway. Surely, he and Azazel will get the job done at our infamous Halloween bash.

Which means—if all goes according to plan—as soon as Violet and I finish our task in the Bay, I'll be truly free. Free from my father's endless punishment. Free to reclaim my throne. Free to go home.

Home.

I've wanted it for so long, so desperately, but now the very word feels foreign in my mind, like a language I once spoke but somehow forgot along the way.

I glance around the rotunda, at the gaudy decor, at the masquerading masses, all of them laughing and smiling, waving at me, complimenting my costume, and my throat tightens.

Hell doesn't even *have* pumpkins. Or ghosts and bats and cotton cobwebs. And it certainly doesn't have these friendly, cheerful, incorruptible people, or costume parties in general, or donuts and cider and mulled wine.

And worst of all, it doesn't have the tea witch. My fairy princess. My sweet, sexy, fiery little mushroom, dancing her awkward dance, laughing with her sisters and aunts, the music casting its spell over us all.

The tempo picks up, bass thumping, and I grab her hands and spin her around, losing track of time and space and everything but the sound of her laugh, the flutter of her fairy wings, the happy din of her sisters and aunts and friends.

I grab her for another twirl, only to be tapped on the shoulder by a rude, insistent finger.

"May I cut in?" the man asks, and I turn to glare.

If it isn't Twenty Watt Dildo, third of his name, popping up again like a rash that no amount of penicillin will cure.

"Thanks, but you're not my type." I wink at Brandt and whisk a giggling Violet away, spin her around and weave deeper into the crowd as one song bleeds into the next, then another, and soon I've lost count, foot-stomping and hand-clapping with her sisters and then the gents from the Saints and Sinners liquor store, an appearance from Ricci from the pottery place, everyone having a genuinely good time I wouldn't have thought possible with the massive amount of clothing and non-alcoholic beverages in the room.

Who knew?

But then, all at once, the music changes. A slow song floats on the air, old and bluesy, dispersing most of the dancers and leaving just a few couples behind.

Tucking her hair behind her ears, Violet smiles up at me. Hopeful. Beautiful.

"Dance?" I blurt out, because apparently I've lost my ability to speak in complete sentences again. "That is, would you like to? I mean, I realize we *have* been dancing, for quite a while, but I meant... Would you like to dance with me? Just us? For this song, specifically?"

Violet's laughing again—a definite yes. With a relieved sigh, I sweep her into my arms and draw her close, one hand holding hers, the other resting on the small of her back beneath the fairy wings, leading her into a gentle sway.

"Fair warning," she whispers, her cheeks pink. "I'm the worst dancer."

"Literally not possible. The record for the worst dancer is held by a gentleman named Caronius from the thirteenth century, who once started a war when he danced himself right off a cliff and dashed his brains on the rocks below, which turned out to be the private beachfront property of his family's mortal enemies, who happened to command their own navy. So take heart, Mushroom. And know that if any wars are waged on account of your footwork tonight, I'll defend you to the bitter end."

That laugh again. The snort at the end. The follow-up apology laugh. "Thankfully, there's no cliff nearby, but I've stepped on your toes at least ten times already."

"You're just getting a bit too far in your head about it." I spin her once, then bring her back to me, closer than before. "I can see it in your eyes, love. The way you fixate on some point in the distance, your smile locked into place as if it's been painted on."

"Painted on?"

"Quite beautifully, of course. Just... not your real smile. You're too nervous you'll make a misstep and—merciful *heavens*!" I tease. "What will the good people of Wayward Bay think if they discover their resident tea maven can't dance? Won't someone consider the *children*?"

"Says the man wearing women's lingerie that barely covers his junk."

"The point remains." I spin her around again, dip her nearly to the ground, then bring her right back. The couple beside us claps, and Violet smiles again, a bit breathless, her cheeks that lovely shade of crimson that's come to haunt my dreams. And my showers. "Close your eyes," I whisper into her hair. "And just... just feel it. The soul of the music has its own mysterious language. You just have to open yourself to it."

She groans but does as I ask, closing her eyes and resting her cheek against my chest, one hand on my shoulder, the other clasped in mine, and we continue our dance.

And my utter downfall.

I knew it was coming. From that very first night under the street lamps, when I gazed into her eyes and made her laugh for the first time.

Tonight, she's softness and light and magic in my arms, an angel who's got no business dancing with the Devil, yet here we are, gliding across the dance floor in our own little world while the rest of the rotunda fades away. Right now, I'm aware of nothing but Violet, every detail in sharp relief, every nuance, every shade of color that paints her. The slight halo of frizz puffing out from her loose curls, tickling my nose as I breathe her in. The lemon-coconut scent of her hair. Her small hand on my shoulder, two fingers tapping out the beat of the music, as if she's afraid she'll lose count and miss that oh-so-crucial step. The swish of her dress as she follows my lead, slowly but surely losing herself to the soul of the music, just as I promised.

I'm so wholly captivated I don't even realize she's speaking until she stops dancing.

"I think the song ended," she says softly, blinking up at me, flushed and happy. Breathtaking.

"I think..." I look around, see the other couples breaking apart. "Right. The song."

The scent of burned sugar and bourbon drifts through the air, and once again her magic envelops me. Entrances me. *She* entrances me. I'm utterly spellbound, no more able to walk away from this than I can walk away from the task of unlocking her heart's desire.

"Mushroom?" I curl a finger beneath her chin, gently tipping her face toward mine, our mouths so close I can taste the apple cider clinging to her breath. "I regret to inform you that despite our prior agreement, I suddenly feel an overwhelming need to kiss you."

A soft gasp. The quickening of the pulse at her throat. The blush I love so much, a deeper shade of crimson, lovelier than the last.

"You do?" she whispers.

"Indeed."

"Well. Since we're confessing things." She swallows hard, eyes glittering beneath the flashing lights. "Despite the agreement, I'm... suddenly feeling an overwhelming need to be kissed by you."

My heart kicks into my throat. Throbs. Makes other things throb. "An odd coincidence indeed."

"Maybe we can work something out?"

"I was thinking that as well, but I'm not sure what. We said this wasn't a date."

She nods vigorously, her wings fluttering. "We swore it."

"What do you suppose we should do about this terrible conundrum, then?"

"The veil is thin, right? So maybe we go for it? I mean, it's almost like it won't count."

"What happens behind the veil stays behind the veil, that's my motto."

"An excellent one at that."

"Mushroom?"

"Yes?"

"Less talking, more kissing?"

"Also an excellent motto. Actually, I like that one better than the what happens behind the veil one, because—"

I cut her off with a kiss, the rest of her words evaporating as she sighs against my lips, her hands twining into my hair, body melting into my embrace.

The taste of her, the silken heat, the feel of her in my arms... I'm gone.

Another soft sigh, and she parts her lips for me and deepens our kiss, the apple cider sweet on her tongue as I lick and nibble and tease. A red-hot spark of desire sizzles down my spine and I pull her closer, my mind swimming, my cock already aching for more, the scent of her magic intensifying as I lose myself completely to this moment, the forbidden kiss I was *never* supposed to want.

It takes me far too long to hear the thunderous applause, and for a moment I think maybe it's for us. But when I open my eyes, I spot the Pumpkinville Mayor sashaying onto the stage, waving to the crowd with her scepter.

The moment pops like a soap bubble. Violet pulls away, looking up at me with dazed eyes and puffy lips, her breathing ragged, glasses askew.

"Thank you all so much for joining us at our seventy-fifth annual Halloween Ball and Shop Crawl!" Mayor Singh begins, and I turn back to the stage in a daze, watching her toss handfuls of candy to the bouncing, squealing children below. The crowd cheers and whistles, and then, all at once, I'm yanked by the invisible leash.

Violet.

She's gone.

I whirl around and spot her beelining for the exit, the limitations of our magical bond forgotten in her haste to escape, leaving me no choice but to run after her, heart pounding, hard-on bobbing beneath the silk like a dinghy on a storm-tossed sea.

CHAPTER TWENTY-THREE

VIOLET

What. The hell. Was that?

My skin is tingling, my heart vibrating, my chest rising and falling like I just mainlined puerh tea and ran a marathon, and I can't. Freaking. *Breathe.*

I bolt for the exit like the building is on fire, completely forgetting about the magical leash. At the telltale yank, I stop just long enough to spy Devlin following, giving me some slack. Slower this time, I head out into the courtyard and duck behind a maple tree, leaning back against the trunk.

Closing my eyes, I press a hand to my chest, sucking in big gulps of air.

That kiss. That freaking *kiss*!

Yes, I've been fantasizing about him for weeks. Yes, every time he touches me during our cat-reading sessions, I catch myself pretending it's real. Replaying those romance stories all the way to the end, alone in my bed at night, wishing against all logic and reason that he'd just bang down the door, strip off my clothes, and give me the *real* Ambrosia Divine play-by-play, no hayloft required. And yes, on *occasion*, when he's in the shower and out of earshot, lesson learned, I take Mr. Wiggles out for a spin, clawing at my sheets and whispering Devlin's name into my pillow as I fall right over the edge.

So you'd think—after all his cheeky innuendos and nonstop touching and flirty *Devlinisms*—I'd be used to it. That my many, *many* X-rated fantasies and multiple battery-induced orgasms achieved in his honor would've numbed me to his charms, to the butterflies in my stomach at the touch of his hand, to the rush of heat between my thighs at the mere sound of his delicious buttery accent, but... *noooo*.

And it's not just the physical stuff, either.

Just when I think I couldn't be crushing any harder, the man does something *genuinely* sweet and sincere, like painting mugs with me, or dancing with my aunts, or saving me from Brandt, or fixing my glasses and showing me how to slow dance.

Then he just hauls off and *kisses* me? Like *that*? Like it's actually *real*?

No. It *can't* be real. No way. But that kiss? Good goddess. I felt it in places I didn't even think existed in real-life female anatomy—places I've only ever read about in Ambrosia's books, painted with words like petals and channels and dark, secret gardens.

We're real, all right! comes the downtown rallying cry, my core still pulsating with shockwaves of molten-hot desire. *Welcome to the funhouse, girl! And thank you, Devil sir, and your Devilish tongue... Can we please have another? Preferably about two feet lower next time...*

"Vi? You okay?" Olivy's voice cuts into my thoughts, and I open my eyes to find her standing right in front of me.

At my nod, she waves at someone in the distance, then flashes the thumbs-up.

"Devlin," she explains. "He's waiting for you on the bench back there. I told him we usually do a quick ritual with Ol' Aggie on Halloween, so he knows you're not trying to ditch him. Unless... you *are* trying to ditch him?"

"I *can't* ditch him. Binding spell, remember?" I remove my glasses and rub my eyes, blowing out a soft sigh. "But I don't want to ditch him, anyway. I just needed... a minute."

"Yeah, I saw you guys run out and got worried. Well, first I saw that *very* hot moment on the dance floor—definitely *not* family-friendly, by the way—then the running. So you can imagine where my mind went." She tucks a loose wave behind my ear. "What happened?"

"Nothing, I just..." I press my fingertips to my lips, still aching from the kiss. Still aching for more. "It was... kind of intense."

"No kidding." She laughs, the light in her eyes dancing. "But you're okay, right?"

At this, a genuine smile breaks across my face. "More than okay, Olivy. *Goddess*, I made a total scene."

"The running? No. The kissing? Definitely. But it was a *good* scene. Trust me."

Lowering my gaze, I bite my lip and mutter, "I think I might actually... like him."

"Like *him*, or like the special Halloween candy he slipped you tonight?"

"*Olivy!*"

"We all saw it, Vi. I'm pretty sure there's a video making the rounds, too. Mayor Singh was especially excited about the prospect of a winter wedding."

"You're all terrible!" I laugh. "She was on stage the whole time!"

"And therefore had the best vantage point."

"Dick or Treat!" comes the giggling call across the courtyard, and I turn to see Emmie, Darla, and Fiona bounding toward us.

"At least *one* of us is getting the good stuff tonight," Emmie teases. "Back me up, Fiona."

"My sources say..." Fiona mimes the act of gazing into her crystal ball, her brows wiggling. "Oooh, yes, someone is *definitely* in for a thorough dicking tonight, and that someone is... our very own fairy princess. May she be blessed with multiple multiples and a man willing to sleep on the wet spot."

"Oh my goddess, shut up!" I crack up at their antics, but

then a new realization dawns. "Oh, no. Please tell me the Aunts didn't see me making out with the Devil on the dance floor. I'll never hear the end of it."

"They've been with Aggie for the past hour." Olivy nods in the direction of Founder's Grove, where I spot my three aunts at the base of Aggie's statue, preparing their annual offerings. "But the Aunts probably know what's going on anyway, even if they didn't see a thing."

"We just *know* things, girls," Darla says in a dead-on impersonation of Joslyn's gravelly voice that has us all cracking up again.

With a bit more room left on the magical leash, I follow my sisters over toward Aggie's statue, turning to catch Devlin's eye.

He smiles at me across the courtyard, and even at a distance, I can feel the warmth in his energy. The lightness.

The intense desire.

Still burning. Not imagined.

Holy Hell.

He waves me on and motions to the bench, indicating he'll wait for me there, and I flash him the thumbs-up and continue on.

Olivy wasn't making excuses with the whole Aggie thing. Since the statue was erected, the sisters and aunts and I have made it our new Halloween ritual—leaving offerings and asking for continued blessings of Wayward Bay, our magic, and each other.

Now, my aunts welcome my sisters and me into their circle. Jos casts me an all-knowing smirk, and Althea squeezes my hand, but none of them say anything about Devlin or the kiss.

Ol' Aggie, though... she knows *exactly* what kind of mischief I've been up to tonight. I can see it in her eyes, just like I imagine she can see it in mine.

I kissed the Devil... and I *more* than liked it.

"Is everyone ready?" Althea asks, and we all join hands around Aggie's statue.

Other Wayward Bay witches have also paid homage to our patron founder tonight, and the base of her statue is a riot of colorful candles and gifts. Non-magical folks tend to leave the offerings in place, believing that Agatha Wayward will curse them to a year of bad luck if they steal from her.

Which is probably true.

Throughout the courtyard, the maple leaves tumble and twirl, the sounds of mischief and merriment floating on the air as the older kids chase the younger ones through the trees and various bands of revelers call out, "Trick or treat!"

It's easily my favorite night of the year, and being here with my aunts and sisters—with Devlin close by, connected by energy and magic and maybe something more—floods me with a sense of gratitude and peace.

Together, in a single voice, we quietly recite our prayer.

Magic above and magic below

Blessings in darkness and light
To witches we love and witches unknown
Blessings on Halloween Night

The magic gathers among us—a little something from each of us that combines into a powerful force of love and protection. It starts as a warm tingle in our fingertips and slowly travels up through our arms, straight to our hearts, connecting us to each other, and to Aggie, and to all the witches who've lived, loved, and died in the Bay.

After a few moments of silence, we each approach the statue, one by one, to leave our offerings.

Beneath Aggie's skirt, Fiona leaves a deck of Tarot cards tied with a silk ribbon. Darla wrote a story—her favorite offering—and tucks the envelope into a small gap under a shoe. From Emmie, a slice of lemon pound cake and a batch of hand-dipped chocolate-covered strawberries. I brought her my Sweet Dreams tea, a peppermint and jasmine blend mixed with rose petals, mugwort, and cinnamon.

"Aggie's having the *best* time tonight," Olivy says, last to place her offerings—a bouquet of lavender and rosemary, along with a small bottle of whiskey, rumored to be Aggie's favorite. "Saucy old girl."

"All she ever wanted was a safe place for us," Althea says, bittersweet tears in her eyes, and the other aunts nod, huddling in close. "A place where women—human and witch-kind both—could live our lives and do what we were born to do, whatever that may be. Nothing would please her more than to see how happy you girls are. How full of joy and love."

At the L-word, all of them turn to look at me. Heat spreads across my neck and cheeks, and suddenly I can't stop grinning. "Okay, okay. Yes, I like Devlin. Fine. But love? Come on! It's not like this thing between us is going anywhere! It's just... just some fun while he's in town."

"Maybe it is, maybe it isn't." Jos cups my cheek, eyes twinkling beneath the witch hat. "Either way, Violet. Don't ever talk yourself out of being happy. Enjoy it, even if it's just for one night."

"Especially on a night like tonight," Lorelei says softly, gazing up at the moon through the trees. "You never know what other kinds of mischief might be afoot."

I follow her gaze and stare at that beautiful silver orb, and somehow, even struggling under the weight of my debts and past mistakes—and *literally* chained to the Devil himself—I feel freer than I have in years.

"Thank you, Aggie," I whisper, pressing a kiss to my fingers and leaving it at her feet.

Then, right there beneath my hand, a Tarot card appears.

Not The Devil this time.

The Lovers.

A choice is coming, my intuition whispers. *Follow your heart's true desire, and you can't go wrong.*

CHAPTER TWENTY-FOUR

DEVLIN

The walk back to the café is silent, but not tense, and I try to enjoy it for what it is—a stroll on a beautiful Halloween night with a beautiful fairy princess by my side.

But no matter how much I try to convince myself it wasn't a big deal, that we both just got caught up in the moment, I can't stop thinking about that kiss. Replaying it. And wishing, above all else, it could happen again.

Ridiculous. Magical moments don't come along that often. Here and then gone. That's what makes them so magical. Appreciate it and move on.

Good advice, arsehole. Top fucking notch.

If only I could follow it.

"Tea?" Violet blurts out the moment we step inside the café, first word she's uttered since we reunited in the courtyard and wished her family goodnight. "I mean, would you like some?"

"Tea would be lovely," I say, if only because I can't bear the thought of this night ending.

"Let me just run upstairs and change, then I'll come back and brew us something special."

"Excellent. It's another non-date."

Her smile falters, and I want nothing more than to kick my own arse into next week.

"Or a date-date," I rush to add, but now she's just crinkling her nose at me. "Or maybe just... tea? Yes, who needs labels, right? Evening tea, that's what it is. Perfect. Go on ahead. I'll... put on the kettle."

And bludgeon myself with it repeatedly until my brain remembers how to function.

"Must you give me that look?" I say to Grumpy and Sunshine the moment the witch is out of earshot, the two of them hopping up on the counter for the express purpose of shortening the distance from which they're judging me. "I'm a bit rusty at this. Forgive me, but you might be more supportive."

Grumpy hisses.

Sunshine lifts a leg and licks his privates.

So much for non-relationship relationship advice from *these* two.

Well. I don't need their help. I've got this.

I may not be a master tea brewer or an empathic witch, but I know what's in Violet's heart—a heart that's full to bursting with the love she has for her chosen family. For her grandmother, Gigi. For her magic and her gifts. For the town that called to her across the years, the miles, the heartache, finally bringing her home.

I saw it in her eyes tonight as she danced with her friends. As she honored the town founder with her family in the courtyard.

As I held her in my arms, wanting nothing more than for her to make room in that heart for me.

So that's what I'm thinking about when I tie an apron round my waist and pull out some of her teas and herbs. I don't know if they go together—vanilla, mint, cinnamon, a pinch of rose petal, a bit of something called essence of selenite—but it feels right, so into the brew it goes.

She returns to me fifteen minutes later wearing a pair of black yoga pants and a long-sleeved shirt featuring unicorns farting out glittery rainbows.

"There you are," I whisper.

"Here I am," she whispers back, and for the span of several heartbeats, neither of us speaks. A hot blade twists inside me, and for a moment I worry everything has changed again. That the Violet dressed in fairy wings who lost herself to the passion between us on the dance floor is *not* the same Violet standing before me now, face scrubbed of makeup, hair twisted back into its usual messy bun, a few loose curls falling around her face, fingerprints marring one side of her glasses.

The magical fairytale costume is off, and perhaps that's all any of this was. Another costume, another role to play.

But then she spots the freshly steeped tea on the counter, and her entire face lights up with a new smile.

Gods, that look. It's everything.

"What's all this?" she asks.

"I took a chance and put my tea brewing skills to the test. No guarantees on taste, but it smells quite good, as far as I know. And before you ask, *no*, I didn't overdo it on the cayenne pepper. Skipped it altogether, actually." I pour two cups from the pot, then hand one to her. "Would you like to do the honors?"

She takes the first sip. Closes her eyes. Sighs.

I wait. And wait. Hours. Eons. And then, finally...

The smile returns. The eyes open, bright and blue and happy. "Devlin. This is delicious."

"Well, obviously." I laugh. "Doubting Thomas. Honestly, Violet. A little trust after all this time would go a long way."

She smiles at me again and sips her tea, and the silence descends anew.

After another excruciatingly long pause, I finally open my mouth to speak, both of us blurting out words at the same time.

"Violet, I wanted to—"

"I've been thinking—"

She blushes. Smiles again. I gesture for her to continue.

"I was thinking about what you said about the grant," she says. "That maybe I should consider it after all. Is that what you wanted to talk about?"

She blinks up at me expectantly over the rim of her teacup, patient and adorable, glasses steamed up from the tea, her mouth parted in a way that has me absolutely ready to confess all of my sins just for one more chance to taste that forbidden kiss.

"Ah, the grant! Yes. So glad you're reconsidering, tops on the list of Important Things We Must Eventually Discuss *but*... Here's the deal, Mushroom, fae queen of the ball, most beautiful witch of Wayward Bay." I remove the cup from her hands and set it on the counter. Then, cradling her face, "If I have to go *one* more second without kissing you again, I'm afraid my immortal life will come to a brutal end, and I'll die at your feet wearing nothing but a woman's negligee beneath a Kettle and Cauldron standard-issue black apron, and you'll have only yourself to blame."

One more smile for the Devil. "You want to kiss me *again*? Seriously?"

"What would ever make you doubt it?"

"I don't know. It all happened so fast, and then the mayor was talking, and all the clapping, and I kind of freaked out and I just thought... I thought maybe you were just... Ambrosia Divining me."

"You thought that kiss was an *act*?"

She shrugs and lowers her eyes, dark lashes fanning across her cheeks. "Not an act, but... I don't know. You're very... *expressive* sometimes. Physically speaking. I didn't want to assume—"

"Look at me, beautiful." I thread my fingers into her silky curls, pulling them free from the bun as I lower my mouth to hers. Then, in a soft whisper, "*Look* at me."

She finally peers up at me again, her eyes wide and searching, full of bewilderment and lust and the barest shred of hope.

"Main Street," I say. "October seventeenth. That first night when we walked to Saints and Sinners. You stood beneath the streetlamp, your eyes so blue, lashes dark from the rain. We were talking about sleeping arrangements and showering. I made a crack about my back scrubber."

She laughs, remembering. "I thought you were talking about something *else* getting hard."

"Yes, and you did your little snort-laugh, and that was it."

"That was what?"

"The very first time I wanted to kiss you."

"It... it was?"

"And in the weeks that followed, I've lost count of how many times I've wanted to kiss you since, as much as I've tried to pretend otherwise, for both our sakes. But tonight, the moment you waltzed into the café, beautiful and sweet and happy... Merciful *Hell*, Violet. All I wanted was to take you into my arms and kiss you breathless. And now that I've had a taste of it, all I want to do is kiss you breathless again. So maybe that makes me a fool, but—"

"Devlin?" She presses her fingers to my lips and smiles again, her eyes misting. "Less talking, more kissing. Excellent motto."

CHAPTER TWENTY-FIVE

DEVLIN

We barely make it up the stairs without falling.

I can't stop kissing her again, inhaling the scent of her, touching her, the damnable farting unicorn shirt thwarting my efforts with a row of buttons in the *back*—who *makes* these bloody garments?—until she finally breaks away and strips the shirt off over her head, revealing a peach-colored bra with tiny daisies.

As cute as it may be, that needs to go as well—far too much blasted fabric between my mouth and her silky-soft skin.

The moment we reach the apartment, I pick her up and carry her to the bedroom, tossing her onto the bed and stripping off the bra, the leggings, the panties until she's finally bared to me, my perfect Halloween gift all unwrapped. I tear off my Freudian slip, leaving the good doctor behind as I climb onto the bed and steal another kiss.

"Wait!" she laughs. "My glasses!"

She tries to remove them, but I grab her wrist. "No, Mushroom. The glasses stay on."

"Naked, with glasses? Devlin! I look ridiculous!"

"You look sexy as fuck, and I'm already addicted, and they're staying on." I cut off her protests with another kiss, and she twines her fingers into my hair, her body warm beneath me, and *fuck* I can't get enough. I'm already out of my mind with desire for this woman in a way I no longer thought was possible—not after so many centuries of meaningless entanglements and utter debauchery.

But Violet... she's so soft and perfect, every kiss like warm honey, the sugar-sweet scent of her ever-present magic an invitation I'll follow wherever it leads.

I bite her lower lip, teasing her with the tip of my tongue as I slowly make my way to her jaw, her throat, the collarbone I've been dreaming about for far too long. Everything about her is so delectable it's an effort not to devour her whole, but I force myself to take my time. To enjoy every sweet and sinful moment the little witch is willing to share.

Because when I finally return to Hell, *this* is the memory I'll return to again and again for the rest of my immortal life.

I lower my mouth to her breast. A long, languid lick, then I suck her nipple between my teeth, nibbling and teasing, making her gasp for me as I slide a hand between her thighs, fingers brushing over her clit, gliding down through her wetness, then back up, a slow, torturous path that leaves her panting and begging for more.

"You're so beautiful when you beg," I whisper. "Do it again. *Beg* me not to stop."

"More," she pants. "I want... more. Please, Devlin. Please don't stop."

I slide a finger inside, then another, stroking her as my kisses wander lower, her thighs parting for me, hips arching closer, my tongue flicking against her clit until I'm drunk on the taste of her desire, fucking *mad* for it, moaning against her hot flesh as my fingers curl in deeper and—

Bzzzz...

Violet stills beneath me, her eyes flying open, cheeks flaming like a sunset.

Bzzzz bzzzz...

"Oh no," she whispers.

Bzzzzzzzz.

Stifling a dark chuckle, I slowly kiss my way back up to her ear and whisper, "Is that who I think it is?"

"Oh, goddess. No." She casts an evil glare at the nightstand and groans. "Not the time!"

"Oh, I beg to differ," I tease. "Now is *precisely* the time."

I reach over and open the drawer, rooting around inside until I find the source of the incessant buzz.

"Mr. Wiggles has a mind of his own," she says. "A dirty one. Just toss him back in and ignore him."

"I will do nothing of the sort. If you think I'm going to let a haunted sex toy intimidate me into leaving your bed tonight, Violet Pepperdine, you are sorely mistaken. And so is *this* ghostly thing." I press the vibrator to her clit and send out a pulse of Hell magic, just so we all understand who's in charge tonight.

The reaction is immediate—the haunting entity relinquishes its hold, the device wholly under my command. Even more satisfying, I feel her reaction, too. My sweet little mushroom shudders at the contact, her back arching off the bed, fingers curling into the sheets at her sides.

I turn up the speed and tease her with the tip, coaxing another sensual moan from her lips.

"Tell me something, my naughty witch," I whisper. "Is this what you were fantasizing about the night I walked in on you?" I dip inside, making her gasp. "Fucking yourself like this, pretending it was *my* cock filling you, *my* mouth on your skin, granting you this *exquisite* pleasure?"

"Oh, goddess. That's... don't stop. Please don't stop."

"I have no intention of stopping. But if you refuse to confess your secrets, perhaps I'll confess mine instead." I kiss her neck, lips brushing the shell of her ear. "Every night when we bid adieu, and you retreat to your bedroom and I to the couch, it's not the television I watch into the wee hours."

"It... it isn't?"

"Oh, I've tried. Binged at least two seasons of your witchy show, but not even the Halliwell sisters can distract me from what's going on in this bed." I bite her earlobe and drag the vibrator back to her clit, giving it another pulse of magic. "Ever since that night, I can't help but imagine what's happening on the other side of your door. Through the gap on the bottom, I watch the light change, your lamp turned off, the candle flames dancing with the shadows. I picture you taking the pins from your hair, each curl springing loose around your face."

I trace a fingertip across her cheekbone and reach for my favorite curl, wrapping it around my finger.

"I hold my breath," I whisper, still kissing her, inhaling her scent. "And pretend I can hear the rustle of your sheets as you slip between them. The buzz of your vibrator as you fuck yourself, just like this, dreaming about all the hot, filthy things the Devil would do you if you invited him in." I glide it in deeper, drag it all the way out, then thrust in once again, angling it *just* right. "Now I'm right here with you, sharing the very bed I've imagined you in night after night, naked and beautiful, and here's *my* fantasy..." I lower my mouth to her ear again. Then, in a hoarse whisper, "I want to hear my name on your lips as I fuck you breathless and make you come for me, again and again and again."

"Devlin..." she breathes, hips rolling, eyes closed, her crimson cheeks bright, so fucking close to the edge. "I'm going to—"

"Not yet, Violet. First, I want another taste."

My mouth descends on her silken flesh, licking and sucking, fucking her with my tongue while I tease her clit with the device, her thighs trembling, her breathy moans making me so hard it aches, and when she finally rakes her nails across my scalp and cries out my name, I nearly come right there.

I can't fucking take it anymore. Not for another second. I need to fuck her, hard and deep. Now.

Ditching the vibrator, I fist my cock, capture her last breath with a desperate kiss, and sink deep inside her.

That's it. All at once, she's falling over the edge, and fucking *hell*, the feel of her. The slow, hot slide into all that softness and heat, her body tightening and pulsating around my rock-hard cock, and I break our kiss just in time to hear her cry out my name once more as she comes completely undone.

"Beautiful," I whisper, because she is—everything about her, sweet with a side of naughty—and when she finally comes back to earth and opens her eyes and reaches up to touch my face, I nearly falter.

It strips me to the core, the closeness of it all. Terrifies and enchants me both, like stepping into the flames to enjoy the view of the fire, oblivious to the danger until you've bloody well incinerated yourself.

I claim her with another fiercely possessive kiss, my hands in her hair as she hooks her heels around my back and urges me in deeper, and *fuck*... I don't care if this is the final act that burns me to ash. I need this too much to stop now—need *her*. Wrapping my arms around her, I flip us so she's on top, wild hair spilling across her shoulders, glasses askew, the dark peaks of her nipples begging to be sucked. I sit up beneath her and take one between my lips, licking and teasing, a gentle bite that has her moaning and rolling her hips, a slow, seductive dance that's damn near got me seeing stars.

Free of my control, Mr. Wiggles buzzes back to life beside us, but we don't stop for him. Or for the curious cats meowing and scratching outside the door. And when we roll again and end up on the floor, tangled in the sheets, it only stokes the flames higher.

My sweet, shy witch has lost all inhibition, begging me to fuck her harder, taking what she wants—all the hot, filthy things I'm more than happy to give her, until I feel her tightening around me once more, that tingling heat racing through my balls. She cries out for me again as she rides me harder, faster, and when the next orgasm takes her, she shudders and tosses her head back and laughs that happy, awkward laugh, and that's it. That's fucking it. I'm gone.

"Fucking *hell*, woman," I growl, gripping her hips and coming inside her in a blissful, white-hot fury that leaves me spent and trembling, no strength left in me to do anything but lie on the bedroom floor, close my eyes, and wait for death to finally claim me.

Still laughing, still panting, Violet curls up by my side on the floor, bare but for the sheets we brought down with us, her cheek warm against my chest, hair a wild mess. I wrap my arms around her and bury my face in the lemon-coconut curls, grateful that death decided to give my immortal bones a pass after all.

"Are you all right, love," I murmur.

She props her chin on her hands and looks up at me, glasses finally gone, lost in the tumble, and smiles. "I'm actually perfect."

"No lies detected." I trail my fingertips up and down her spine, making her shiver. "Call it irony if you will, but in the old days, witches were thought to be the Devil's consorts."

Her cheeks flame and she averts her gaze, but not before I catch the light dancing in her eyes. The teasing grin gracing her lips.

Draping a thigh across my hips, she says, "Is that what I am? The Devil's consort?"

"Oh, Mushroom. You are so much more than that."

"Good. 'Cause I'm not ready to give you up just yet."

Fuck. Me.

I've *never* felt this way before. This sudden, overwhelming need to make her happy—not just in the bedroom, but everywhere. To keep her safe. To promise her the world and do my damndest to deliver it on a silver fucking platter.

To *not* saw off my own arm to escape.

What *is* this madness?

"Gigi—my grandma?" she says softly. "She knew you were coming. She tried to warn me, but I didn't want to listen."

She tells me about her grandmother's magical Tarot cards, the often unexpected messages from across the veil.

"Anyway," she continues, "your card kept showing up—The Devil. For two days straight, I couldn't get away from it. I tried to make it disappear, chase it away, set it on fire, and yet... you were relentless."

"I've been called worse." I laugh. "Did you really think you could destroy a magical Tarot card? The Devil, besides?"

"It was more like a symbolic gesture."

"Symbolizing *what*? Your desire to murder me?"

"No. I was trying to convince myself that I had even a *shred* of control over my life."

"Control is an illusion peddled by a capitalist society that does everything in its power to convince you you're losing it, just so it can sell you something to convince you you'll get it back."

"Is that why you don't bother with it?"

"Capitalism?"

"Control." She reaches behind my head and retrieves her glasses. Pops them back on, her eyes searching my face. "Everything you do is so... I don't know. Spontaneous. Inspired. I wish I could be more like that."

"No, you don't." I offer a sad smile, then shake my head.

"Spontaneous or not, none of us has any control. Just influence. However, if you're saying you're ready for your own pitchfork tattoo, I'll happily and spontaneously make the arrangements." I grab her backside, sending her into a fit of giggles that doesn't settle until I roll on top of her and pin her down, already hard as fuck for her again.

She opens for me at once, and I sink deep inside her and kiss her breathless, grateful that of all the witches who could've summoned and bound me, I ended up in the arms of this one.

∽

Later, when the impending sunrise has turned the sky pink and we're both showered, re-hydrated, and happily exhausted, we collapse into her bed, her back against my chest, my face buried in the crook of her neck, the cats finally allowed back inside, everything about the moment fucking perfect.

I'm just drifting off to sleep when I feel her turn over in my arms.

"What is it, love?" I whisper, opening my eyes to find her watching me intently.

"I'm not sorry I summoned you, Devlin."

"No?"

"I mean—I'm sorry I magically kidnapped you against your will, and I'm sorry for all the inconvenience it's caused you. But all that aside... I'm really glad our paths crossed. For all that I tried to ignore Gigi's signs, I just... I don't know. I can't imagine going my whole life without ever getting an opportunity to know you. That's all."

She smiles again, brighter than the dawn, and I run my thumb across the lower curve of her mouth and sigh. After all the flirting, all the kissing, all the *incredibly* hot sex, it's this moment, this simple confession that strikes at the heart of me. That makes me wish, for just another fleeting moment, that it really could go on forever.

"Devlin?" she whispers, dazed and drowsy, nodding off. "Do you really think I've got a chance? With the grant, I mean? Even with Brandt calling the shots?"

"I think, Mushroom..." I steal one more kiss, slow and soft and perfect, then cup her face. "You and your many, many spreadsheets will blow the competition out of the water, leaving the cunt-mollusk weeping and gasping for air and wondering what in the bloody hell just happened."

CHAPTER TWENTY-SIX

VIOLET

"Holy shit, Violet! You're wearing a skirt!"

I startle at Emmie's sudden proclamation, nearly dousing the skirt in this morning's energizing Get It, Girl brew.

"Emmie, jeez!" I dry off my tea-splattered hands and step out from behind the counter. "Well, don't keep me in suspense. How do I look?"

Dropping a box of scones on the closest table, she walks a circle around me twice, taking in my transformed appearance—wild curls tamed into a sleek twist at the base of my neck, my breezy jeans-and-tee style swapped for a borrowed navy pinstriped blazer and skirt courtesy of Darla, a pair of Aunt Jos's pantyhose that are absolutely squeezing the life from my limbs, and ankle-breaking heels from Olivy that I spent two hours traipsing around in last night—first, to practice. Second, for Devlin, in a slightly different context, the after-effects of which I'm still feeling on my inner thighs.

Which haven't even recovered from the night *before* the heels. Or the night before that. Or any of the nights we've been setting on fire together since Halloween.

Not that I'm going to think about that right now.

Focus, Violet. Focus!

After what feels like a decade, Emmie finally comes around to face me again, her grin stretching wide. "Brandt fucking Remington, third of his boring-ass name, won't even know what hit him."

"Unless I *actually* hit him, which is a distinct possibility."

"And a well-deserved one at that, but not one we're going to entertain until *after* the grant money is sitting in your bank account. And when that happens—*when*, not if—I'll be locked and loaded with another dozen powdered donuts to pelt at his stupid smug face, for old times' sake. Deal? Deal." She whips out a tube of lipstick and gives me an unsolicited touch-up. "You could use some color, though. Maybe blush. Do you have—"

"Yes." I pat my purse, where I just dumped in all the old makeup from my nightstand. I hardly ever wear it, but there's bound to be at least a few useful jars or tubes of something colorful in there. "I'll do it on the ride over—Devlin's driving. I know it's a short walk, but between the heels and the hair, I didn't want to leave anything to chance."

"Plus," Devlin says, popping out of the kitchen with a to-go cup of the Welcome brew he loves so much, "it gives me a chance to feel you up across the console, and who on *earth* would pass up an opportunity like that?"

He winks at me, his eyes sparkling with that mischievous glint I've come to know and love, his hair still kind of messed up from having my hands in it all night.

All week.

Since Halloween, we've only left the bedroom to work at the café, order food, shower, and prep for my pitch meeting with the grant committee. And three out of four of those tasks are easily accomplished naked, so when it comes down to it, no. We haven't really left the bedroom much at all.

Goddess, he's just so amazing. The way he touches me, the things he does with his mouth, the words he whispers in my ear...

My thighs clench at the memories. Conditioned response at this point.

Sometimes, when he's looking at me like he is now—the eyes, the raised brow, the barely perceptible smirk that tells me he's got some filthy, sexy comment perched on the tip of his tongue—I wonder what it would be like if he stayed. If our time together didn't have that pesky expiration date.

But there's no more room in my life for impossible dreams. So for now, I'll take Aunt Joslyn's advice and enjoy every moment, for however long it lasts.

And also have some really, *really* hot freaking sex.

"Speak of the Devil." Emmie grins at me. Then, "Oh, I almost forgot!" She reaches into her bra and pulls out three crystals. "Citrine, green aventurine, and pyrite. For abundance and opportunity, and a little luck too." She shoves them into my bra, still warm, then says confidently, "You've *got* this, Vi. You're going to do great. And don't worry about K&C. I've got everything in order here, and Darla said she's on standby if I need backup."

I lean in for a hug. "I'll be back to set you free before the Sweet-N-Savories afternoon rush."

"Take your time. We've got you covered."

"Thanks again, Em."

Other than Olivy, my family doesn't know just how desperately I need the grant. They just think it's a great opportunity for me to upgrade the shop, so I'm letting them roll with it. Devlin still thinks I should tell them what's going on, but after today, I'm hoping I won't need to.

It will all work out.

It has to.

"Oh!" I turn back to Emmie. "There's a clipboard hanging on the back wall with some of the most common blends. Cinnamon and vanilla can be added to just about any of the black teas, although I've been experimenting a bit with nutmeg and it—"

"Violet, my love, my sweet sister, my favorite tea witch and all-around badass? Don't take this the wrong way, but..." Emmie ties on an apron and shoves me toward the door. "Make like a tea... and get the fuck out of here. You've got committee stiffs to impress!"

THE DEVIL MADE ME BREW IT

∽

"Any questions so far?" I ask brightly, my colored pie charts beaming down from the big screen at the head of the conference table as I walk the length of it, making eye contact with each of the committee members.

But ten minutes in, I can already tell.

The committee stiffs are most certainly *not* impressed.

Not by my rock-solid business plan or my ace spreadsheet game. Not by the binders Devlin and I meticulously assembled with enough sections and colored tabs to earn my Virgo-of-the-Month award a dozen times over. Not even by the basil- and vanilla-enhanced charm infusing me from today's Get It, Girl brew.

I don't understand. Devlin and I combed over the application together for days, crossing every t and dotting every i in triplicate. I've got all the required paperwork, the licenses, the appropriately business-boring outfit, *and* my tea-infused zest for life. But despite my efforts, I've yet to garner so much as a *single* smile or nod of encouragement from the lot of them.

Least of all from my stupid ex, who spent my introductory pitch scrolling through his phone, undoubtedly checking his investment portfolio.

Just like he used to do in bed.

"I'm surprised at the lack of a social media footprint," the woman next to Brandt says—Elsie Cunningham, the new teen lit librarian at the high school, not that far out of high school herself. "I did some sleuthing before our meeting and couldn't find much about the Kettle and Cup on any of the major apps."

"Cauldron," I say.

"Is that a new app? I haven't heard of it, but—"

"No, the name of the café is Kettle and *Cauldron*, not cup."

She sets down her phone, her glossy smile twisting into a frown. "I think you're proving my point. You have no brand, no presence. A kitschy name will only get you so far. You need to get the word out about your business, or how will anyone know you exist?"

"I don't have much time to be online. Most of my time is spent in the café, perfecting brews and interacting with my guests." I tap my phone and the next slide appears—a clever bit of tech magic Olivy hooked up for me. "But the grant will help me invest in additional marketing and—"

"Have you thought of hiring an influencer to help promote your brand?" she presses. "Influencers are known to help juice the algos and increase reach across key demographics..."

She's rambling on, speaking an entirely different language Devlin and Olivy would definitely understand, but all I hear is the sound of a giant toilet flushing my dreams down the drain.

"Thank you, Miss Cunningham," I say. "That's a great

suggestion—I'll look into it. In the meantime, I'd love to tell you more about my specialty blends, and the cozy experience we offer our patrons, including our very own Mayor Singh, who's one of Kettle and Cauldron's most loyal customers." I tap to a photo we shot yesterday featuring the mayor holding up her teacup to the camera, a huge smile on her face. The photo opp was her idea. She thought it would help.

Unfortunately, she's not on the committee, and judging from the looks on their faces, I'm pretty sure she just lost their vote in the next election, too.

"Miss Pepperdine," Brandt says stiffly, as if he didn't spend the better part of last year assaulting my left labia like a scratch-off lotto ticket while asking me repeatedly if I was, quote-unquote, almost there. "Your passion for tea is admirable, but passion is not collateral. Not for the kind of financing we're looking to invest."

I want to ask him what kind of financing *would* allow me to use passion as collateral, and by the way, do you even know what passion is, and furthermore, *you're lucky my witchy zone of genius is magical tea instead of ex-hexes, or you'd wake up tomorrow with a worm in place of that glorified cocktail weenie currently dangling between your legs...*

Also, I'm 99% sure he just likes throwing out words like "collateral" because he thinks it makes him sound smart and impressive. This is a grant presentation, not a loan application.

Swallowing back my annoyance, I tap to the next slide and say, "I understand your trepidation, but if you'll take a look at my projected revenue forecast, page three, section six, you'll see some of the ways in which the grant can help the business thrive into next year and beyond. I think you'll all agree—"

"Next year is not *this* year." Brandt taps a manicured finger against the still-unopened binder before him. "Let me be frank, Miss Pepperdine. Your application wasn't as outstanding as some of the other businesses we're considering. Not by a long shot."

Dread drops in my gut like a hot rock. He's icing me out. Just like I thought he would.

"I agreed to attend this presentation as a courtesy to you," he continues, "given our previous... association, and the fact that you are a valued member of our community. But you're asking this committee to pass up on other viable business applications and invest a sizable amount of money in a business that after two years running has yet to turn a profit. A business that's still very much in debt with no clear-cut path to solvency."

The others nod their agreement—Miss Cunningham, who's now smiling at something on her phone, only half paying attention to my slides. Former Police Commissioner Wembly, who's only on the committee because his wife got tired of him moping around at home after retirement and forced him to join something. The mayor's assistant, Margo

Kip, a closeted vampire who's been gunning for her boss's job for the last three years. And a middle-aged witch whose name is a mystery, even among magical circles, because she allegedly only speaks to animals.

So. Not great odds here, with Brandt manning the ship.

"The grant *is* the path to solvency." I fight to keep my frustration in check as I tap to another slide. "As I've outlined here, with multiple levels of Roman numerals and bullet points, this grant will allow me to pay off the café's debts while providing additional capital to invest in a new employee or two, lease better equipment, and expand our offerings to include—"

Bzzz. Bzzz bzzzzz.

"—a new lunch menu and late-night café service on weekends, to start."

Bzzzz.

All heads turn to my empty chair, and the purse I draped over it, from which the strange, insistent buzzing emanates.

Bzzzzzzzzz.

"Do you... need to get that?" Brandt asks, clearly annoyed. Then, showcasing his mastery of air quotes, "It might be your new... *friend*."

It's not. Devlin is right out in the hall waiting for me, and he'd never call me during this meeting. No way. Besides, I could've sworn I silenced my phone on the way here, right after I touched up my lipstick. I *know* I did.

And... *hello*. I've got my phone in hand, using it to control my slides. So what the hell is—

Bzzzz! BzzzZZZ! BZZZZ!

I strain to listen again. So familiar, yet so...

Oh, goddess. No. No no no no no!

Realization crashes down on me like a ton of bricks. My makeup bag... Goddess, I was running late this morning. Wasn't even paying attention when I grabbed the stuff out of the nightstand. Just scooped and dropped, claw-game style. Blushes and eyeshadows I probably got from Jos's old stage makeup kits back when I still lived at the house. Mascara one of my sisters left in my bathroom. Lipstick from who knows where. And apparently—desperate for more attention than he's been getting at home since Devlin's tongue took center stage—Mr. Wiggles.

And today, he *definitely* wants his truth to be heard.

BZZZZ!

"It's... my phone," I mutter, forcing a smile. "Sorry about that. As I was saying, the—"

"But you're holding your phone," the keenly observant Mr. Wembly says.

"Am I? I mean, I am! I meant my *other* phone. My... emergency one. Just ignore it."

Bzzz bzzz bzzzz....

"If it's an emergency phone, shouldn't you answer it?" Miss Cunningham wants to know. "It might be... an emergency?"

"Please continue with the slides, Miss Pepperdine." Brandt gets up from his chair and heads for my purse. "I'll just get that and silence the—"

"No!" I practically leap across the table to stop him, and in my not-so-athletic haste, I launch two of the three crystals from Emmie out of my bra and clear across the table. They spin to a mortifying stop right in front of the nameless witch, who just looks at me and winks.

The social-media-loving librarian snaps a picture. Me, sprawled halfway across the table. The crystals. The spectacle.

Buzzzzzzzz bzzz bzzz bzzz buzzzzzz! goes Mr. Wiggles.

I call up my magic, willing it to cut the power. To short-circuit the damn thing. To dampen the sound, at the very least, but it's no use. I'm too frazzled to concentrate on even the simplest spells.

Meanwhile, back inside my purse, mortification HQ, Mr. Wiggles suddenly downshifts like a pickup truck cresting a steep hill, growling and grinding, dropping into a gear I've never even heard before, pressing his pulsating pink-headed glory against the side of my handbag. Repeatedly. I mean, he is absolutely winning at life in there, which on a normal night in my bed I would encourage, but right now in front of all the committee members, including my ex...

Buzzzzzzzz. Bzzzz bzzzz.

I stare up at the ceiling. *Really, universe? Really?*

"Whoever that caller is," Margo the bloodsucker says, a knowing twinkle in her eye, "they sure are persistent!"

I fake a smile right back at her and soldier on, directing attention to my next slide—a description of some of the healing properties of the herbs and spices I use in my blends, leaving out the magical stuff, of course—but it's no use.

I've lost them.

Damn it. I gave up my overalls and cute T-shirts for a power suit and pantyhose, for the love of the goddess. I'm wearing heels! And lipstick! I deserve a fighting chance!

Two seconds from hurling the bag out the window, along with my whole disastrous self, I clear my throat and raise my voice to be heard over the grand finale buzzing on behind me. "In conclusion, with generous funding from the Keep the Bay Beautiful for Business grant, Kettle and Cauldron can expand our café offerings, boost the local economy by creating new jobs, and continue to play an important part in keeping the Bay... um... really beautiful. Thank you for your time and—"

Bzzzzzzzzzz bzzzzzz bzzZZZZZZ!

Okay, that's *it*. Sentient Mr. Wiggles is totally fucking with me, and I'm done. All out of chill, I grab the purse from the chair, swing it over my shoulder like an axe, and smash it onto the conference table.

Three times.

The buzzing slows to a muted whine, then grinds to a halt.

Silence descends.

Sadly, my precious emotional support vibrator is no more.

But the tears for our fallen comrades will have to wait.

Forcing a great big smile, I click off my presentation, beam at the wild-eyed committee, and say, "Any further questions?"

CHAPTER TWENTY-SEVEN

DEVLIN

As soon as she exits the conference room, I know the news isn't good. The defeated look in her eyes says it all.

My heart sinks, and all I want to do is storm into that room and blast the entire committee to Hell, but I can't, because Violet's already marching off toward the exit.

"I don't want to talk about it," she says when we get into the car, slipping off her borrowed heels and tossing them into the backseat.

"Understood," I reply, though it kills me not to ask what happened, not to demand the names and addresses of all those responsible for dimming the light from her eyes. "Is there anything I can do?"

Sever a few heads? Display them on pikes as a warning to all who dare cross you again?

She shakes her head, curls falling out of the twist, every one of them breaking my heart.

And securing a few new spots in Hell for those committee members...

Back at Kettle and Cauldron, Violet puts on a bland smile for her sister, giving a few tight-lipped, one-word responses to Emmie's inquiries about the presentation before scooting upstairs to change clothes.

Fifteen minutes later she returns, dressed in the familiar overalls and a long-sleeved shirt covered in teapots and biscuits, her hair in a loose braid over her shoulder.

"Feeling any better?" I ask.

"No. But at least I'm not feeling hopeless *and* wearing pantyhose, so... win?" She heads back behind the counter to relieve Emmie and gets right to work—grating ginger and cinnamon, chopping mint, crushing one thing or another.

Across the street, the ongoing Mean Beans crowd has finally begun to thin. We haven't seen lines in days, and sure enough, the tea business is ticking back up. Today, a somewhat steady stream of customers keeps us both busy—Violet preparing her magical brews, me clearing tables and sweeping floors and generally trying to stay busy, lest I fly into a murderous rage and burn something down.

Still, not even the slow-drip return of her regulars is enough to brighten her spirits today, and when the last customer of the evening finally heads out, Violet locks the door and turns off the main lights, tosses her apron into the wash pile, and drops onto the couch with a sigh that could sink ships.

Giving her a moment to regroup, I step behind the counter and brew her a cup of chamomile tea—one ingredient, hard to mess up—because seeing her in pain and knowing there's nothing I can do about it is a torment so brutal even the King of Hell can scarcely endure it.

"If you'd like to be alone, I'll leave you to it." I hand her the cup and saucer. "But I'm here if you'd like to talk."

"What's there to talk about? If you looked up 'epic disaster' in the dictionary, it wouldn't even mention my name. That should give you a clue." She sips the tea. Sets the cup back in the saucer, china clinking and trembling until she finally gives up and abandons it on the side table. "You might be tempted to try 'hot mess express,' or 'human wrecking ball,' or 'pathetic failure playing the sad trombone,' but you won't find it there, either. In fact, you won't find it *anywhere,* in *any* dictionary, online or off, slang or classic. Why? Because they haven't actually invented a phrase to encompass the complete and utter shitshow that Violet Pepperdine performed at that presentation today."

"Oh, Violet." I sit next to her, drawing her feet into my lap. "I'm so sorry, love."

"I totally bombed," she continues. "All the slides, all the facts and figures, my colored pie charts... and all I got was a *no.* A big, fat, irreversible no with a side of better-luck-next-time and a don't-let-the-door-hit-ya-where-the-good-goddess-split-ya garnish. I can't believe they didn't ban me from ever stepping foot inside the Town Hall again. It was *that* bad."

I know she's upset, but... None of this makes any sense. Sure, I expected her to be nervous. A bit shy at first, maybe. But this is her dream. Her passion. She knows the tea business better than anyone, and she knows how to talk about it, no matter who's in the room.

"Did they actually tell you Kettle and Cauldron is out of the running? They're still hearing pitches, aren't they? I thought they weren't supposed to announce winners for another week or two."

"They didn't *have* to tell me. I could read it in their energy, Devlin. They were completely disinterested. And Brandt?" She shakes her head, teeth clenching. "That smug bastard. As I was gathering up my things, he had the nerve to offer me a fifty-dollar bonus if I opened up a new business checking account at his bank!"

Remind me to get that rotisserie fire and pole ready for him...

"That wasn't even the worst part. I was in such a rush this morning, somehow I tossed Mr. Wiggles into my purse with my makeup. Well, he must've felt left out, because he gave everyone quite a show." She tells me the rest of the story, a blush creeping up her neck that darkens a bit more at every turn of the tale, right up to its tragic end. "Maybe I'll be able to laugh about it one day, but today is not that day."

"Surely they didn't turn you down because of a haunted

vibrator. That's grounds for a discrimination suit or... something."

That something being me shaving Brandt Remington from head to toe, tarring and feathering him, parading him down Main Street, and *then*—finally, dreams really do come true!—roasting him alive.

"I told them it was my phone." She reaches for the abandoned chamomile and scoffs. "Pretty sure Brandt Remington the *Third* has never even *seen* a vibrator. It's like you said—that man wouldn't know a good time if someone *literally* shoved it up his ass. He'd probably think it was some newfangled at-home proctological exam and thank me for being so concerned about his preventive health screenings." She sips the tea. Rolls her eyes. "Great. Now I'm thinking about that puckered asshole's puckered asshole. Could this night get any worse?"

"Not anymore. We've hit a new low. But getting back to the disaster with the vibrator—"

"It wasn't *just* the vibrator, Devlin." She gazes into her teacup, shoulders sagging. "Even before Mr. Wiggles crashed the party, I was already toast. I blew it five minutes in. It was like they'd already made up their minds about me before I even queued up the first slide. I should've known better than to think I could compete with Brandt's ego."

"If it's any consolation, I've already phoned in his reservations to Hell. Presidential suite. *Very* nice accommodations."

At this, she finally cracks a smile. "I appreciate you trying to cheer me up."

"Oh, that wasn't the cheering-up portion of the show. That was just an FYI." I wink at her and rise from the couch. "But I do have something that *will* cheer you up if you're game. Two somethings, actually. Sit tight."

I retrieve the box from under the counter and reclaim my seat next to her. "First thing: Ricci dropped off our mugs while you were upstairs changing."

Her eyes light up—victory at last—and her grin stretches wide—double victory. "You didn't peek at them, did you?"

"No. I wanted us to open them together." I pop open the lid. The mugs are wrapped in white tissue, and I peer beneath an edge to find mine, then pass it over. "For you, Mushroom. I fully expect you to display it up front. No relegating me to a dusty shelf in the kitchen."

"*None* of my shelves are dusty. But it's a deal. Front row placement at all times." She unwraps the paper to reveal my masterpiece—a white mug painted with the Devil's horns and tail swishing over the words, *The Devil Made Me Brew It*. Inside, I've left her a tiny black pitchfork.

"Aww. Now that is quite... *cheeky*." Violet wriggles her eyebrows. "Get it? Cheeky?"

"Oh, I get it. As will *you*, if you insist on being cute."

She laughs. Miracle of miracles. Then, "Thank you, Devlin. I love it. It's not going on a shelf *ever*—I'm going to use it every single day. Now open yours."

I tear into the paper, unwrapping a mug painted inside and out with her signature red-capped polka-dotted mushrooms. It's thoughtful and adorable and for some reason brings tears to my eyes, which I quickly blink away.

"Just a little something to remember me by," she says softly. "When you're home, I mean. If you even drink tea at home. It's... it's silly. I'm sorry. I know I'm—"

"It's not silly, Violet." I finally meet her gaze. "It's lovely. Truly lovely."

Heat floods my chest, racing through my veins. Suddenly, there's so much more I want to tell her—that no one has ever given me a gift so freely, without expectation, without strings attached. That I don't need a mug to remember her by, but in the thirty seconds since I've opened it, it's already become my most cherished possession.

That some small, insistent voice inside me is growing louder by the day, shouting down the terrifying truth I can't seem to face:

I don't want to go back home. I don't want to leave her.

Violet's eyes shine with intensity, her lips parting in a gasp, and I realize she can sense my emotions. That in letting my guard down, I've already revealed so much more than I meant to. Than I should have.

"Devlin." She reaches for my hand. "I didn't—"

"Oh, but we're not done yet!" I blurt out, forcing myself to shore up my walls. Plaster on the smile. Get this show back on the road, post-haste, before I say something that dooms us both. "The mugs were just the first thing on the cheering-up agenda, and I promised two."

Violet sighs, and I don't have to be an empath to feel her disappointment. "You don't have to keep—"

"Oh, but I do." I retrieve my phone, queuing up a video from a particularly crazy party last summer. "Here. Watch this."

I tap the play button and hand it over.

Violet sighs again, but ultimately turns her attention to the video. I see it all unfolding, reflected in her glasses—a memory come to life. Me, Finn, Azazel, the foyer full of ridiculous people.

The horse.

"See?" I lean in to watch over her shoulder. "And this is just the *tip* of the mortification iceberg. I've been making a fool of myself for an audience for longer than you've been alive, and I promise you, your botched performance was not as bad as you believe. From this day forward, whenever you're in doubt, I want you to think back to this *very* special video of the Devil himself riding a horse through the middle of a crowded foyer wearing nothing but a cape and a silver g-string, launching himself into the infinity pool over a burning pyre, and remember... it could *always* be worse."

The momentary heaviness that fell between us dissipates in the wake of her laughter. "You've definitely set a new bar."

"A *low* bar."

"Basement, if I'm being honest. Sub-basement. Although, you *do* look pretty cute wearing almost nothing."

"No lies detected."

"I'm still not a huge fan of the pitchfork, though."

"Lies!" I pull her close, snuggling her against my chest and kissing the top of her head. "You *love* the pitchfork. You've loved it from the very start."

Violet continues scrolling through my greatest hits, laughing at some of them, gasping at most of them. But when she finally returns my phone, the light in her eyes has dimmed.

"That was supposed to cheer you up, Mushroom. Why are you not cheered? Do I need to further lower the bar? Because I've got more. *Lots* more. Sub-sub-*sub*-basement more."

She tries to smile, but it's pained, and when she speaks again, her voice is soft and sad and full of regret. "It's just... kind of hitting me."

"What is?"

"That I took you away from all this. I had one bad night, got drunk, and cast a spell that stole you away from... from everything. Finn and all your friends, all these beautiful, glamorous people, the gorgeous house and the parties and... *goddess*, Devlin. I had no idea this was your life."

"No one has any idea," I say softly. "Because this *isn't* my life, Violet. It's merely the face I present to the world. The show I've been putting on in one form or another for centuries." I scroll through the recent videos again, see myself in all of them—surrounded by drunken revelers, laughing and hollering, all in various states of debauchery, all having the times of their lives, drinking away their nights as if they have an eternity of them to go through. As if they're not heading straight for Hell.

But nothing about it feels familiar anymore. It's as if I'm watching someone else play the part. Someone I've never before seen and have no interest in *meeting*, letting alone *being*.

"Devlin?" Violet lifts her head from my chest, peering up at me over her glasses, her hand on my heart. "What's wrong?"

I smooth back the hair that's fallen into her eyes. "Tell me what you feel."

"Regret."

"Regret," I echo, my voice heavy with it. With an honesty I've never once shared, never once been comfortable revealing. "It's a strange thing to be surrounded by people, yet feel so desperately alone, you wonder if you might literally disappear. Or worse—if you already have."

The fire pops, casting us in a bright glow. Violet gets to her knees beside me and reaches for my face, her palms warm on my cheeks, tears glittering in her sapphire-blue eyes.

"I see you, Devlin," she whispers. "I won't let you disappear."

And there, in those words, in the depth of understanding in her eyes, in the silence of the night and the soft warmth of the fire, it hits me—one more truth I can't escape.

I'm bloody well in love with this woman.

CHAPTER TWENTY-EIGHT

DEVLIN

I pull Violet onto my lap, and she straddles me and slides her hands over my shoulders, her gaze never leaving mine. She smiles now, a sweet and bashful thing that's so very Violet it breaks my heart to look at it.

I don't know how much time passes, me staring at her, falling deeper into her eyes, her searching mine for a soul that may very well not exist, but then the logs shift again and sparks cascade from the fire, startling Grumpy and Sunshine out from beneath the couch, and Violet sighs and traces a delicate fingertip across my brow and whispers, "What I wouldn't give for a peek inside the Devil's mind."

"Very scary. I don't recommend it."

"Can't be all *that* bad. I mean, not like g-string-on-a-horse bad."

"No, not quite. I was... thinking about home, actually."

"I've heard California has the best sunsets. Is that true?"

"It *is* true, but I was thinking of my *first* home."

"Hell?"

I nod. "Specifically, the Desolation Mountains. It's a region of Hell reserved for the worst demons guarding the worst souls who've ever existed—men condemned to eternal torture. The darkness there is endless—jagged black peaks as far as the eye can see, black sky, black rivers so poisonous even the most battle-hardened demons avoid them. The creatures who roam those peaks will tear a man limb from limb, wait for the body to regenerate, and do it all over again, because no one ever dies. Suffers, but doesn't die. There's no sound, either—not even a whisper of wind or the screams of the damned. Just a maddening, all-consuming silence. Near complete sensory deprivation punctuated by the most unimaginable pain and anguish. But in the very center of the region exists a lake the color of the deepest sapphires, ringed in flame. No one knows how it was formed, for it's far too breathtaking to have come from Hell's creators. It simply... exists."

"Is that where you live? When you're there, I mean?"

"No. I've only seen it once."

"What made you think of it now?"

"Your eyes." I trace my fingertips along her brow. "The color, the fire behind them. Beautiful and fierce. A quiet rebellion that defies all expectations."

A tear slips down her cheek.

"You asked me once why I left Hell," I say, my voice

barely a whisper in the fire-lit dim, one more confession I've never before shared. "It was my family who asked me to leave, Violet. My father, mostly, but the rest quickly fell in line."

"I thought... I thought you were cast out of Heaven, not Hell. At least, that's the story I've always heard."

"That bit is true. I *was* cast out. Then they gave me free rein in Hell, which seemed to satisfy all parties, as it kept me out of their precious homeland and allowed my father to keep a foothold in the lower realms by proxy."

"What happened to make them cast you out of Hell, too?"

"I committed an unforgivable sin." I shake my head. A bitter smile dawns. "Many, *many* centuries ago, I fell in love with a witch."

Violet gasps.

"Not just any witch, either. But an ancient sorceress glamoured to ensnare me at every turn. I fell for it, too. I was so enraptured by her, I truly believed she loved me. But it was all a ruse she concocted to get close to Hell's upper-level guardians. Witches aren't permitted in Hell unsupervised because of their association with Hell's demons—together, they're a force too powerful to contain. That's why so many of them attempt to summon demons to the material realm, but a demon is most powerful in its home realm. So any witch who enters must be escorted by me or a member of my family."

"Did you escort her? The sorceress?"

"I'll spare you the details, but yes. She wanted to see my home. And I, being significantly younger and ever-so-slightly less discerning than I am now, wanted to impress her. So off we went. Long story short, she spelled me, left me for dead, and seduced the guards, tricking them into freeing the worst demons of the lot. They returned to the material realm and started a war with the God of Death. Humans got caught in the crossfire, scores of them died, all blamed on some natural disaster or another. My father had to intervene, which he despises—his favorite pastime is watching humans destroy each other in his name. In the end, it was determined I was at fault. That I was reckless, selfish, irresponsible. That I would never be fit for Hell's throne—never be fit to be anything but a jester, eternally mocked. Utterly discarded."

Tears fill her eyes, but I force myself to keep going.

"To further humiliate me—and to profit from my desperate need to please him—my father granted me the opportunity to earn my way back. Sign one million corrupt human souls to Hell in a thousand years' time, and I'm free to return, with the caveat that I can never leave Hell again. Fail to sign them, and I'm banished *forever,* cursed to die here as a mortal man. Those were his terms."

"What do you mean by signing souls? How does that even work?"

"Essentially, my demon companions and I find the most

corruptible, reprehensible humans, give them an encouraging nudge toward the dark side, and ask them to sign away their souls. It's really that simple. Most of them do it without batting an eye, not even realizing they're pledging themselves to eternal demonic servitude." I stare into the flames, shame gnawing at my gut. "My father deemed it an impossible task."

"Is it?"

"According to my last call with Finn, we've only got one left. Then I'm free to return to Hell. Free to take up the throne and rule over the kingdom of the damned once more, my immortality intact, my fate sealed."

"But that's... not what you want," she whispers tentatively, her touch compassionate, not a shred of judgment or fear in her eyes despite my vile confession. "It's... it's your father."

"What of him?"

"All this time, you haven't been chasing your throne or your immortality. You've been chasing the affection of a man who's wholly incapable of loving you." At this, her tone turns sharp. "I don't care *what* mistakes you made in the past. Any parent who abandons their child and intentionally sets him up for failure is just doing it for the gratification of their own warped ego, and I'm sorry, but they don't deserve *anything* from you. Not your obedience. Not your apologies. Not your right to happiness. And *certainly* not your eternal life."

I nod. As usual, she sees right through it, right down to the rotten core.

"You've given him so much of it already," she whispers, her thumbs brushing the tears from my cheeks—tears I didn't even realize I'd shed until I felt her touch. "You deserve to be happy. You deserve to be... to be loved."

"There was a time—not so long ago, really—that I wouldn't have believed you. How could I dare to want happiness or love after spending so much of this immortal existence just... just *ruining* things? Mostly on purpose. I mean, I get why I did it. I'm not proud of it, but I get it. Why bother trying, right? If you never do anything right, no one can be disappointed in you for fucking up. You're just meeting the expectation. But that's... not a way to live."

"And it's not who you are, Devlin." She presses her hand to my heart again. "I hate that anyone made you doubt it. Especially your own family."

I take her hands in mine. Bring them to my lips. Kiss each one of her fingertips. Close my eyes and try to breathe through the crush of emotion in my chest.

"Centuries of anger and resentment have nearly stolen my capacity for anything else, Violet. And I swore to myself—swore it on my very throne and the family I so desperately wanted back—that I'd *never* love another. Least of all a witch." I open my eyes again. Gaze into hers, still shining with understanding, with hope, my beacon in the all-consuming darkness. I smile. "The thing of it is, Mushroom... I've gone and fallen in love with you anyway. Accidentally, but completely. And I'm not quite sure what to do about it, because when I look into those beautiful blue eyes, I can't help but think of a day on the near horizon when I'll no longer be able to, and I can scarcely *breathe* because of it."

"Devlin," she whispers, those endless sapphire pools nearly drowning me, and I swear my bloody heart stops beating as I wait for something more—more words, another touch, anything.

It feels like a day, a year, an eternity before I finally see it, but then... merciful *Hell*, there it is. The dawn of a smile, the smile that heals me, that tells me that maybe—for once in my fucked-up immortal disaster of existence—I really *do* deserve something better.

She's still in my lap, knees bracketing my hips, and now she leans forward with a kiss, powder soft at first, feathering my cheeks, erasing the last of my tears. She moves on to my mouth, a gentle brush against my lips, and then her kiss turns passionate, fearless, a promise that holds the entire world inside it.

I twine my fingers into her curls and deepen our kiss, claiming her as she has claimed me, and then she's shifting down, her mouth blazing a path along my chest, my stomach, unbuttoning my shirt as she moves lower, lower still, every hot kiss making me harder for her, aching, until finally she slides a hand inside my pants and frees my cock, stone-hard and throbbing at her touch.

She's on her knees in front of the couch, her head in my lap, my hands in her hair, and when the devious little mushroom finally glances up at me over those ever-smudged glasses, her eyes full of mischief, I gasp. It's my red-hot shower fantasy come to life.

I tighten my grip in her hair, holding her back, if for no other reason than to take this opportunity to freeze this moment, to sear it into my memories.

"Let me taste you, Devlin," she whispers, her breath misting over the tip as she grips me, strokes me, melts everything inside me. "*Please.*"

I'm already trembling for her, my resolve breaking. "As much as I love hearing it, Violet, this is one thing you will *never* have to beg me for."

One more smile, shy but determined. One more mischievous flare in her eyes. And then she lowers her mouth and her tongue darts out, swirling around the tip, and *ohhh fuck*...

Without warning, she takes me in deep—so fucking deep I can't even see straight anymore. I bury my hands in her hair again, guiding her into a perfect rhythm as she sucks and licks, moaning against my flesh, unraveling me one desperate kiss at a time until I'm certain I won't survive this. Won't survive *her*.

She draws back, teasing the tip once more, then taking me in so fast she nearly gags, and...

"Fuck, yes. Right there... Right... *fuuuck*... Violet..." I clench my teeth and hold my breath and fucking shatter for her, spilling down her throat, shuddering against her lush mouth as she takes it all in, every fucking drop, and when she finally pulls back and gazes up at me one more time, her eyes dark with lust, her lips swollen, and *demands* that I take her upstairs—right fucking now—I know there's no more denying it.

Ancient oaths be damned. I'm wholly at her mercy—the sweet, formidable, beautiful witch who has the Devil utterly bound.

First by magic, second by love.

And I'm quite certain it will be my downfall.

CHAPTER TWENTY-NINE

VIOLET

It's half-past three in the morning—the witching hour. Here in Anxietyville, it's also known as the endlessly-staring-at-the-ceiling, wondering-how-my-life-went-so-far-off-the-rails hour.

But tonight, for the first time since I was a kid living under Gigi's magical roof, I don't feel so lost and out of control.

I feel... happy.

I hardly even recognize the word.

Devlin just snuck down to the café to raid the day-old pastries from Emmie's, and I'm here in bed, finally alone after several hours of panty-melting debauchery that started with me on my knees and ended with Devlin on his, my poor cats cowering in the pantry to escape the primal howls coming from my bedroom (yes, I howled like a she-wolf, I'm not ashamed to admit it).

But an anxious mind has its own kind of dark magic—the undeniable power to poison even the most joyful moments. One minute you're floating on air, butterflies dancing in your stomach, your heart about ready to burst with the exciting possibilities of it all... and the next, you're curled up in the fetal position, hyper-focusing on all the ways it can and most likely *will* go wrong.

And just like that, the happy feeling inside me pops like an overinflated balloon.

Don't get too comfortable, my brain says now. *Happiness is too elusive. Too easily shattered.*

I try to counter it, Devlin's whispered confessions stirring those butterflies back to life. *I've gone and fallen in love with you anyway. Accidentally, but completely...*

But here in his absence, sheets rapidly cooling, all I can think about is what happens when he leaves for good. When he goes back to Hell, cursed to remain, or gets stuck here, cursed to die.

Happiness is an illusion, says my oh-so-helpful brain. *And the happier you allow yourself to feel, the harder it is when you make that inevitable face-plant. The one you* always *make, Violet, because no matter how hard you try, you can never, ever be perfect...*

Goddess, I can't stop thinking about him. Of our first dance on Halloween that eventually led to our first kiss. Of our first *everything* that came after (came being the operative word, multiple times, in multiple ways).

That night, I was nervous and exhilarated and yes, *extremely* turned on. It was its own kind of happiness—one my brain actually let me keep.

But tonight?

The poison inside me is already spreading, his words twisting into weapons for my anxiety to wield against me.

I've gone and fallen in love with you anyway. Accidentally, but completely...

He meant it. I felt it in his energy, in his fevered kisses tonight.

But no matter what he says, no matter what he *believes*, this thing between us *wasn't* an accident.

And it wasn't love, either, my brain says. *It was magic, plain and simple. A binding spell that he's confusing with the real thing...*

"I hate you," I whisper to my brain, to the anxiety that's been poisoning me since I was a kid, making me terrified of losing every good thing that comes my way.

Another fifteen minutes pass, and Devlin's still not back. I try to get used to it, knowing I'll have to soon enough.

But all that does is make my chest hurt.

"Please, Gigi," I whisper, the panic simmering again, old insecurities rushing in hot. "I just need a sign. What do I do? How do I know if this is real?"

My phone pings from the nightstand, and I startle. Flick on the bedside lamp. Put on my glasses.

There beneath the phone, three Tarot cards rest, all in a row.

The Devil card—my familiar companion, reminding me only of Devlin, of the first night he came to me and all the wild, hilarious, intense moments we've shared since.

The Fool, young and carefree, about to walk right off a cliff—an invitation to leap without looking, to embrace a new adventure with wild abandon and childlike wonder. But the Fool offers a warning, too, and now I see only the cliff, the long fall to the bottom, all the ways life can shove you right over the edge long before you even notice the drop.

And then, finally, the Lovers. Reminding me, just as it did on Halloween when it appeared at Aggie's statue, that a choice is coming.

Follow your heart's true desire, my intuition echoes, *and you can't go wrong.*

"But what if my *heart* is wrong?" I whisper, and the phone notification pings again, urgent and insistent. *Read me. Read me. Read me.*

Outside the door, my floorboards creak.

Phone in hand, I glance up and finally see him in the doorway—my Devil limned in moonlight, the dark fallen angel who's somehow fallen for me.

"Violet?" he asks, tone heavy with concern. "Is everything all right, love?"

"I'm... I don't know." I glance at the notification.

It's not a text, but an email.

Oh, no.

No one ever emails me—only my suppliers, but this is way outside normal business hours for them.

Which means it can only be one thing.

With trembling hands, I tap the icon and load the message.

From: Wayward Bay Town Council Advisory Board

Subject: Wayward Bay Small Business Grant - THE KETTLES CAULDRON

Great. They can't even get the name right. That doesn't bode well. Heart pounding in my throat, I read on.

Dear Miss Pepperdine:

Thank you for submitting THE KETTLES CAULDRON for our first annual Keep the Bay Beautiful for Business grant program.

After careful consideration of your presentation and submission materials, we regret to inform you that the committee has chosen to decline your application.

As this will be an annual program, we encourage you to apply again next year.

Until then, we wish you much success in your business endeavors!

Sincerely,

Brandt Remington III

President, Remington Capital Group

Co-Chair, Committee to Keep Wayward Bay Beautiful for Business

~

That's it. Four sentences. Four lousy sentences and a stupid exclamation point to really send the point home.

"Violet?" Devlin is by my side now, knuckles brushing my cheek. "What is it? You look as though you've seen a ghost."

I can't speak past the lump in my throat. Past the crushing disappointment. I hand over the phone, unable to meet his eyes.

"That fucking prick," he says. "That utter fucking spineless waste of space."

"They didn't even take a full day to make their decision. That's how bad my presentation was."

I didn't expect to win—not with Brandt in charge, and

definitely not after my disastrous presentation this morning. But still. Seeing it in writing—written by Brandt, of all people—is a gut punch of the highest order. Especially since I *just* asked Gigi for a sign.

Well, I asked for it, and I got it. No coincidences, right? That's what I get for allowing myself to be happy. I've made too many mistakes already. Who the hell was I to think I could have it all? Who the hell was I to think that any of this could actually work?

That I could earn the money to save the shop, to keep on doing what I love most?

That a man summoned from the depths of Hell, whose kisses taste like sin and whose whispered promises make me dream of an impossible future, could truly fall in love with me?

That somehow, together, we could build something real?

I gulp in a shuddering breath, everything inside me suddenly hot and itchy.

"Violet?"

"Sorry. I just…" I throw off the blankets and push past him. Snatch my bathrobe from the hook on the door. "I… I need to go."

"What? Where? Violet, I—"

"It's not you. I can't… I can't think straight. I need to figure something out. Things. All the things."

"I'll help you. I'll put on the kettle and we'll—"

"No! I mean… no." I suck in another deep breath, panic

and regret clawing at my heart, threatening to tear me apart. "I need to be alone tonight. As alone as the bond will allow, anyway."

The bond. The magic. The connection Devlin is confusing for love.

The connection I almost let myself believe was real, too.

Suddenly, I want nothing more than to banish him. To shatter that bond. To know, once and for all, if there's anything else tethering us together.

Anything real.

Devlin puts his hands on my shoulders, steadying me. Calming me, just for a moment.

"Stay here, little Mushroom." Pain and helplessness flood his energy, a dark contrast to a night full of love and passion, of secrets laid bare. "This is your home. I'll spend the night downstairs."

"Devlin, I can't ask you to—"

"It's *fine*, Violet. Just like old times." He offers a smile that doesn't even reach his eyes. And I know I should say the word—the one tiny word right on the tip of my tongue.

Stay.

But I can't.

Devlin nods, as if he can hear my thoughts. Then, with a deep sigh, he kisses my forehead and whispers, "Get some rest, Violet. We'll figure it all out in the morning."

CHAPTER THIRTY

DEVLIN

There *is* no figuring it out.

Not in the morning, while Violet busies herself in the café inventing new blends for customers that never seem to materialize and we stealthily avoid talking about anything that matters. Not in the afternoon, much the same as the morning. And not, as I'd hoped, in the long, lonely stretch of evening that bleeds into a darkness so complete, I feel as though I'm right back in the bowels of Hell.

By the second day of walking on eggshells, when I feel I'm losing her a bit more with every passing pleasantry, with every minute that ticks by when I can't touch her, can't kiss her, can't bury my face in her hair and promise her things will work out—somehow, some bloody way—I finally decide to take matters into my own hands.

She won't like it. But I can't just sit here and watch her light fizzle out over a fuckstain in a cheap suit who isn't worth the expense of breath it requires to tell him to go fuck himself.

∼

It's after midnight when Brandt Remington, third of his name, enters the café. And though he's here at my request, it's with no small effort that I withhold my full wrath at the sight of him, this imposter, this worm, this worthless wad of gum beneath my shoe. To think that he ever uttered a single word to cause her pain, let alone *touched* her...

"Thank you for meeting me here, Brandt," I say congenially, escorting him to a table at the front. "I'm so sorry for the short notice and the hour, but I'm on a deadline and can't spare a moment away. Also, discretion is of the utmost importance, as I'm sure you can imagine."

"Absolutely." He smiles across the dim space as if seeing me in a whole new light. "I'm always happy to make time for an investor."

"Care for a drink?" I pour myself a bourbon, and at his nod, one for him as well.

He takes the offered glass. Smirks at me over the rim. "Did I call it, or did I call it?"

"Call what?"

"The moment I laid eyes on you, Devlin, I knew you weren't really interested in Violet." He laughs. "Cute girl, pretty good lay, but not a lot going on upstairs, if you get my drift."

"Oh, I get your drift, Brandt." *I'm about four seconds from drifting my boot up your arse and kicking my way out through your teeth...*

"So tell me." He smacks his lips, sets down the drink. "What, exactly, can my associates and I do for you and your millions?"

Another laugh.

Another urge to rip out his throat.

But that particular reward will have to wait.

After seeing Violet so upset the other night—because of the dim bulb wet-napkin bastard gloating in front of me—I knew there was no way I'd let it go. I also knew there was something not quite above board about the grant application process. Violet suspected as much from the moment she entered that conference room, and their all-too-quick rejection letter was further proof.

So that night, relegated back to the café couch, I contacted Olivy, who—after making me promise she could indeed sell my severed appendages should any harm come to her sister—put her dark-web sleuthing skills to work, coming through for me in a big way.

After printing out the evidence for the judge and jury—me serving in both esteemed capacities—I called his personal cell number, also uncovered by Olivy, and requested the meeting. Millions of dollars to invest, I said.

Looking for a trustworthy partner who understands how to cut through the red tape. How to get creative with the legalities. All for the greater good of lining our pockets.

Brandt didn't even question it. Not the odd hour, not my sudden interest after mocking him at every previous interaction. Ah, well. Greed has a tendency to dull the edges of even the sharpest tacks, and as we've already established—quite thoroughly—Brandt is certainly not one of those.

Now, I place my dossier on the table and scoot my chair around so I'm seated *right* next to him, so close my knees touch his thigh, so close I can smell the bourbon on his breath. Awkward as a first-time threesome, that—not knowing exactly where to look, what to touch, which tab goes into which slot.

Fuck, I love making lesser men squirm.

And squirm he does. "Wh-what's going on here?"

I drink my drink. Drink *his* drink. Lean in close. Smile. "One chance, Brandt."

"Chance for... for what?"

"I'm going to ask you a question, and you're going to answer it. If you lie to me, you'll suffer consequences the likes of which someone of your limited mental capacity can't even *begin* to imagine. Hence, one chance. Any questions?"

"I... I... I'm not—"

"Why was Violet's grant application denied?"

"*That's* what this is about?" Confusion clears from his eyes, his brow furrowing. I swear the bastard almost cracks a smile, as if he'd ever get off the hook so easily with me. "She's not up to snuff, Pierce. It's that simple. That's why she lost the grant."

Oh, but I *love* when they test my patience.

"*Wrong.*" I let my true form emerge, horns twisting out of my skull, the red glow of my eyes reflecting in his dark pupils, fear paralyzing him in place. "She lost it because her jealous arsehole needle-dick ex decided, in his infinite wisdom—which wouldn't even fill a fucking *thimble* if I tipped his head sideways and poured it out his ear—that she didn't qualify. And why did you make this decision, the jury might ask? Because..." I flip open the dossier. Run my finger down the first page, then the next. "Ah, yes. Here it is. You've already awarded the grants a month ago—long before the program was even announced—to five out-of-state firms posing as local businesses on paper. Firms your institution has been financing with shell loans for years. Firms headed up by men—and I use the term *very* loosely—you attended college with. Pledged a fraternity with, as a matter of fact. A fraternity which also includes... drumroll, please... Nathan Pike, reprobate realtor to bottom-feeders the world over."

Brandt's face turns the color of sour milk, his lip quivering, the scent of his fear nearly overpowering the scent of the booze, but I'm just getting warmed up.

"There's also the matter of your so-called financial institution's practice of denying business loans for legitimate businesses all over town without even reviewing their applications, adding illegal fees and rate hikes on the few businesses who get a foot in the door, closing lines of credit without cause, and generally being an abusive dickhead to your staff."

"That's not... this isn't what it... Where did you get all that?"

"It's an interesting scheme, I'll say that much. Drive up the cost of doing business for the locals until they're forced to abandon ship. Then your man Nathan swoops in, convincing the leaseholders to sell the storefronts at a loss—on paper, anyway, since the buyers are none other than the rest of your college pals, who are more than happy to offer up a payoff on the back end. Works out wonderfully for all involved, doesn't it? They get prime real estate for a song. You and Nathan get kickbacks. Everyone wins! Except, of course, your friends and neighbors, but hey, what's a few lost livelihoods and broken dreams in the grand scheme, right?"

Brandt mutters something unintelligible.

"Didn't quite catch that, Brandt. Care to give it another go?"

"Who... who are you?" He blinks rapidly, licks his meaty lips. "Wh-why? Why are you doing this?"

"I think you know who I am. As to the why... Well, I'm nothing if not fair and balanced, despite the rumors, and I appreciate when justice is served. I also believe in the people of this town and their right to make a living doing what they love. Finally, because you're a flaming cunt, and it's fun to watch you cower. By the by, did you know Violet calls you 'the mollusk?'"

"I... I don't have to sit here and listen to this." Finally finding what he believes to be his backbone, Brandt stands up and tries to grab the dossier, as if I haven't made multiple copies and digital backups.

I lift a hand and hit him with a blast of Hell magic, knocking his arse right back onto the chair.

"Oh, I beg to differ, Mr. Remington, third of your name. You *do* have to sit here and listen. And watch, too. I'm more of a visual learner myself, so I get it." I press a fingertip to his forehead, unleashing a vision of his near-term future in Hell. A future he cemented long before I came into the picture—long before he even met Violet.

But for what he did to her, I'm adding a few bonus items not on the regular menu. Some *special* tortures crafted just for him. I'm no empathic tea witch, mind you, but I do what I can to ensure my clients receive *exactly* what they most deserve.

"You've lied, cheated, and conned your way through your entire life." I hit him with a mind-movie of unimaginable terrors even the most gruesome horror flicks can't top. "You've used and discarded people. Hurt those who've helped you. Carved up this town like a slice of cherry pie and redistributed it to your grubby-fingered cronies, collecting hefty kickbacks along the way."

"I... I only did the same as anyone would!" he cries.

"Took advantage of the opportunities that came my way. It's just... just good business!"

I remove my finger. Let him come back to the moment. "Is that what you tell yourself so you can sleep at night? That hurting people is good business?"

"I'll... I'll pay you. Please. Name the amount and it's yours!"

"You'll pay me with the money you've bilked from your so-called friends and neighbors?" I laugh. "Hard pass."

"What can I do to change it, then? I'll do anything... anything! Name your price!"

This is, admittedly, my favorite part. The useless groveling. The whimpering. The bargaining, ah, such sweet music.

Poor, deluded Brandt Remington, third of his name, last in line the day they handed out the brains. He doesn't realize there's no changing the destiny of a man whose deeds have marked him for Hell.

That doesn't stop me from naming my price anyway.

"Your blood and signature on the dotted line, if you please." I grab his hand, make a quick slice across his finger with a knife, then produce the contract—same as the one my guests sign in L.A., only this twat doesn't get the luxury of ignoring the fine print. I don't even *show* him the fine print.

The blubbering mollusk does as I ask.

Signed, sealed, delivered.

He would've ended up in Hell anyway. But he signed the

contract, so as far as my father's accounting goes, this one counts as mine.

My one millionth soul. A monumental achievement in its own right, cue the applause, cue the confetti.

"Excellent doing business with you, Mr. Remington." I tuck the contract into the dossier and escort him out the door. "Now go ahead and slither on back to your office. I believe there are a few clerical errors you need to correct on those grant letters—starting with Violet Pepperdine's."

CHAPTER THIRTY-ONE

VIOLET

My bed is an icy wasteland in Devlin's absence, and my heart isn't fairing much better, the special combo-pack of anxiety, loneliness, fear, and confusion keeping me tossing and turning until the wee hours.

Eventually, after two nights of barely snatching any sleep, I give up and head downstairs in search of the only thing that can soothe me now. The one thing I still have, despite the fact that I'm about to lose it all.

Tea.

It's still dark outside when I don my favorite mushroom shirt and a pair of well-worn jeans and creep down to the café, the chilly air a reminder of autumn's last hoorah, the fire nothing but ash.

I sense Devlin's energy—frenetic, but asleep—and slip past the purple couch without looking at him. I'm still not ready to see him. To deal with everything that happened between us. His confession from the other night. My ensuing freakout.

What any of it even means.

He told me he loved me, but how can I accept that? How can I allow myself to return those feelings when my failure to earn the grant—to get out of my own way and save my life's dream, my heart's desire—has doomed him to a mortal life in Wayward Bay? Doomed him to die?

That's not love. That's a death sentence.

Sniffing back tears, I turn on the kettle, find a clean teapot, and get to work. It's either that or lose what's left of my mind.

Put On Your Big Girl Panties and Get Over Yourself. That's the name of today's blend. Black tea, hawthorn berries, dried rose petals, elderflower syrup, and a dash of lavender-infused honey—a blend to help my grieving heart move on.

The kettle whistles.

My phone pings.

My heart clenches—more bad news on the way. That's all I can think.

With one eye closed, I glance at the stupid screen. Another email.

Goddess, I don't want to read it. But I've already lost the grant. Lost my last shot at saving the café. Stole Devlin from his friends and his home and the life he built, long before I came along and kidnapped him.

At this point, what else have I got to lose?

I tap the icon. Spot the committee's email address in the sender field.

Take a trembling breath.

And read.

Dear Miss Pepperdine:

Due to an unfortunate computer error that had nothing to do with me or my staff, you were mistakenly informed that your business THE KETTLES CAULDRON did not qualify for the Keep Wayward Bay Beautiful Small Business Grant Program. The committee would like to rectify that error and inform you that THE KETTLES CAULDRON has been awarded one of this year's coveted small business grants in the amount of $75,000 USD.

A member of my staff will be in touch later this week with further instructions on completing the appropriate tax forms and receiving the funds into your designated business bank account via electronic transfer.

Congratulations, and as always, thanks for doing your part in keeping Wayward Bay Beautiful!

Regards,

Brandt Remington III

President, Remington Capital Group

Co-Chair, Committee to Keep Wayward Bay Beautiful for Business

∽

I read it three times to be sure.

Then I chug my tea, make another mug, chug that one too, and read it again now that I'm fully under the influence of life-affirming caffeine.

The words are still there, all in the same order, all saying the same thing.

I got it. I got the grant.

Holy hell, I got the *freaking* grant!

"*Devlin!*" I race out to the fireplace, heart galloping in my chest, my smile so wide my cheeks hurt. I don't even care that he's still sleeping or that I've just terrified my poor kitties or that I look like a crazy person who just got kicked off the crazy train for being too crazy. "Devlin, get up! Get *up!*"

"Hmm?" He blinks at me. Smiles. Yawns. Closes his eyes and goes right back to dreamland. Three seconds later, he bolts upright and stares, taking in the full sight of me. Wild hair. Backward shirt. Bouncing on my toes. Laughing.

He rockets to his feet and grabs my arms. "What is it? Did something happen? Are you hurt?"

I shove the phone toward him, everything inside me buzzing from the news. And the caffeine. And the crazy. Complete package right here, folks. "It's from the committee. Well, Brandt, but on committee business. Read it. Read it!"

I can't even wait for him to read it. At the first glimpse of his morning smile, I shove the phone in my pocket and pounce on him, uncontainable excitement propelling me into his arms. Devlin doesn't hesitate—just wraps me in a hug and spins me around, holding me tight enough to set the world back to rights.

"Tell me what we're celebrating," he says with a laugh, its rich timbre vibrating through my chest. "Not that you need a reason to throw yourself at me, but it *is* a bit unexpected. I thought you wanted... space."

"I thought so too, but I..."

He finally sets me down and looks into my eyes, his gaze searching, hesitant but hopeful, still holding the echo of his confession.

I've gone and fallen in love with you anyway...

I suck in a sharp breath as the realization dawns.

Of all the people I could've called with this news, of all the open arms that would've welcomed me with a congratulatory hug—the Aunts, my sisters, Mayor Singh, even Grumpy and Sunshine—I chose *this* person. *These* arms. This man whose every touch makes me feel cherished and safe and wholly accepted, even when I thought I was a complete failure who didn't deserve to be happy. To find love.

In that moment, looking into his soulful eyes, feeling the hope and warmth of his energy, it hits me. Like a jolt of high-octane yerba mate straight to the heart.

I, Violet Pepperdine, empathic tea witch, romance bookworm, spreadsheet queen, grilled-cheese connoisseur, and rule-follower to the end...

Have fallen ass-over-teakettle in love with the Devil.

My heart sputters into an erratic dance, a wild beat I'm certain Devlin can hear, but all I can do is smile. Tears spill down my cheeks.

"It's all right, love." He cradles my face, swiping my tears with his thumbs. "You don't need to tell me if you don't want to. I don't need a reason to hold you. I'm just grateful for the opportunity."

I stretch up on my toes and kiss him, full on. It's so perfect, so sweet, so electric I almost forgot why I ran out here in the first place.

The news hits me all over again, and I break away and hand over my phone once more, forcing myself to hold still. "It's from the committee. I got the grant, Devlin. There was a mixup or a glitch... whatever... it doesn't matter because I got it! I can pay off my rent and most of the debts and hire some help and... Devlin, I don't have to close! Do you know what this means?"

He brushes the curls from my forehead and grins. "That you're an amazing, incredibly smart, hyper-capable, downright *formidable* witch who's going to take this town by storm again and again and again as she accomplishes everything she's set out—"

I don't let him finish. *Can't* let him finish. Because I've never been so honest-to-goodness happy before. So complete, so hopeful about the future, so full of promise and joy and sunshine and... goddess, all I want to do is celebrate it.

Really, *really* celebrate it.

With the man I love.

"Devlin?" I loop my arms around his neck and flash my most sinful grin—a grin that wasn't even in my arsenal until the Devil crossed my path and taught me all the best tricks. "Less talking, more kissing."

CHAPTER THIRTY-TWO

DEVLIN

The Devil is evil incarnate. That's what they say, isn't it? A fallen angel cast out of Heaven and sent to the fiery pits, forced to rule over the reprobates and degenerates, the worst of men and monsters alike. Sentenced to an immortal eternity of torture, depravity, the kind of unimaginable loneliness that hollows you out inside. No escape, no rest for the wicked.

Tainted.

I'm not supposed to remember what Heaven feels like. I'm not supposed to want that paradise for myself because I don't deserve it and even if I did, I could never earn my way back anyway.

And yet...

Somehow, despite all my missteps and misdeeds, I've found my paradise. In Violet's arms, I'm home. The only home that's ever really mattered.

Her kiss is my Heaven. Her embrace is my eternity. And when I carry her upstairs, lay her on the bed, and sink deep inside her as I have on so many nights before, I find the salvation I've been chasing for centuries. Understanding, not rejection. Love, not cruelty. It cracks me wide open, shatters me, and puts me back together again with nothing more than her gentle touch. A look. A cry of unbridled ecstasy sealed with a kiss that offers me a gift as rare as love itself.

Hope.

"I love you, Violet Pepperdine," I whisper. "Gods be damned, I love you so much it makes me ache to see your tears, even when they're happy ones." I kiss her cheeks, the salt coating my lips, tethering me to her. To this moment. To us.

Whatever the spell that bound us, please don't let it be broken...

She threads her fingers into my hair, gazing up at me with those impossibly blue eyes, a smile curving her lips. "I fell in love with you too, Devlin Pierce," she whispers. "Accidentally and completely. And I'm sorry, but I'm *not* letting you go."

I claim her mouth in another kiss, arching against her body, taking her deeper, harder, making her writhe for me, making her gasp and moan until she shatters around me like the brightest star, and I come inside her, claiming her as mine, marking her, wanting nothing more than to make our fairytale fantasy real.

When I finally draw back and break the kiss, I meet her hooded gaze and she smiles again, and something between us shifts, the air in the room expanding, then contracting, the sugar-sweet scent of her magic saturating every molecule.

Then, all at once, I feel it. A loosening in my chest, like the shedding of a too-tight jacket. The cutting of a rope.

The breaking—I realize with a start—of a witch's binding spell.

"Devlin?" she whispers beneath me, and I watch the same realization sweep over her face, her blue eyes widening.

"The spell," I whisper. Amazed, awestricken. Terrified. "It's... it's broken."

My portal magic—dormant since my fated arrival—rushes back through my veins, a long-dead battery fully recharged. And thanks to the deal I made with Remington, the last soul in the collection plate, the pathway to Hell is free and clear.

Centuries. Millennia. I've been waiting for this moment for longer than I remember living my old life. Ruling upon that throne. Cowering before a father who never saw me as anything but a failure.

I did it. Bested him. Broke the spell trapping me in Wayward Bay, too.

Yet somehow the victory rings hollow. Like winning the

championship tournament only to realize the gleaming golden trophies you once admired from the other side of the glass are no more than plastic trinkets.

"So I'm *not* dreaming about the grant." Violet wriggles out from under me and sits up in bed. "We really did it, Devlin. We unlocked my heart's desire and saved the café, and now the spell is broken."

She smiles, her eyes full of conflicting emotions. Wondering, undoubtedly, what this means for us now that we're no longer magically bound.

"We did it," I confirm, trying to keep my own emotions neutral. My own secrets intact.

The space between her brows creases, and she reaches for her glasses on the nightstand, pushing them onto her face. The haze of our lust is fading, the tide of pleasure and love finally receding.

Her logical mind clicks back into gear.

"I still don't understand what happened," she says, and I know what she's thinking about, know where those thoughts will lead her, know that the tender, all-consuming moment between us is already unraveling.

I'm losing her. Fucking *Hell*, I'm losing her, and all I can do is sit here in pained silence and wait for her to come to the natural conclusion.

"With the grant, I mean. What changed?" Violet pulls the sheet up, tucks it under her arms, covering herself. "They turned me down, then suddenly I'm in the winner's circle? They said it was some kind of glitch, but come on. Every person on that committee knows me. Knows everyone who applied. This was no glitch."

"Does it matter?" I sit up beside her and kiss her shoulder. "You've earned the grant, that's the main thing."

"Have I, though?" She peers at me, her eyes narrowing. Filling with questions. Confusion. A flicker of hurt.

An unfamiliar heat simmers in my chest, spreading outward like living fire.

It takes me a beat to realize what it is, for it's been far too long since I've felt it.

Guilt.

A hot, sticky ache that quickly gives way to anger. Why should I feel guilty for helping her? That's why I was summoned here, after all. She *needed* me. Not her sisters, not her own magic, not the gods or goddesses or even the worst of Hell's demons.

For this task, only the Devil himself would do.

Only *me*.

"Devlin?" she asks, her voice cracking.

Too late, I realize my mistake. The most recent one, anyway.

Violet can feel my emotions—the stronger they are, the easier it is for her to interpret them.

In the case of my flaming-hot guilt, I may as well be wearing a neon sign around my neck.

"Did you... have something to do with this?" Her eyes fill with tears—most assuredly *not* happy ones this time—and her mouth parts in an unspoken accusation.

"I didn't... I mean, it's not what you think. It... it was merely a conversation. A long overdue one, at that."

She doesn't respond. Just stares at me with that wounded look. Sadness, at first. Then shock. Then rage, all of it flickering through her eyes in a heartbeat.

I fold my arms across my chest. "He's not a good person, Mushroom. You must realize that."

"What did you *do*?" she demands.

"Nothing too horrifying, I assure you. Brandt and I merely had a conversation about some of his recent indiscretions, of which there are a great many. Actually, I was hoping we could talk about that later. With Olivy's help, I discovered—"

"Olivy? You dragged my sister into this, too?" She reaches for her phone, presumably to call the spooky witch, but I stay her hand.

"Your sister merely did some digging into Remington's business dealings. She has nothing to do with my meeting with him."

"Business dealings?"

"As it turns out, Remington's been signing off on all manner of shell loans for companies headed by his college cohorts. The realtor is involved as well. Nathan? Oh, yes.

They're as thick as thieves, that bunch. Literal thieves. And they've been stealing from Wayward Bay for years, Violet."

She gapes at me, an incredulous fire in her eyes, not giving me an inch.

"There's a folder!" I exclaim, as if this can somehow redeem me, can somehow bring her back to me. "It's down in the café. All the evidence of his wheeling and dealing, leading this town to ruin. Remington is at the helm of a—"

"Tell me *exactly* what you said to him."

"Just... let me get the files, Mushroom. You—"

"*Don't* call me that."

She's so upset she's shaking, her curls trembling, her eyes wild.

I reach out to take her hand, and she recoils.

The guilt and fear roiling inside me shifts into righteous indignation. No, blackmailing her ex wasn't the most *heroic* deed of the century, but my heart was in the right place. Can't she see that?

"I *showed* him," I say, my voice rising, "what an eternity of being roasted alive in Hell looks like, and I should think you of all people would be pleased to know he accepted my terms without—"

"Pleased. Right." A bitter laugh. A deadly glare. "And what were these so-called terms you set forth, undoubtedly out of the kindness of your bottomless, selfless heart?"

"I..." *Damn* it. I can't admit it. Don't have to, anyway. She already knows the answer. It's written all over her face. "Violet, please let me explain. I thought—"

"You *knew* I wasn't comfortable applying for the grant, Devlin. Not just because I didn't want to deal with Brandt, but because I didn't think I had a chance—not with all the other great businesses and eager entrepreneurs in the Bay."

"But you *did* apply!"

"Yeah, you know why? Because of *you*. *You* thought I had a chance. *You* thought I could win. That's how you made me feel. Like you truly believed in me at a time when I didn't quite believe in myself, and that's all I needed."

"I *did* believe in you. I *still* believe in you. You deserve this grant more than—"

"No, I don't. And you just proved it. If I *did* deserve it, I would've been able to earn it on my own merits."

"But—"

"They turned me down, Devlin. With the same stupid form letter they sent to all the other rejects, mere hours after my presentation. Because Brandt and the other committee members know the one thing you can't seem to get into your stubborn, impulsive, devil-horned head. The one thing I haven't been able to admit to myself, either." She shakes her head, tears welling. "Kettle and Cauldron is not a viable investment, and neither am I."

The tears shimmering in her eyes finally spill, each one carving a tortured path through my heart. Never before have

I wanted so badly to smash something, set it on fire, and piss on the ashes.

That something being Brandt Remington, third of his name, first on the reservations list for a demonic hot-stone torture session, use your imagination.

"They turned you down, Violet, because your ex is a lying, scheming, conniving—"

"You're right. He's all those things. Worse, even—I'm not surprised Olivy found all that dirt on him. But you know what? *He's* not the one who resorted to fear tactics and blackmail when he thought the woman he claimed to love couldn't hack it on her own. That was all you."

"I was trying to right a wrong!"

"The committee made their decision, and I didn't make the cut."

"Precisely the wrong in question. Remington denied your application out of spite and because he'd already awarded the money to out-of-state businesses as part of a complex scheme to—"

"Really? What about the other committee members, then? The school librarian? The retired police commissioner? Are they all in on this conspiracy?"

"One corrupt man can be *very* persuasive, and perhaps—"

"Perhaps nothing. It doesn't matter. There's no way I can take the money now."

"Yes, you can. You got the confirmation. Fill out the tax papers, and the grant is yours."

"You don't get it. I thought you were different. I thought..." She rises from the bed, sheet wrapped around her trembling body.

"Violet?"

Nothing.

"Violet, please. Please look at me, love."

When she finally meets my gaze again, all the fight drains out of her in an instant, shoulders slumping, glasses sliding down her nose, hard-won confidence evaporating.

"Can we just—"

She cuts me off with a shake of her dark head and points to the door. In a soft, broken voice that damn near breaks *me*, she says only, "Leave."

"The bond—"

"Is broken, remember? We unlocked my heart's desire. A pointless endeavor, as it turns out, but we fulfilled the conditions of the spell, so you're free to go."

I cross the room, hunting for the clothing I discarded on the way in. "I'll give you space if that's what you want. We'll talk more later, after you're—"

"No. No more talking." She sighs and climbs back into her bed alone, turning away from me. "You got what you wanted, right? Corrupted your final soul, broke the binding spell, paved the way back to the throne."

"It's not like that, Violet. Please. Let me—"

"You're not tied to me anymore, so that's it. Go."

"But... This isn't... Where do you want me to go?"

She turns toward me with one last glare, cheeks flushed, eyes on fire, the very last look she ever intends to give me. "I want you to go to *Hell,* Devlin Pierce. I never want to see you again."

CHAPTER THIRTY-THREE

VIOLET

Wrapped in a fleece blanket on the purple velvet couch, my café closed for the night, no company but the two goofball cats whose love and loyalty *never* wavers, I finally let myself have a good cry.

About all of it. My crushing debt. The eviction letter from Nathan, his impossible deadline mere days away. The small business grant, lost and won and lost again, because I've got no choice but to refuse it.

But mostly, I cry for Devlin. My dark prince. My unexpected champion.

Summoned, spellbound, and then...

Poof, just like my dreams.

The pity party is pathetic and endless, not even a cake to cry into, my exhaustion so complete I start to wonder if I'll ever be able to get up off this couch again. I'm stuck in the same spot for so long I watch the sky change from sunset to moonrise to sunrise, golden morning light filtering through the nearly bare trees outside, a cardinal tapping on the front window.

The fire has burned down to embers, and I raise a lazy hand and call it back to life, staring into the flames until they're nothing but a blur.

Get up, Violet.

But I can't.

"I don't know where to go from here," I whisper, the admission eating through my chest. My heart.

Losing my shop feels like a failure.

Losing Devlin feels like death.

My heart is broken, my dreams shattered, and the worst part of it is... I still miss him.

Am I enraged that he went behind my back, that he undermined my efforts with dark magic and threats, that he truly *didn't* think I could earn the grant on my own after making me believe I could, that he didn't have the courage or respect to tell me about what he and Olivy found before he went after Brandt? Hell yes.

But... goddess. Devlin literally changed my life. Inspired me to be wild and spontaneous and a little reckless, too. Showed me that I could break out of my hyper-perfectionist prison and do something crazy, like...

Like stand up to my ex and slow dance in front of the entire town at the Haunted Halloween Ball.

Like go before a committee that included said ex and prove to them that *yes*, my tea shop *is* amazing, that it deserves their investment.

Like keep on trucking, all the way to the end of a disastrous presentation, despite the unintentional sabotage of a haunted vibrator.

Like fall in love with the Devil himself, and believe—for a little while—that the Devil could love me right back.

Oh, Devlin...

He was right. I see that. About so many things. Me, getting in my own way. Losing sight of my so-called *why*—the spark behind everything I do. Turning my passion into a job and forgetting that it's actually what I love to do more than anything.

Forgetting that no matter *what* happens to the physical shop, no one can take my magic away. My inspiration. My love and talent for tea blending that started with a kind, beautiful, ass-kicking grandmother who loved me fiercely and taught me how to turn my personal magic into a gift I could share with the world.

A lone butterfly swirls through my stomach, and I smile. I actually smile.

Maybe Devlin and I failed in our mission to save Kettle and Cauldron—Hell, maybe it was doomed from the get-go. Maybe *we* were doomed. I mean, come on. Mixing mojitos and magic? Drunk-summoning the Prince of Darkness with a *spreadsheet*? Not exactly laying the bedrock of a lasting relationship.

But that doesn't mean I need to spend my final days as the proprietress of Kettle and Cauldron sacked out on the couch, crying into my tea leaves over a lost dream and a lost love.

You ruined it for us, chimes in the Downtown Pep Squad, still reeling from her own terrible loss. *We could have had it all, but—*

"You shut up."

You're the reason we can't have nice things. You know that, right?

"And *you're* the reason we can't walk straight, you insatiable little beast. So get it together, girl. We've got shit to do today."

And we *do* have shit to do, I realize now. As long as there's still time, there's still a chance. Right?

I shake my head, clearing the cobwebs from my sleep-deprived, overworked brain. Just because I've suffered a few setbacks doesn't mean it's time to clock out of my own life.

The lone butterfly swirls again, bringing another smile to my lips. A flutter to my heart.

If Devlin taught me anything, it's this:

The show must go on.

Pity party officially over, I rise from the couch like a revenant, a ghoulish monster resurrected for a singular purpose. With cold, stiff limbs, I lumber over to the kitchen and put on the kettle.

I need something strong today.

Not Get It, Girl.

More like... Beat Their Asses, Rip Out Their Hearts, And Leave No Traitors Alive.

I get to work mixing the brew—black puerh tea, grated ginger, two whole cinnamon sticks, dark chocolate shavings, a pat of butter because I fucking deserve it, and a hint of crushed red pepper to *really* send the message home.

Then, steeping the heady mix, I recite a new spell, all my own.

> *From ashes I rise, my purpose now clear*
> *I call on my magic, no longer in fear*
> *My strength is within, but help I may need*
> *To follow my heart, wherever it leads*

The tea swirls and shimmers in the pot, infused with my magic, my intention, the force of my will. The moment it touches my lips, I feel it working, fueling me with a shocking clarity and determination I haven't felt in...

Well, since I first opened Kettle and Cauldron.

With steady hands, I reach beneath the counter and retrieve the folder. The one Devlin left with all the so-called evidence against Brandt. The one I've been ignoring because I was butt-hurt and too freaking stubborn to realize—despite his sneaking around, despite the underhanded way he went about things—that Devlin really *was* trying to help me.

That he's helping me *still*, from wherever he is now.

"Thank you," I whisper, my heart cracking, but still beating. Still surviving, just like it always has.

Then I whip open that folder. And there, right on top of the stack, a new Tarot message awaits.

No, not one of the charging Knights preparing me for the battle ahead. Not one of the Queens reminding me to be fearless and wise. Not even the Devil himself.

But the gentle, inspiring Ace of Pentacles.

And this time, as I gaze at the image on the card—a hand outstretched from the sky bestowing a golden pentacle to a young witch, her face alight with hope and possibility as she reaches out to take it—it's not the voice of my intuition whispering in my mind.

It's Gigi, as clear as if she were standing right beside me, squeezing my shoulders and sending me out into the world to face another day with grace and determination.

Every day is a gift, Violet. Find the joy in this one. Do that every day, one after the other, and your entire life will be filled with beautiful blessings.

She said it to me often. Whenever I was struggling at school, or trying to make sense of my confusing magic, or resenting the parents who abandoned me, or feeling like I was running out of reasons to stick around, even for myself.

Gigi reminded me that there was *always* a reason. Big,

small, it didn't matter. I had only to find it. To acknowledge it. To accept the gifts inherent in every new day.

I close my eyes, and again, I think of Devlin.

For better or worse, everything he did—from the moment I served him his first cup of Welcome to Wayward Bay tea—he did it for me.

All the times he tested my boundaries or pushed me out of my comfort zone, he was teaching me how to truly live. How to break out of my own limiting beliefs and trust myself. How to jump like the Fool of the Tarot right off the cliff, with a smile on my lips and joy in my heart, and trust that whatever awaited me at the bottom would be better than whatever I left behind.

You've got this, Violet. You always have.

It's his voice in my mind now, bolstering me, encouraging me.

I open my eyes and finish the last of my tea. From the bottom of the mug, a little black pitchfork winks up at me, and I laugh. I was so distracted when I first poured the tea, I didn't even realize I was drinking from his mug all along.

The Devil Made Me Brew It, it says. In so many ways, he *did*.

Now, he's going to help me *keep* brewing it. Keep showing up. Keep Kettle and Cauldron alive, just like we set out to do on that first golden-dawned, post-magic morning oh so long ago.

I spread out all the paperwork on the counter, my heart

pounding faster with every new detail revealed. Pages and pages of them—Brandt's shady deals, ties to shell companies, foreign bank accounts, laundered funds. And the names—some I recognize from Remington Capital. Others straight from the headlines—CEOs of all different companies, mostly chains, the kinds of stores always in the news for squeezing out the mom-and-pop shops and treating their employees like absolute garbage. These men are all associates, all members of the same fraternity, all colluding to put Wayward Bay's small business community in the ground.

The businesses they've targeted are listed here, too—every real estate transaction traced back to Nathan Pike. Corto's Curiosities—the shop Mean Beans took over. Second Chance Romance, the old bookstore. And the places still on the chopping block—Kettle and Cauldron. Glaze for Days. Dozens upon dozens of others.

Fueled with a new rage, enhanced by my magical brew, I grab my phone and call Ricci.

"This is going to sound completely out of left field, but… what do you know about Nathan Pike?"

"That fucking guy," she says with a scoff, and that's all the confirmation I need. "He owns my building. Bought out my lease from Fran Solomon a few months ago. At the time, he assured me nothing would change, but I just went to negotiate the renewal, and the jerk is *tripling* the rent. When I tried to push back, he said he's got plenty of other tenants lined up, willing to pay top dollar."

"Seriously?"

"Same thing happened to Mavis over at the dog grooming place. And Paul Aberg's hat shop. Nathan's saying we can either pay up or move out. Technically, it's within his rights to change the terms of a lease before renewal, but... I don't know. Something's fishy about the whole thing."

"Ricci? You have no idea."

The Ace of Pentacles gleams at me from the counter, reminding me that today is a gift. That I'm *blessed* with gifts —lots of them. Not just my magic. Not just my talent for teas. But my voice. A voice I've let other people silence for too long. People like Nathan, who tried to scare me into giving up my business without a fight. People like Brandt, who tried to make me feel like a useless bimbo with a cute little hobby that didn't deserve to succeed.

People like *all* the men on this list, trying to silence the folks of Wayward Bay. Good folks. Witches, vampires, demons, fae, humans. All of us trying to build something special. Something meaningful.

"I was thinking about bringing it to the mayor's attention," Ricci says. "I'm not sure if there's anything illegal going on, but maybe she can do some sniffing around. Seems like she'd want to know about all this, especially since she's spearheading the small business initiatives."

At the mention of Mayor Singh, a plan begins to crystalize in my mind. In my heart.

Going through with it means... *Goddess*. It means standing up in front of my friends and neighbors and admitting that I've failed, again and again and again. It means asking for help. From Ricci and the other business owners getting shafted. From everyone else who cares about the Bay as much as I do. From Olivy, too; she's the one who found all the dirt on Brandt, so I want her at my side when I blow his ass out of the water.

I tremble just to think about it. And part of me—a very loud, very persuasive part—is telling me to run upstairs, queue up a new season of Charmed, and forget all about this taking-a-stand nonsense.

But I can't just sack out on the couch and hope for the best anymore.

I will *not* let Brandt Remington the Third and the other members of Club Douche Bro carve this town into pieces and destroy its very soul.

"Ricci? I've got an idea."

"I'm listening."

"Can you get a hold of Mavis and Paul? And anyone else who's had a run-in with Nathan or anyone at Remington Capital, and meet me at the Town Hall in an hour?"

"Sure thing," Ricci says. "Should we bring anything?"

"Yes. Your ass-kicking boots." I sweep the files back into the folder. "I'm going to expose these bastards for the lying, conniving assholes they are. And I'd love to have a few allies on my side."

"You already know I'm in. And Violet?" Ricci laughs, rich and warm, and something in my chest loosens up, just enough to let a little hope in. "I'm pretty sure this is the start of a beautiful new friendship."

CHAPTER THIRTY-FOUR

DEVLIN

The acrid smoke hangs in a gray haze before me when Finn steps into my throne room, rolling his eyes and sighing as if I've unleashed a plague upon the world of men.

Again.

"Did you seriously just smite Azazel?" he demands.

"*Azazel* touched my belongings without permission. You know how I feel about that."

"Over a coffee mug?" He reaches for the mug clutched in my hands, but I snatch it away before he can mar the glaze with his filthy fingerprints.

"It's a *tea* mug, you daft bastard. And don't get any ideas unless you'd like to join Azazel in Oblivion."

He raises his hands in surrender and backs away, his judgmental green eyes boring right through my bloody skull. Unable to withstand the scrutiny, I gaze out across the polished obsidian expanse of the throne room, waiting for the inevitable lecture.

But for the first time in our long, long friendship, Finn remains silent.

"Was there something you needed," I snap, "or are you just going to stand there and gloat about my millennium's worth of poor life choices?"

"Not sure you need me for that, Dev. Doing just fine on your own."

Still not taking the hint, he helps himself to a drink from my bar and saunters over to the balcony, taking in the view of the Fire Rivers of Eshtock.

He doesn't say anything else, and soon the only sounds are an occasional fiery explosion from the rivers and the constant din of tortured souls.

One drink, he finishes. Back to the bar for another. Finishes that one too. Pours a third and returns to watch the rivers.

Then, finally, when I swear we've been ignoring each other for so long the rivers have changed course four times over, he says, "Are we talking about this, or—"

"There's nothing to talk about." I rise from the throne, fix myself a drink in my mushroom tea mug. Head to the balcony. Contemplate jumping, for all the good it would do me.

"Your girlfriend is—"

"What in the seventeenth bowel of Hell makes you think she's my girlfriend?" I snap.

"Oh, I don't know. The pining, for one. The brooding. Not to mention all the shagging before that and the—"

I glare at him, horns out, full-terror mode engaged.

Finn laughs. "I'm just saying you seemed to really like this one, mate."

"Like her? *Like* her?" I scoff. "Violet Pepperdine is the least likable woman I've ever met. She's stubborn as a two-headed demonic mule, refuses to listen to reason, has no idea how self-righteous she is... Bloody nuisance, if you really want to know."

"Stubborn and self-righteous, right." Finn sighs, sarcasm dripping from his tone. "I can only imagine how difficult that must be for you."

"Fuck *off*," I say, but the fight in me fizzles right out. "She's just... she's gone, Finn. And it's my own fault."

There's no ire in my words. Just the deep resignation that comes with knowing you've lost something precious. A thing you never even knew you wanted, never believed you deserved, and when you finally got it, you cocked it all up anyway.

It's been an eternity since she sent me away. An eternity since I returned to Hell, not even bothering with a stopover in L.A.

And I've never before felt so utterly lost.

My family was not here to greet me. My father was not

waiting with open arms, ready to admit he was wrong. There was no red-carpet welcome, no tearful reunion. No redemption for the Prince of Darkness and his band of loyal demons.

Only a cold and empty throne, crumbling from centuries of disuse, and a destiny I'm no longer sure I understand, if I ever understood it at all.

A single hour on the mortal plane feels like a lifetime in Hell's unending sameness, and no matter how many nights pass, no matter how much I try to distract myself with the underworld reunion tour, with the simple pleasures of torture and ruin, nothing has dimmed the memory of her touch from my skin. The taste of her kiss from my lips. The pain of her parting words from my ears.

Gods be damned, how did it even *come* to this? From the very instant she summoned me to Wayward Bay with her ridiculous drunken spreadsheet magic, all I wanted to do was find a way to escape.

Until one day, I didn't.

Now, it hurts to envision a future—*any* future—without her. Without that snorting laugh serving as the soundtrack of my morning and her soft sighs as the soundtrack of my nights. Without her bottomless blue eyes shining from behind those enormous glasses. Without the tea and the grilled cheese and our beloved Ambrosia Divine. Without Grumpy and Sunshine, the feline friends I never knew I needed.

It's not just Violet, either. Thinking of Wayward Bay fills me with a fierce longing too. The Aunts. The sisters. The Mayor. The pottery-painting woman. The fae and demon couple who own the liquor store. The kids in their silly goblin masks. The apple-scented air and the autumn leaves and the stately trees and the silver-blue bay glittering in the distance.

It was my home, for a time. A place where I felt welcomed. A place where even the Devil was allowed to belong.

A new ache blooms in my chest for all the things that could have been. All the things I held in my hands, in my heart, and then swiftly lost.

Now, as I look out across the vast rivers of molten fire that cut through the black landscape in gleaming ribbons of orange and gold, all I can think about is how much—for the first time in my immortal existence—this place feels like my *own* version of Hell. An inescapable torture of my own making.

"I'd forgotten how beautiful they are," Finn says beside me, and it takes me a moment to realize he's talking about the rivers. "This place... it's deceptive, isn't it? Endless torment for the ones who sell their souls. A supposed paradise for those who broker the deal." He sips his drink, his tone uncharacteristically melancholy. "Ever since your father banished us, all you wanted was to come back home. It's what you—what *we* worked for all these long centuries.

Days, years, all of it blurring together in a mind-numbing replay of sex and drugs and parties and... *ugh*, the people. The desperate, depraved people."

"That's all over now, Finn. We did it. Achieved our impossible ends. Corrupted a million souls, earned our way back, and here we are."

"And yet?"

"Yet I can't for the life of me remember why it ever even mattered."

Finn sighs. We've been friends for so long, he can read my thoughts almost as well as Violet could read my emotions. "If you leave now—for a mortal witch, besides—your father will *never* let you return. You'll be forfeiting your position, your power, your throne. Your immortality. All of it, gone. No more impossible tasks, no more deals. Just gone. You know that, right?"

"For fuck's sake, Finn. What good is an immortal life when the woman you love is bound to the mortal realm? When all you've got in front of you is an eternity of misery and loneliness and a broken heart that will never heal because the only one who can mend it has cast you away?"

His eyes widen, and I mirror the shocked gaze. It's the first I've ever admitted it to anyone but the witch herself.

"Yes, I'm bloody well in love with her. Is that what you needed to hear? The kind of love that makes you do crazy things. Take big risks and fail even bigger. Now *she's* in the Bay and *I'm* here and I've got everything I'm supposed to want—everything I sacrificed and killed and deceived and danced and fucked for—and I've never felt so bloody hollow. So utterly dead inside. So you know what? I'm done. Done with this existence. With this place that feels like a stranger's home. I want something better, Finn, and I'm daring to say it out loud. I want a quiet life. A good life. One where I can make the same woman laugh every single night, over and over and over until we collapse in our bed, tired and happy. I want to grow old with her, as ridiculous as that sounds, watching her brew her magic teas and joke with her sisters and take care of her aunts and maybe have a few adventures together along the way."

"It sounds like a nice dream," he says, no mocking in his tone. "But what about your family?"

"Family." I scoff. "The so-called family who continues to reject me even after I've spent centuries trying to make amends for a crime I didn't even commit? The so-called family who will continue to punish me for eternity simply because they all got together one day and decided I was the prized fuck-up of the bunch? And remind me again what terrible crime I committed? Loving the wrong woman? I was practically a child."

Finn puts a hand on my shoulder, his eyes full of a sincerity and understanding I've never seen before. Or maybe I just wasn't paying attention.

"Love isn't a crime, mate," he says softly. "Even when you fall for the wrong person." He tips back the last of his drink.

Stares back out at the rivers. Sighs. Turns back to me. And then, at long last, the old smile slides back into place. "But now that you've fallen for the *right* person, I assume you've got a plan to get her back? Preferably one that *doesn't* require me listening to any more of your weepy blathering? Devil's balls, mate. You really did step right out of a Hallmark movie on this one. I tried to warn you, didn't I? As a matter of fact, do you still *have* your balls? Or did you let your witch boil them up in a tea for the good neighbors?"

I cast him a deadly glare. "Don't make me smite you. I'm still in a mood and you're pressing your luck, demon."

"I'm touched, Devlin. I can feel the love. Should I fetch us some tissues? I sense a good cry coming on. But not a sappy one. A manly cry. Very becoming. Now, about that plan? What do I need to pack, and who do I need to kill along the way?"

CHAPTER THIRTY-FIVE

VIOLET

I haven't been back to the scene of Mr. Wiggles' murder since my botched presentation, and the sight of the Town Hall fills me with a dread that threatens to send me bolting back to the safety of Kettle and Cauldron. To the familiar comfort of a nice, stress-relieving cinnamon tea, Stevie Nicks on the playlist, a crackling fire, the soft purr of the cats as they stretch out on the hearth and...

Poof.

The moment the vision coalesces in my mind, it's gone. Because that's exactly what will happen if I don't see this through. If I don't find a way to set one foot in front of the other, march into that meeting, and demand justice. Not just for me, but for Ricci and Paul and Mavis. For the shop owners those monsters have already run out of town. For my sisters and aunts who run their own small businesses too—

businesses that Brandt and his cronies are already plotting to crush under their filthy boots.

"Violet?" Ricci asks, her hand warm on my elbow. "You ready?"

I take a deep breath. Ground and center. Send out a pulse of magic—a silent spell for clarity and guidance and success.

And in return, the Devil card flashes through my mind. A reminder of what we had. Of who I am when I'm with him. Stronger, somehow. Less inhibited. Less afraid.

Devlin and I are over. I know that. But I feel him with me now anyway, whispering in my ear. Cheering me on. Reminding me that I *can* do this, that I have a voice, that people will listen if I'm willing to take the risk.

He was my friend before I fell for him, and it's that friendship I think about now, drawing on his strength, borrowing a bit of his charisma. His Big Devil Energy.

I smile at Ricci. Nod. Take one more deep breath.

Together, we march through the mayor's office—ignoring the half-hearted protests of her vampire assistant, Margo—and straight into the mayor's private conference room. The place where she holds the budget meetings.

All heads turn to us. The Mayor herself. Brandt. A half-dozen other members of the town council—some of them owners of businesses on Brandt's list, completely unaware that their fellow council member is working to sabotage them.

"Violet?" Mayor Singh rises from her seat. "Ricci? I'm sorry, I didn't realize we had an appointment. I'm in meetings for the next hour, but—"

"We don't." I heft up a stack of folders filled with the copies I made on the way over. "But you're going to want to hear this."

"Miss Pepperdine," the mollusk blubbers, "if this is about the grant, we've already straightened out the clerical error with your—"

"Oh, this *is* about the grant, *Brandt*. And so much more."

The fear in his eyes is real. The sense of power that comes with knowing I'm the one who put it there? Absolutely priceless. No wonder Devlin is so good at this sort of thing.

Ricci and I quickly distribute the folders.

"Take your time," Ricci says as the committee members flip through the pages, brows knit, their initial confusion quickly turning to anger. "There's lots to digest."

"I brought donuts," comes the call of a familiar voice, and I turn to see my sister Emmie heading through the door, a whole gaggle of witches filing in behind her. Olivy, who's got her laptop and another stack of folders. Darla and Fiona. My aunts, Josyln and Althea and Lorelei.

"We're the three sisters of Three Sisters B&B," Lorelei announces. "And we're here to roast Brandt Remington's nuts."

Mavis and Paul—the folks Ricci called—join us next, a

trail of others streaming in behind them. More friends and neighbors and fellow business owners. Members from other committees. A tidal wave of support that floods the meeting until it's standing room only, all of us elbow-to-elbow.

"Was this your doing?" I whisper to Olivy.

She shrugs. "You said you needed help taking him down, so I called in the Calvary."

"I'm going to kill you later. You know that, right?"

"Oh, I'm looking forward to it. After you thank me, of course." Then, with a squeeze of my hand and a genuine smile, "You've got this, Vi. And we've got you."

I nod. Clear the knot of emotion from my throat. And then...

"My name is Violet Pepperdine," I begin. "I own Kettle and Cauldron. For a few more days, anyway."

Tears fill my eyes. With a voice that trembles but doesn't break, I tell them my story, admitting—for the first time in history—that I screwed up. That I'm in trouble. That I need help.

I tell them about the debts. Nathan's eviction notice. The grant. Everything that led me to this, standing up in front of what feels like half the town and laying myself bare.

Everyone on the committee is watching me, their energy an overwhelming soup of confusion, compassion, anger, empathy, sadness, guilt.

"Miss Pepperdine," Brandt tries again, but I hold up a hand, silencing him.

Not with magic. Not with a cup of hot tea to the ballsack, the idea of which delights me to no end.

But with my determination. My will. My refusal to back down just because someone else thinks I don't deserve to be here. That I don't have a right to take up space. To be loud.

"Remington Capital Group," I continue, locking him in my gaze, "under the leadership of Brandt Remington the Third, along with realtor Nathan Pike and several of their college fraternity associates, have been conspiring with large out-of-state corporations to keep small businesses in Wayward Bay struggling through the use of several underhanded tactics, including charging significantly higher than average interest rates on business loans and credit cards, turning down new loans without cause, and sneaking in junk fees."

"As businesses falter under the weight of these debts and fees," Ricci says, "Nathan Pike comes in with high-pressure sales tactics, using fear and manipulation to convince struggling property owners to sell while raising rents and other costs on the properties he and his associates own."

"We... we've done nothing of the sort," Brandt stammers, all eyes on him. "Remington Capital is a small business as well, j-just like yours. We need to v-v-vet our clients for the best fit."

"It's all there in black and white," I say. "Read the evidence—all of it can be verified. You're charging double the rates for local clients, then offering low-interest loans to several companies registered out of state."

"Funny thing about those companies," Olivy says, passing around another set of copies. "They're all owned by one Westfield Holdings, a company registered to Nathan Pike's aunt, Beverly McKee."

"Beverly is an investor," Brandt insists, his face turning redder by the minute. "One of our best clients."

"Really?" Olivy scratches her head. "Because I reached out to Beverly this morning, and she had no idea she owned these so-called businesses. Why? Because her nephew has been committing fraud in her name for years, all at the behest of Remington Capital. Not only that, but he and his so-called associates, including the CEO of Mean Beans and the owners of the other businesses who've recently relocated here, have a web of connections that spans the entire country—New York, Seattle, Boston, Miami, San Francisco. They've been picking off the surrounding small towns the same way they're trying to do here—driving out small businesses, selling off the properties, bringing in the corporations to rebuild on the ashes."

"And reaping the kickbacks," I add. "Including half the grant money. Grants they awarded to out-of-state companies posing as local businesses, taking a healthy cut to line their own pockets."

"You're just a vengeful woman," Brandt hisses. "Full of spite because you couldn't make your own business work.

You failed, Violet. You failed, and now you're trying to retaliate, refusing to take responsibility for your own ineptitude, and—"

"You know what? I *did* fail," I say plainly, shocked to realize the dreaded F-word doesn't sting as much as I once feared. Doesn't send me cowering into the corner, full of shame and self-loathing. "I tried to run a successful business doing what I love. What I'm good at. And I couldn't turn a profit. But you know what? I learned a hell of a lot along the way. And I *will* figure out how to make it work. Maybe not this week, maybe not this year, but I'm not giving up again. No matter *who* tells me I should. Because when you're blessed enough to find something you love in this world, something that makes your heart sing, something that has you jumping out of bed looking forward to every new day— even when it's rough, even when you falter, even when you fail—you find a way to get back up and try again. Whatever it takes, you find a way."

Emotion is thick in my throat, and I no longer know whether I'm talking about Kettle and Cauldron, or my magic, or Devlin. All of it is nearly inseparable for me now— my loves, my passions. My whys.

"You're not seriously listening to this woman," Brandt says, casting a desperate gaze at his fellow committee members. "She's not well. She... she got herself into debt with that worthless tea business, and now she's—"

"Now she's presenting the evidence," Mayor Singh says,

putting a warm, supportive hand on my shoulder, "to lock you up for a very, *very* long time."

Goose thoroughly cooked, Brandt leaps from his chair and attempts to storm out, but there are too many bodies in here blocking off his escape routes.

"Sit down, Mr. Remington," Mayor Singh says. "We are *far* from done here." Then, pressing a button on the conference phone, "Margo? Get me the police."

~

"We told you," Emmie says when we're finally dismissed. "If anyone can handle a little competition, it's Violet *Fucking* Pepperdine."

I laugh. "You also said I was a witchy, formidable, tea-slinging badass."

"And you proved it in spades today."

"The donuts played a big part."

"Hey. Always happy to help my sister kick some evil bootie." Emmie leans in for a kiss. "I need to get back to the bakery, but I'll see you guys later? Witch-N-Bitch happy hour?"

"No booze for Violet, though," Olivy says. "From now on, she's all about the tea. Maybe a little seltzer, if she's feeling wild."

"Agreed." Grinning, I hike my bag over my shoulder, following Olivy out through the rotunda. Gone are the

Halloween decorations from the ball, replaced now with the first signs of whatever Thanksgiving shenanigans Mayor Singh's cooking up. Plastic turkeys, wicker cornucopia, more haystacks.

Hard to believe it was only a couple weeks ago that I danced with the Devil on this very floor.

That I kissed him.

That I fell in love with him.

"You know, Vi." Olivy slings an arm over my shoulder. "After that little display, I'm pretty sure you're on track to unlock your heart's true desire after all, no assistance needed."

I laugh, but it fades fast. "We already unlocked it, Ols. I turned down the grant, but we still got it. It counted. Long enough to unlock the spell, anyway."

"Thanks to Devlin's unscrupulous means."

"Don't remind me." I sigh. "The point is—oh, shit. Wait."

Something dawns on me, kicking me right in the heart.

Oh, goddess...

Saving the café was everything I ever wanted, but...

Is it possible it *wasn't* my heart's truest desire?

I stop at the exit and turn to face her, panic rising.

"Olivy. You told me there could be no shortcuts with my spell. That Devlin had to help me without using his Devil mojo."

"Right, because that would've been a cheat, and the magic forbade it."

"But..." I squeeze my eyes shut, desperately trying to remember that day. The timeline. "The spell was broken as soon as I got the news about the grant."

"Like you said, it counted. You got the money to save the shop. Heart's desire unlocked, spell broken, off into the sunset you ride."

"But... no. That can't be right. The only reason I got the grant was that Devlin used his influence on Brandt, so that automatically negates it, doesn't it?"

"It... oh. Shit, Violet. You're right." She ponders it a bit more, then shrugs. "I'm not sure what loophole he found, but obviously it worked out. The spell was broken when you found out about getting that money."

"But that makes no sense, either. If it was just about the money, why didn't the spell break the moment Brandt sent the second email? Or when Devlin convinced him to give me the grant in the first place, which happened the night before? The money was a done deal at that point."

"Violet, I see your number-crunching wheels turning, but... I don't know. Maybe I misunderstood something about the spell. It was complex magic."

"No, you were right about the spell. It couldn't be broken without a genuine, non-manipulative unlocking of my heart's desire. That much, I could feel."

"So what are you saying,? That Devlin *didn't* use his influence to save the café?"

"No. I'm saying my heart's desire—my truest heart's desire—wasn't to save the café. It... it was love."

"*What?*"

"I remember it now. I'd just gotten the email saying I won, and I ran to Devlin to share the good news. We ended up... celebrating. Horizontally celebrating. And I realized I was in love with him. I confessed it. *That's* what broke the spell."

I fell in love with you too, Devlin Pierce. Accidentally and completely...

Tears fill my eyes, my heart pounding. "I fell in love with the Devil, Olivy. And unlocked my heart's true desire."

Olivy squeezes my hand, her eyes shining—*very* out of character for my typically stoic sister. "This is a good thing, isn't it? I mean, I still want to flay him alive for hurting you, and may do just that, but... you love him. He loves you. There's gotta be a way to figure this out."

"But... but what does it say about Kettle and Cauldron—my life's dream—if Devlin was my true heart's desire?"

Olivy smiles, her energy so full of love and happiness it has me tearing up again. "It says that you're a witch and a woman who deserves to find true love, and *also* has big, important, amazing dreams. These things are not mutually exclusive, Violet, and I'm sick of society trying to tell us that they are. You don't have to choose between them. You just have to choose what you want, and ruthlessly go after it." She tugs on one of my curls and laughs. "A wise witch once said that even when you falter, even when you fail—you find a way to get back up and try again. Whatever it takes, you find a way."

"That *is* pretty wise." I nudge her in the ribs. "Maybe I should write that down."

Olivy's grin stretches wide, that all-knowing spark shining in her eyes. "I *did* call this, remember."

"No, you said Devlin and I would—and I quote—*bone*. You never said anything about falling in love, because if you *had*, I would've saved everyone the trouble and kicked him out right then and there."

"You are so full of cow shit, I'm surprised you're not mooing."

"I am *not*. I'm done with love. All it ever does is get people in trouble. They say magic has consequences? No it doesn't. Love has consequences. From now on, I'll be smartly avoiding them. Not worth it, I'm telling you."

"No?"

"No freaking way. See this face?" I point at myself with both thumbs. "This is my no way, no how, no love face."

"Well, I'm so glad we had this little chat, Violet, because *you've* got a visitor. And to think... This time, you didn't even have to get drunk and screw up your spreadsheet to summon him!"

I follow the direction of her gaze to the courtyard, where I see—sitting on the same bench where he patiently waited for me after my post-kiss Halloween freakout, dressed in a charcoal gray suit and crisp white button-down that has every passerby swiveling for a better look—the man with the power to steal my breath, my heart, and the entire downtown pep squad with a single raised eyebrow.

The Devil himself.

CHAPTER THIRTY-SIX

DEVLIN

Violet enters the courtyard like a vision in dark jeans and a pink blazer, her "Make Like a Tea and Leaf" shirt peeking out from beneath the lapels.

I miss those birds. The gnomes. The mushrooms.

I miss *her*.

When she reaches me, my heart stutters.

I haven't stopped thinking of her since we parted ways. Haven't stopped dreaming of her, haven't stopped revisiting my memories of her as I walked the dark and lonely corridors of Hell, night after endless night.

So how is it possible that I forgot just how unabashedly beautiful she is?

"There you are," I say softly.

"Here I am," she replies.

And then we just stand about for another wasted eternity, staring at the ground between our feet, two clumsy teenagers both at a loss for words.

But this is my wrong to right. My turn to cross that invisible line and say all the things I was too bloody scared to say before. Too bloody stupid.

"I was hoping for a meeting with Mayor Singh," I begin. "I decided I needed to share the evidence with her about Brandt. But when I arrived, her assistant told me I'd have to take a number on account of you and several other irate business owners storming the meeting."

She nods. Takes a step closer. Finally meets my eyes again, and my heartbeat kicks back into gear, thank the fucking demons for small favors.

"You were right about his shady dealings," she says. "They went even deeper than we realized. Not just in Wayward Bay, but all over the country. That guy we saw at Three Sisters that day? Another of their college friends—CEO of that crappy burrito chain that keeps getting shut down everywhere for health code violations. They were trying to drive Ricci out of business, hoping to take over her building."

She tells me about the additional evidence Olivy uncovered. The other men implicated in the scheme. The support and testimony of dozens of other neighbors and business owners.

"The good news is, now they'll all be wheeling and dealing in prison," she says. "The police have already detained Brandt and Nathan. Mayor Singh is waiting to hear back from the FBI. I'll probably have to give an official statement."

"And what of the grants? Are they discontinuing the program?"

"Nope." She smiles. "The town wants to move forward with it. They're going to start from scratch, though—new sponsors, new committee. They want us all to re-apply."

"That's great, Violet. I really hope you will. You deserve a fair shot."

"Oh, I'm definitely applying. Ricci too. We're in this together, now." She laughs, but a sigh quickly chases it away, emotion glazing her eyes. In a whisper that nearly breaks me, she says, "I'm sorry. I just... I don't know how to do this, Devlin."

"Do what?"

"I don't know what to say to you. You were right about Brandt, and I'm grateful for the evidence. And while I know I could've handled things better, it still doesn't change the fact that what you did... It sucked. Totally and completely sucked. I can't... I just... *Damn* it."

She stalks out of the courtyard, and I've got no choice but to follow.

I let her walk away once—let her slip right through my hands like water. I'm not about to live through that a second time.

"I never meant to hurt you, Violet," I say, jogging to catch up. "First and foremost, please know that. I truly believed I was helping you."

"And what about helping yourself?" She turns around to face me, tears staining her cheeks, each one breaking my heart. "Or are you seriously going to tell me you didn't force Brandt to sign away his soul?"

"I did force him, yes. Though his fate was sealed long ago. Signing it over was just a technicality at that point, as most of them are."

She glances up at the sky and shakes her head. Says nothing.

"Violet, you have a right to be upset with me, but please don't tell me you're losing sleep over that man's fate."

"Is that what you think I'm losing sleep over? Seriously?" She looks at me again and laughs, bitter and cold. "No, Devlin. You don't get off that easy. I'm upset because you knew how important it was that I earn the grant fair and square. No magic, no supernatural complications—just on my own merits. Yet you went behind my back anyway with your... your twisty horns and glowy eyes and that... that *Devil* mojo and—"

"I beg your pardon," I say, defenses rising. "It's not *mojo*. It's—"

"It's *wrong*, that's what it is. I don't care what name you give it, it's wrong. You manipulated and blackmailed him into giving me the grant after he'd already turned me down.

And I just don't know how to get past that." She turns away again, stomping off toward the café.

Once more, I'm right on her heels, shadowing her every step. "Yes, I *did* manipulate and blackmail him. Terrified him to the bloody core—you should've seen him. I wielded my dark influence, my power, everything at my disposal, all to make him tremble and squirm and bend to my will. Guilty as fucking charged." I reach for her hand and stop her just outside the café door, forcing her to turn and meet my eyes, knowing damn well this might be the very last of it—the last time she ever looks at me from behind those big glasses, the last time I ever get the chance to speak all the words from my heart. "But even knowing the outcome, Violet, I wouldn't change what I did. Because while I'm sorry for hurting you—more than you'll ever realize—I'm *not* sorry for trying to save Kettle and Cauldron by any means necessary."

"By threatening my ex with eternal Hell? Why?" She unlocks the door and storms inside, dropping her bag on the counter and retreating behind it. "Why would you think that was even *remotely* okay? Why would you *do* something like that?"

Why. That's the question, isn't it? And as I follow her behind the counter, desperate to touch her, to hold her in my arms, to make all of this right, a thousand answers spring to mind.

Because I don't like Remington's stupid name and his smarmy look and the cheap suits.

Because his mere *existence* offends me.

Because the idea that he once placed his filthy hands on my soft, sweet, perfect little mushroom incites within me a murderous rage the likes of which I haven't felt since the betrayal that banished me from Hell in the first place.

Because I'm the fucking *Devil*, darling, and I do whatever I damn well please.

But in the end, all the bluster and fury fade away. The mask of lies I once so easily donned is gone—she shattered it the night I took her into my lap and confessed my love, leaving the old Devlin Pierce behind.

So now, I take what remains and offer it to her without expectation, without demand, hoping only that she'll accept it for what it is.

The truth.

"Because for the first time since the dawn of Hell, you and your family allowed me to be part of something infinitely smaller yet unfathomably bigger than I'd ever experienced before or since. Because Wayward Bay needs the café, just like it needs Glaze for Days and Emmilou's Sweet-N-Savories and Darla's magical stories and all the other gifts its residents have to offer." I take a step closer, gazing down into her face. Risk a touch, tugging on one of her curls—my favorite one—and looping it around my finger. "Because on one rainy autumn night, a shy, awkward, all-powerful, curly-haired witch drunk-summoned the Devil with naught but a candle, a Tarot card, and a spreadsheet function, and I stupidly, madly, irrevocably fell in love with her. Which means there's nothing I wouldn't do to support her, nothing I wouldn't do to *destroy* the man who stands in the way of her dreams. And you can be mad at me all you want—you have every right to be. I'm sorry I went behind your back and went against your wishes. I'm sorry I caused you to doubt my unwavering faith in you, even for a moment. But hear me, Violet Pepperdine. I would do it again without a thought. I would fight dirty, I would manipulate, I would terrify, I would cross lines so forbidden they don't even exist yet. I would do *all* of that, again and again and again, just to keep you from feeling an *ounce* of pain or rejection. Just to keep that smile on your lovely face, because the world is a cold, dark place without it. So, fine. Maybe that makes me evil, just like the stories would have you believe. Maybe it just makes me a regular old arsehole desperate to do the right thing, cursed to cock it up time and again. But it also makes me a man in love with someone he'd do *anything* to protect. To cherish. To make her understand the depth of his feelings because in all his immortal years, no one else has ever held a candle."

Tears spill down her cheeks, the silence simmering between us, her eyes as blue and fiery as the sapphire lake in the Desolation Mountains, and in them I see the interplay of every emotion she's feeling—sadness and anger, frustration and regret, fear.

And then—right there at the end, just when I think I can't bear it another moment—love.

"How do you know it's real?" she finally asks, her voice breaking. "You say you feel all these things—all these intense, amazing things—but the magic bound us first, Devlin. What if it's all just... just a remnant from the spell?"

"Ah, Violet." I tuck the curl behind her ear, searching her face. Her heart. "Have you ever watched a storm approach?"

She nods. "There's a spot at the Aunts' place. Top floor balcony. You can see all the way to the Bay from there."

"It's only at a distance that we can appreciate the beauty of something so powerful, so chaotic. But up close?" I shake my head, fighting back a shiver. "I feel as if I've spent my whole life with that storm right on my heels, desperate to outrun it. I was terrified if I slowed down for even a *moment*, the chaos of my own pain would finally catch me and devour me whole. But then I met you. And for the first time, I wanted to stop running. I didn't care that the storm was still on my heels—in some ways, it always will be. But it no longer matters. You're my calm, right in the chaos of everything else. From the very start, you saw me. The truth behind all the lies. The man behind every mask I've worn. Behind every delusion I've so desperately tried to cling to. You saw all of it and made me feel like I could finally stop pretending. Stop running. Stop everything and just... just *be*." I cradle her face in my hands, catching every tear with my thumbs, whispering against her lips. "The magic bound us first and foremost. That is true. But everything that came after? That was you and me. You ask how I know what I feel for you is real? Because for the first time in this impossibly long existence, *I* want to be real. Real *with* someone. *For* someone. *Because* of someone. And it's you, Violet. It's always been you. I'm in *love* with you, and that's all there is to it."

She's crying again, her eyes so big and blue, her tears endless rivers. "I... I don't know what to say."

"Say you want me to stay here in Wayward Bay. Tell me I'm yours. Tell me you feel for me even a *fraction* of what I feel for you, and I'll spend the rest of my life making things right between us. Earning back your trust. Proving to you that I really *do* believe in you, that I've got your back, that I'll *never* give you a reason to doubt me again."

She closes her eyes, her sigh as heavy as the end of the world.

"What's the point?" she whispers. "You can't stay here anyway, Devlin. You have to return to Hell, or you'll be turned into a mortal man, cursed to die just like the rest of us."

"Cursed to *live*."

"If you call a few more decades living."

"The expiration date is precisely what makes it so worthwhile. It makes every day a gift." I laugh and roll my eyes. "Fine, put that on a greeting card if you must. But it's true."

Violet smiles through her tears. "Gigi used to say that. 'Every day is a gift, Violet. Find the joy in this one. Do that every day, one after the other, and your entire life will be filled with beautiful blessings.'"

"Smart woman."

"Very." Violet wipes away her tears and exhales slowly, the gears of her logical mind already churning. "I know you're saying this is what you want, but giving up your immortality isn't something you can just wake up and decide to do. I can't ask you to make a sacrifice like that for me, Devlin. It's—"

"Already done," I say softly. "After innumerable centuries trying to get back to Hell, I've gone and cast myself right out again."

"But... what?"

"I told you—once I went back to Hell, I wouldn't be able to leave. Not without relinquishing my throne and my immortality." I shrug. "So I did."

Violet gasps.

"It was the only way I could leave on my terms," I say. "And I *had* to leave. I had something very important to attend to today."

"You... you gave up all of that just to tell Mayor Singh about Brandt's dirty deals?"

"No. I gave up all of that just for a *chance* to see your sapphire eyes again. To hear your laughter. To wrap my favorite curl around my finger and whisper against your lips and make you blush that lovely shade of crimson. You've already given me that, Violet. You already made the trip worthwhile." I smile, my heart breaking all over again. "Cast me away now, and know this: it was still worth the trip. Still worth the sacrifice."

She turns away from me to collect herself. Giving her space, I step out from behind the counter and take a seat, watching the rise and fall of her shoulders as she steadies her breath, my heart pounding like an ancient drum.

Violet doesn't speak after that. Just reaches up to her shelves, pulling down canisters and bottles and jars, chopping and grating and stirring, losing herself in her work, her home, her happy and safe place. For a moment she disappears into the kitchen and puts on the kettle, then returns, making a few more selections from the shelves, stirring a bit more, still not meeting my eyes.

The minutes tick by. The kettle whistles. Violet heads to the kitchen, returns with the water. Steeps the tea. Pours a cup.

After what feels like another ageless endless bloody fucking *eternity*, she finally turns to face me again. Steam clouds her glasses, veiling her eyes. She slides a cup and saucer across the counter.

"Drink," she says plainly.

"What did I tell you about my personal policy?"

"Don't worry. It's not a banishing tea."

"Hmm." I give it a whiff. Cardamom and cinnamon. Hint of rose. I've seen her make enough brews now to know what that means. "Are you putting a love spell on me, Mushroom?"

I wait for her answer. And wait. And fucking die a thousand times over.

And then, miracle of bloody miracles, she smiles.

"It was always you for me too, Devlin," she says softly. "My true heart's desire. Not the shop, not the money. But love. You."

"Are you saying...?"

"I'm saying that I'm in love with you. I'm saying I want you to jump off the Fool's cliff with me and trust that it's right." She tucks her curls behind her ears, her smile bright, her tears gone. "I'm saying... I want you to stay, Devlin."

"Oh. Well, in that case, no offense to the tea brewer, as I'm sure this is a delicious blend that would absolutely cure at least seven of the many, *many* things that ail me, but Violet?" I set down the cup and lean forward. "I would *much* rather spend the afternoon with a mouth full of *you*."

One more smile, that's all I need. That's all I *get*, because I don't wait for a response beyond that. Just haul her across the counter and claim her in a kiss that obliterates every last fear, every last doubt, every last regret.

I'm working my way down her neck, enjoying the soundtrack of her soft, sensual moans, when she suddenly stops, unleashing a gasp that I somehow know isn't meant for me.

"Why are we stopping?" I demand. "I was just getting to the good part."

"Sorry, but it looks like your unquenchable carnal desires will have to wait." She grants me one last all-too-brief kiss before hopping back behind the counter, eyes glazed with happy tears, a shocked but ecstatic grin gracing her lovely mouth.

Then, tossing me an apron, she nods at the crowd gathering outside the windows: the mayor, the pottery painting woman, all four of her sisters, the Aunts, Maleek and Jovahn from the liquor store, her landlady, the crowd of adoring women from my very first week here—the whole damn town of Pumpkinville, it seems.

"Violet," I whisper. "Do you see them?"

She laughs, and snorts, and laughs again. Then tightens her apron strings and says simply, "Devlin? It's time to put that kettle back on. We've got customers."

CHAPTER THIRTY-SEVEN

VIOLET

One Month Later

The snow has just started falling in earnest when the cats and I put the finishing touches on Kettle and Cauldron's Winter Solstice window display.

Not to brag, but it's pretty epic. White and silver lights, cottony snow drifts, hand-painted evergreens in a ceramic village—a miniature version of our very own Main Street, the café front and center. A twinkling star hangs above it all, reminding me of the Star from the Tarot.

Reminding me how far we've come.

With the impending blizzard, we had to close the shop a few hours early today, boxing up treats and putting teas in to-go cups, hustling everyone out the door in their fluffy coats and hats and mittens so they could get home before the roads turn bad. The new police commissioner has been making the rounds on the TV and radio all morning, warning us to prepare for a record-breaking snowfall.

I'm kind of excited for it. Kettle and Cauldron is in full-on festive holiday mode, twinkle lights twinkling, my favorite Celtic Christmas music floating through the speakers, holly and ivy adorning the mantle over a roaring fire, a simmer pot full of juniper berries and pine boughs steaming on the stove.

'Tis the season for gathering around the fire with a hot beverage, and we've been filled to capacity every day.

What a difference a month makes, huh?

Since our historic takedown of Brandt Remington and company, the town of Wayward Bay has blossomed in ways we never could have imagined—not in our wildest dreams. Ricci and I won the next round of grant funding, along with three other local businesses—Small Notions tailor, Flowers on Main, and Dark Escapes, a new chocolatier that opened up around the corner from us. But after the awards ceremony, the five of us owners put our heads together and came up with a new plan. Something that will—with hope and patience and a bit of magic—make Wayward Bay even more beautiful.

So, with the blessing of Mayor Amalie Singh and the grant's sponsors, we decided to pool the grants into a fund for *all* the Bay's small businesses, available to use as needed. Sometimes, that means awarding a smaller grant. Other times, a low- or no-interest loan. And in times of prosperity, it means donating back to the fund to keep it growing for years to come.

We also set up a small business advisory board helmed by me, Ricci, Emmie, and Mr. Corto, who was able to return to the Bay after Mean Beans was forced to close its doors for good and lost their rights to the building. Together, the board has launched new initiatives to help businesses partner with one another for even greater opportunities.

The Kettle and Cauldron is now proudly serving chocolates from Dark Escapes. Emmie hooked up with Flowers on Main to offer Valentine's and birthday packages pairing roses and cupcakes. All of us are working together for the first annual Wayward Bay Busy Business Holiday Extravaganza, featuring gift baskets stuffed with our wares and gift cards that can be used interchangeably at any participating Wayward Bay establishments, from the laundromat to Glaze for Days to the movie theater and yes, Kettle and Cauldron too.

I've still got a ways to go in paying off my debts, but things are looking up on the financial front. When Beverly learned what her nephew had been up to—nearly swindling her entire estate right out from under her—she was eager to press charges and cut all ties. Together, we worked out a new payment plan for my back rent, and with the way business is going lately, I'll be back in the black before I know it.

And now, I have a new dream. It won't happen overnight. In fact, it'll probably take me a few years to save up the capital, but I'm not going to lease this space forever. I'm going to buy it. Beverly and I have a plan for that, too. It's an investment. Slow and steady. Totally worth it.

I also have my new employee. Still a little green, needs a *lot* of supervision and hand-holding, but...

Yeah. He's worth the investment, too.

"Devlin, we talked about this." I sigh, shaking my head as he emerges from the kitchen.

Some things never change.

"You don't like the Santa hat?" He shakes his head, disappointment flashing in his eyes. "Violet, I know you're a witch, but surely even *you* can spare some love for Santa."

"It's not the hat."

"What, then? I've washed my hands. The apron is freshly laundered and pressed, as requested. Employee of the Month, right here."

"Seriously?" I look to the cats, both watching us with wide, curious eyes from their perch on the counter stools, their tails swishing. "Back me up here, boys."

"You're the one with the frowny face, Mushroom." Devlin picks up Grumpy and kisses him on the head, making the traitorous cat purr. "So if I've broken one of your *many* rules, you'll need to be more specific. *Very* specific. Still new at this whole upstanding mortal citizen thing, if you recall."

"*Pants*, Devlin! You need to wear pants!"

"In public, yes. That's what you said. But..." Flashing his signature mischievous grin, he releases the cat and hauls me close. "Pants would only get in my way. As yours are doing right this very instant. If anyone deserves an eye roll and a lecture, Mushroom, it's you."

He doesn't give me a chance to respond. Just plants a kiss right on my mouth, his cock growing hard against my thigh, fingers already working to open the button on my jeans.

I laugh, squirming out of his hold. "Do you ever get tired of stalking me?"

"Do you ever get tired of being stalkable?" He kisses me again, hungry and relentless as we make our way toward the fireplace.

"Why are you like this?" I tease, my entire body already aflame from his touch, burning with the same desperate need I feel in his energy. The same desire.

"Because I'm the Devil, darling. I've seen it all, done it all, gotten *all* the T-shirts. I was quite certain nothing could work me into such a state, yet here you are. *Working* me." He crowds me against the wall, tucking a finger under my chin and tilting my face up toward his. "From the moment I crash-landed in your quaint little tea shop and laid eyes upon these crazy curls, I've been in a semi-hard to fully-erect state every time I look at you."

"*Every* time?" I narrow my eyes. "Not statistically possible."

"Then blame the magic if you must, but it's true. See exhibit A." He grabs my hand. Presses it to the rock-hard bulge of his apron.

"Correlation doesn't mean causation. Maybe you're just easily turned on."

Devlin laughs. "By the new Police Commissioner's winter storm preparedness speech. Really."

"I don't know. Maybe you've got a thing for short, domineering bald men in fur-lined hats?"

"I most certainly... Oh, wait." Devlin's nose wrinkles. "That was a *very* brief phase during the Renaissance. So, fair point, but in this *particular* instance, wrong."

I'm cracking up again, as usual.

"And what about knitting circle?" he goes on.

"You had a hard-on at *knitting* circle?"

"Always. Surely you can't think I've got a septuagenarian witch fetish."

"Actually, I *did* think that. The first meeting, when Aunt Jos kept hitting on you and you were all, 'Oh, I'll take you on a few dates, Joslyn. I'll be your escort, Joslyn. Unpaid, of course, as I'm no longer in that line of work, but I'll happily bone you for free because I'm such a stellar gent!'"

"Mushroom?" He lowers his mouth to my throat, kissing and murmuring his way to my ear, every dark whisper sending a pulse of red-hot desire to the downtown pep squad, who's more than forgiven me for the brief hiatus. "What I've got a *thing* for is adorable, clever, curly-haired witches who drive me absolutely wild at every turn."

"Do you know a lot of curly-haired witches who drive you wild?"

"Actually, no. Just the one. Which leaves you in quite a bind, doesn't it?"

"How do you figure? You're the one with a raging hard-on in the middle of a snowstorm."

"And *you're* the one—the *only* one—who can satisfy this desperate, aching need. Unless, of course, you're willing to risk disappointing the Devil himself, which is not something to take lightly."

"No?"

"There are consequences, my lovely little tea witch. Lots and lots of con—ohhh, that is so not fair."

Hand beneath his apron, I stroke his hard cock, soft and slow, brushing my thumb over the tip, making him shudder.

"No, don't stop now," I tease, slowly getting to my knees. "I want to hear *all* about these so-called... consequences." With that, I flip up the apron and take him into my mouth, sucking him slowly, reverently, watching him lose control, one lick at a time.

"You are *not*... playing fair," he pants.

I pull back and glance up at him over my glasses, the picture of innocence. "Does the Devil want me to start playing by the rules?"

He grips my chin. Drags his thumb across my mouth. Then, in another dark whisper that sets my soul on fire, "*Never.*"

He drops to the floor and takes me down, pinning me to the rug in front of the fireplace. Gone is the apron. The dress shirt. The Santa hat. He tears off my clothes too, leaving me bare before the crackling flames.

Cupping my face, he presses the softest, sweetest kiss to my mouth and whispers, "I love you, Violet Pepperdine."

I return the kiss, certain my eyes are shining with the very same light I see in his. The very same love. "I love you too, Devlin Pierce."

One more smile, and then he descends, claiming me with his kiss, plunging between my thighs in a long, hot stroke that has my hips rolling, urging him in deeper, every cell in my body begging for more.

There's no dirty talk this time, no flirting, no teasing. Just us. Together. A perfect dance, his mouth hot on my throat, my collarbone, my nipple, everything in me wound tight, buzzing in the best way.

He draws back, cupping my cheek in his big, strong hand, thumb skating across my lips as he fills me again and again, driving me right to the very edge of that high, beautiful cliff.

I arch my back and take him in deeper, harder, faster, and when he kisses me again, I fall, a wild unrestrained tumble right over the edge.

I come for him with tears in my eyes, a joyful laugh bubbling out of me, the inevitable snort for the big finish, but I don't care. I'm so freaking in love with this man, nothing else matters. And when he whispers my name and buries his face in the crook of my neck and shudders against me, coming inside me hot and hard and yes—Ambrosia Divine knew what she was talking about after all—*furiously*, I close my eyes and send up a prayer of gratitude.

To my grandmother, who gave me my first home, my first safe place in a world that was anything but.

To my sisters and aunts and the people of Wayward Bay, who gave me my next home.

And to Devlin, my Prince of Darkness, my fallen angel, the Devil with a heart of gold who believed in me when I wasn't sure I remembered how to do it myself.

Now, when I look into his eyes, when I inhale his peppery, dark chocolate scent, when I hear the rich butter of his accent and feel the rumble of his laughter through his chest, I know I've finally found my *forever* home. My heart's truest desire unlocked. Embraced. Celebrated. And cherished, for the rest of our messy, beautiful, wild, mortal lives.

"It's really coming down out there," he says softly, pressing a kiss to my shoulder and nodding toward the windows, where Grumpy and Sunshine laze on the sill, tails swishing. "Cozy, isn't it?"

Outside, the snow falls in fat, heavy flakes, a beautiful white ballet. It feels like we're in a cabin at the center of our own private snow globe, safe and warm while the storm blankets the world beyond our door in a winter wonderland.

"Super cozy," I say. "Just needs one more thing to be absolutely perfect." I rise from the floor and reach for my clothes, exhausted and happy. Truly, unapologetically, deliriously happy. Then, leaning in for one more kiss, I say softly, "I'll go put on the kettle."

∽

Thank you so much for reading Violet and Devlin's story in The Devil Made Me Brew It! I've got lots more books planned for The Witches of Wayward Bay, so if you loved visiting this magical town and hanging out with all the sexy, sassy witches you've met so far, be sure to follow along at patreon.com/sarahpiper for updates (you can join for free to get all the book news, or sign up to one of the paid tiers for extra goodies), and come hang out in our Facebook reader group, Sarah Piper's Sassy Witches!

JOIN THE COMMUNITY

Want to get even more up-close-and-personal with me and all these naughty, sexy characters? Come join the fun in our online communities—we'd love to see you there!

PATREON

Over on patreon.com/sarahpiper, you can get fun stuff like early access to new stories and serials, bonus content, behind-the-scenes updates, Tarot readings, live virtual hangouts, fan polls, and so much more!

FACEBOOK READER GROUP

Pop in to our private Facebook group, Sarah Piper's Sassy Witches, for sneak peeks, cover reveals, exclusive giveaways, book chats, group therapy to deal with those killer cliffhangers, and plenty of complete randomness from your fellow fans!

LOOKING FOR AUDIOBOOKS?

A New Way to Get Your Audio Fix...

Audiobook lovers, you can now buy audiobooks directly from my author store at **SarahPiperBooks.com/shop** for early access and huge savings!

The books will still be available on other retailers, but buying direct means you can:

• **Save big.** Author store prices are 30-60% off retail prices.

• **Be the first to listen.** New releases will typically be available for direct buy for advanced release 1-2 weeks before they hit other retailers.

• **Directly support your favorite authors and narrators.** Your support means the world to me, and helps ensure I can continue to partner with the best narrators in the industry to bring these stories to life!

Visit SarahPiperBooks.com/shop to get started!

MORE SERIES FROM SARAH PIPER!

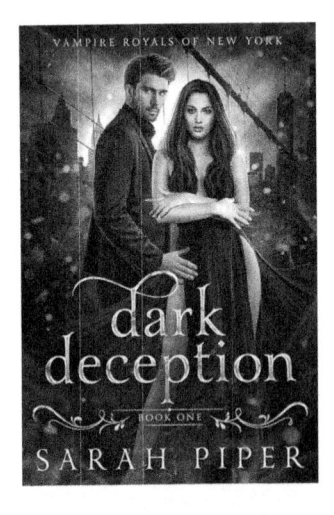

VAMPIRE ROYALS OF NEW YORK: Love a dirty-talker? Of course you do! Check out this scorching hot paranormal romance trilogy featuring a commanding, dirty-talking British vampire king and the seductive mortal thief who might just bring him to ruin... or become his eternal salvation.

TAROT ACADEMY is a paranormal, university-aged reverse harem academy romance starring four seriously hot mages and one badass tea witch (yep, if you loved The Devil Made Me Brew It, this series is a must-read too!). Dark prophecies, unique mythology, steamy romance, and plenty of supernatural thrills make this series a fan favorite!

ABOUT SARAH PIPER

Sarah Piper is a witchy, Tarot-card-slinging paranormal romance and urban fantasy author. Through her signature brew of dark magic, heart-pounding suspense, and steamy romance, Sarah promises a sexy, supernatural escape into a world where the magic is real, the monsters are sinfully hot, and the witches always get their magically-ever-afters.

Readers have dubbed her work "super sexy," "imaginative and original," "off-the-walls good," and "delightfully wicked in the best ways," a quote Sarah hopes will appear on her tombstone.

Sarah lives in New York with her husband, where she spends her days sleeping like a vampire and her nights writing books, casting spells, gazing at the moon, playing with her ever-expanding collection of Tarot cards, and obsessing over the best way to brew a cup of tea.

You can find her online at SarahPiperBooks.com, on Patreon at patreon.com/sarahpiper, and in her Facebook readers group at Sarah Piper's Sassy Witches! If you're sassy, or if you need a little *more* sass in your life, or if you need more Dean Winchester gifs in your life (who doesn't?), come hang out!

Printed in Great Britain
by Amazon